William Warren Humble (A. J. Warren) was born in Houghton-Le-Spring, Co Durham, England, and moved to Berlin in 1997. Whilst working there, he studied German and later in life was persuaded by a friend to take up writing. The 22 years spent living there allowed him to explore the corners and the culture of the city in detail. The culmination of these events led to his first detective book.

For Lilian
and
our two daughters

A. J. Warren

THE FLOWER PRESSER

AUSTIN MACAULEY PUBLISHERS™

LONDON ★ CAMBRIDGE ★ NEW YORK ★ SHARJAH

A CIP catalogue record for this title is available from the British Library.

ISBN 9781398421325 (Paperback)
ISBN 9781398421332 (ePub e-book)

www.austinmacauley.com

First Published 2022
Austin Macauley Publishers Ltd®
1 Canada Square
Canary Wharf
London
E14 5AA

Writing a book is an idea that takes you on an adventure. There are many twists and turns. The people who you meet have an effect on the outcome. Unknowingly they have all contributed.

The first person to thank is my wife who asked me to write a gruesome detective novel after watching numerous television murder investigations. Secondly, my two daughters, they planted the seed for an English detective who originally worked behind the Berlin Wall. I thank also my mother, who pushed me to publish my book and my father who is no longer with me.

Marina Jones who introduced me to Clärchens Ballhaus and then the summer Monbijou park dance scene. It was one night when I parked my car near Ebertbrücke, scene of the third murder, on my way to Monbijou that the inspiration for this book came about.

I thank especially Ursula Kierzek who encouraged me to write again. I am forever grateful to her and her sister Susanne. Their families always made me feel welcome and part of their home.

All my former work colleagues who listened to me harp on about my book and my long-term friend Holger with whom I shared a few beers and discussed ideas.

There is one further person and that is Allison Ballie, author of *Sewing the Shadows Together* and *A Fractured Winter* for her encouragement. We met accidentally in a fish and chip shop at the Ijmuiden ferry terminal whilst waiting for the Newcastle ferry. She introduced me to Newcastle Noir.

Lastly, as I mentioned at the start, writing a book is an adventure and a journey. The last two parts of the chain are the publisher who believes the story is worthy to take forward and the reader.

Thank you to all.

Chapter 1

The simulated sodium orange glow of the electric street lights reflected on the Berlin cobbled street. Argentinian tango music wandered across the river from the Monbijou Park, where people were dancing and intertwining to the passionate beat. Young couples enjoying the summer night, sat on the steps of the Bode-Museum and the bridge parapet opposite; they were puzzled by the police presence. They watched but were unable to see the mutilated half torso, which had been pulled out of the river. Am Weidendamm, a link street connecting two tourist areas, was cordoned off to protect the murder scene. Tonight, the two faces of Berlin were in stark contrast.

Warren had scheduled a relaxing Thursday evening at home with a bottle of wine, until Judith phoned. He stared at his glass of Pinot Noir red wine as he placed the mobile phone back onto the table. It would be a long night and he wondered if this corpse would transpire to be the third victim. The temptation to drink the wine was there, but he knew there would be grief from Judith. She had phoned from her car and would shortly be in front of his flat to pick him up. Warren cursed his job as he poured the wine back into the bottle and pushed the cork in. He headed outside to wait for Judith.

Judith drove along Oranienburger Strasse to the crime scene and Warren looked with envy at the tourists, sitting outside, enjoying the summer evening.

"This was my first night off in two weeks, Judith: glass of wine, sit on the balcony, relax, unwind and enjoy the summer evening. Someone has pissed me off tonight, but I'll get over it, eventually."

"You always do. You should have been a tourist, Warren, instead of a detective. Change your job."

"And miss this unhealthy stress; the sight of another dead body, a late night and feeling exhausted the next day. I couldn't cope with that level of relaxation; my body would probably go into shock and give me a heart attack. Do you have a bottle of water by any chance? This evening heat is killing me. It is five weeks without rain and anything over 27 is too much for me."

"It is on the back seat, but it will be warm. It's a no-win scenario with you. You complain when it's minus ten in winter and too hot in summer. We can turn left here, and now is the start of our long hot night."

"Let's see what condition the body is in, Judith. My feeling is that we have a third murder on our hands and we still have not solved the last two."

"The seniors will be pissed off, as you say. It seems to be your word of the night."

"It comes naturally to them, they are never content. It's part of their genetic makeup and a requirement for promotion."

Judith drove over Ebertbrücke and Warren saw the police boat, indicating the crime scene. It was 22.00 when they pulled up in Judith's grey VW and stepped out of the car. The crime ghouls had already gathered at the edge of the scene, hoping to satisfy their morbid interest in death. There was no doubt in his mind that it was already posted on social media. The urgency for people to be the first to tell, with no respect for the dead or the victim's family, puzzled Warren and social media had only made the race faster.

Judith and Warren pushed through the ghouls, showed their ID cards to a junior officer and crossed over the line into the crime scene. He stomped over to the duty officer and curtly spoke to him.

"Move the barriers and tape further back, seal off that bridge and the thoroughfare opposite. Also, inform the ghouls if anyone takes a photo or sends a message, they are liable to be arrested for interfering with a police investigation."

Warren looked over to the crowd leaning on the bridge parapet like spectators at a pop concert.

"This mobile selfie generation should be more concerned with life instead of their experiences, Judith."

"Getting old and irritable, are we, Warren? What will you be like tomorrow after a late night?"

"It's only tonight. I had opened a bottle of good red wine. Besides, my senses tell me, we have a third body on our hands, which makes, whoever is doing this, a serial killer. Don't forget, you're a similar age to me, old enough to be grumpy on the odd occasion."

"But not tonight, you have won that prize."

"You were not off duty. Let's find Doc, Judith, and obtain the macabre details."

Judith peered over the steel fence and saw him struggling to walk up the steps from the police boat. "Come on, you can make it."

Doc's white bushy eyebrows and bearded face looked upwards at Judith and he smiled at her. Slowly, he appeared over the edge and refused help as he clambered onto the street. "Judith, good evening, thanks for the sarcastic offer of help, I've ten years more on my knees than you. At least you offered, evening, Warren. All the years of cycling, when I was younger, to keep fit left me with arthritic knees. When was the last time that we discovered a corpse at a respectable time? Some murderers have no respect, do they, Warren? I see you've put your hair into your usual ponytail style, Judith."

Judith looked bemused and stared at him unsure how to answer.

"Doc is right; you normally put your hair up at a crime scene."

Judith shrugged her shoulders, "I've never realised it."

"What's not suitable tonight, my two favourite colleagues, is what I have just witnessed. I've seen many things in my life, tonight, it is not pleasant and I'm being diplomatic. I feel sorry for the young officer below; poor lad has only been out of training school and in the real world for three months. This is not the sort of case to be baptised on. He's white as a ghost, I have no doubt his mum will look after him tonight and tuck him up in bed."

Warren and Judith glanced at each other, wondering what the hell was to come.

"You seem to be certain, that it is murder."

"I am Judith, I have yet to see a suicide where the person has managed to cut himself in half and then throw each half into the river. That's why, I'm convinced. Over the years, I have seen bodies mutilated by propellers; this was no boat accident. The police are currently searching up and downstream for the other half. And Warren, please don't ask for an accurate time of death until the post mortem is complete."

"What do you mean, mutilated, Doc?" said Warren.

"From what I have seen, the person was mutilated as well as, cut in half."

"Where's the body now, is it still down there?"

"No, I was on the boat to finish some paperwork, Judith. The corpse is in the tent, I'll show you, but I would say, prepare yourselves."

The gentle summer breeze carried the faint pungent smell of rotting flesh as they walked over to the pristine white tent. The smell swirled around their nasal sensors. Judith and Warren looked at each other, the thought of what awaited them on the other side turned their stomachs. Warren fought to hold the retching down and Judith noticed.

"Are you okay? You've gone white."

"Sort of, not really, lack of wine, but I'm holding it down."

Doc looked at Warren.

"He never had much of a stomach for graphic crime scenes, Judith, but somehow he survives. Before we go in, I must warn you, it's not pretty. The mutilated decayed half corpse is the bottom half, male. The torso was separated above the pelvis. It's the most obvious place to separate a body, all flesh you see, except for the spine."

"What was responsible for the separation of the torso, Doc? I mean what type of instrument?"

"No formal idea, Warren, but it looks like he was hacked in half, not sawn, the edges of the corpse are uneven. We will be able to tell more at the post mortem, usual answer, I'm afraid. Hopefully, the vertebrae, where the separation took place are still intact. If there are cut marks, we should be able to suggest a type of instrument. Since the body was in the river for several weeks, we will also analyse, what has entered the corpse. Astrid will provide you with more detailed information, tomorrow. I will also provide a prelim report of the initial findings of tonight."

Judith and Warren looked at each other with apprehension, at the thought of viewing the body.

"Are you two ready? You'll need to get suited up first."

Judith looked bemused at Doc.

"I can see, you are wondering what I am talking about. I'm warning you in advance, the poor guy suffered before he was killed and I've also the feeling that he didn't have an early death. If the other half of his body suffered as much, I do not want to see it, but I am afraid there is no other option. Quite simply put, it's my job. Here's a couple of face masks. Judith, if you have any perfume, spray it on; it will help to mask the smell. The smell of corpses pulled from the river can hang around your nasal passage for weeks. Warren, if you are going to throw up, please, leave the tent."

Judith looked at Warren, who shook his head to decline the spray.

"We'll pass, who knows the smell may be important."

"That is the main reason Judith, why I don't use a suppressant cream under my nose."

Judith and Warren braced themselves as they entered the tent. The pungent, musty decay of death swirled around the inside of their noses. The taste of death clung to the back of their throats. It was obvious from the body bag, that there was only one half of a decomposing corpse. Doc leant over and unzipped the bag; the warm evening air intensified the pungent smell within the tent. Judith and Warren fought to hold the vomit back. It was a case of who would give in first and they both looked at each other.

"The torso, as I mentioned was cut in two and by the size of the cuts, I would anticipate something like a butcher's cleaver. As I said, we will learn more. The other wounds are older and some have healed more than the others. His Achilles tendons were also cut."

Doc partially lifted each leg and pointed to the cut marks at the back of the ankles.

"Whoever did this ensured the victim could not run away. There are marks around the ankles, indicating that he was bound. From the size of the marks, I would say tie wraps were used, first guess, of course."

Doc looked up at the two, very ghostly, ashen white, pale-faced detectives.

"Are you both okay?"

"No, carry on."

Judith nodded her head in agreement.

"This is where it gets weird, and I've never seen this before. The areas on the upper thighs are partially skinned and they have slightly healed. You can see the difference in the texture. In summary, whoever did this kept our man alive and tortured him, for how long is the open question."

Judith noticed Warren flee from the tent to avoid vomiting and contaminating the corpse. She could hear him retch and the noise of vomit as it splattered onto the surface of the river. Luckily, the police boat had moved.

Warren was still leaning over the parapet, when Judith joined him.

"Here's a Tempo tissue, you're still dribbling and luckily, that bit has just missed my shoe."

He smiled back and wiped the residue from his mouth.

"Sorry, do have you that bottle of water, by any chance in your bag?"

"Sure, here you are. Keep the bottle. I don't want it back after you have had your mouth around it. I still have another two in the car."

Warren leant on the steel parapet; his hand shaking as he swigged the water and emptied the bottle. Judith noticed the colour of his sapphire blue eyes had faded.

"I'll be okay. I need a few minutes, Judith. The sad thing is that humans can be so cruel, a mind-set, which I will never understand. We all live in this world only once."

Warren, looked across the river to the coloured string of lights at Monbijou Park, Rumba music was drifting in their direction. He knew people were having fun and he struggled to come to terms with the two contrasts of the night. He knew that he and Judith were in charge of a case where few people would wish to be. Their seniors respected their experience; they both knew this third murder would stretch their patience and the public's.

"You've drifted, Warren."

"I am clearing my mind, Judith. This is our third murder in two years. The last two had marks on their ankles and wrists where they had been bound. The first one had small slit marks over his body and his neck had been sliced open, all his blood had been drained. The second one had his tongue cut out, his stomach split in four and his intestines were removed, like some sort of hung, drawn and quartered medieval torture. That body did not surface in Rummelsburger Lake, until the ice thawed. There is still a family somewhere wondering where their son is. Now, it looks like the killer is honing his art, each one is progressively worse. Whoever did this is sick, but that person will have logical reasoning in their world to justify what we have seen. I've never come across a serial killer of men. What must go through a person's mind when they are in such a position?"

"Look back in history, how people were tortured; brutally and some survived. What the human body can cope with astounds me. My whole sympathy goes out to these victims what they went through, not only the physical but the mental torture they endured. Whatever they did, they did not deserve this ending."

"Depending on the reason they were killed, Judith, some people may disagree, but we will…"

Their discussion was interrupted by a young uniformed officer who stood and looked at Warren.

"Spit it out man, I'm not in the mood for guessing games tonight."

"They've found the rest of the corpse."

"Where?"

"The locks, at Mühlendamm."

Warren saw Judith stare at him for his unacceptable manner to the young officer. He knew an apology would be in order rather than face the wrath from his partner.

"Apology, for my curt manner, we're all tense tonight with what we have found."

He looked at the young officer; his head was pounding from throwing up and thanked him for the information. He turned to Judith just as Doc wandered over, stroking his beard and leaned against the steel parapet on the river wall. Judith looked at him.

"Are there any pictures of you when you were younger without a beard? I'm curious."

"It's a long time since this face has seen daylight, Judith. It's probably paler than Warren's face. That smell can have an effect on many people with a weak stomach. The whole body is a chemical reaction, over thirty different chemicals at work to produce that smell. Do what I do, bin your clothes; it's the easiest option rather than trying to get rid of the smell. The smell and taste in your nose and throat, as you know will last a few weeks."

Warren's expressionless face said it all to Doc.

"I have just heard the locks next to the Direktorenhaus, Juedenstrasse."

"That's right, Doc."

"Shit, it'll be closed; can we open it as part of the investigation. I've always meant to visit it after they'd renovated the building. We could have a private tour, free of charge, at the expense of the Berlin taxpayer."

"I like your humour, Doc."

"It's a deflection of the reality; we need as much as we can tonight to distract us from this sick, twisted nightmare. By the way, you suit your hair in a ponytail, I forgot to mention earlier."

Doc looked at Warren, who was still ashen white.

"I would rather not see the rest of the corpse tonight, but we don't have that luxury; it's the tougher side of our job."

"There is one advantage; I've nothing left in my stomach to bring up Doc, so let's get on with it. Hopefully, the team can sort it out before dawn. There are office blocks down there and tomorrow the tourist boats will be queuing up to go through the locks. The last thing we need is a bunch of tourists tweeting like birds in a dawn chorus. This guy is becoming more confident or twisted at what he's doing. He would probably call it, skilled. I've no doubt, there will be a fourth."

Judith looked in apprehension at Warren, knowing he was right, but she had the sinking feeling in her stomach that they would find a fourth.

"You've drifted, what are you thinking?"

"Sorry Judith, it's the thought of not being able to prevent another murder. So far, we've failed three people and their families. Another worry is keeping tonight's details out of the press."

"It's a modern world we live and some people with a smartphone feel like they are a roving reporter. They need to tell the world and claim their moment of fame as being the first to report. Sometimes, they do more damage than good."

"Warren, Judith, when you have both finished pontificating about people's freedom of rights to report, I've another half of a body to examine. I'll meet you both there."

"Apology, Doc, we'll see you at the crime scene. We'll walk, it'll give you time to inspect the corpse."

"Whatever."

"Doc seems on edge tonight, Warren."

"We all are, Judith. It's a long day; people are already tired and torture is not the run of the mill murder. Those images, in our head…we will carry to our grave."

Judith felt miffed at Warren making the decision on how to arrive at the next crime scene. It was already past midnight and tired nausea was starting to set in.

"You walk and do what you normally do, peruse the area and collect your thoughts, here, take the water and these headache tablets. Me, I'm not interested in walking back to collect my car and I would appreciate it, if you don't decide how I arrive at a crime scene. I'll see you there and I'll run you home later."

Warren walked along the edge of the river and noticed the night sky had clouded over the ball of the Alex Tower. The thunderstorm from hell was arriving, the only question was, where would it strike in Berlin? Alone, with his thoughts, the twenty-minute walk in the cooling Berlin night was a welcome distraction from what he had witnessed. Warren could see the lights of the crime scene in the distance as he approached the steps next to the Mühlendamm Bridge. Judith was busy talking to a uniform policeman as he approached her.

"I see, even at this time of night the ghouls are here, it is as almost some people can smell death out. What has uniform to say?"

"The body was noticed by a man, who had finished work and was on his way home. At least, we know it was put there tonight or it had surfaced late evening."

"It makes sense, Judith; these locks are regularly used during the day and into the late evening. Hopefully, the post mortem can pin a more accurate date as to when this poor soul was put in the water. Can you get in touch with the head of public communications to limit the damage? I know it is late, but I don't want any reports until we have all the information."

"It may be a bit late now, but I'll try. There's Doc, coming out of the tent now, he looks shaken. I've never seen him like that before."

Judith, approached him, placed her hand on his shoulder and caressed him like an old friend. She always had a soft spot for him.

"Are you okay Doc?"

"Not really, Judith. The smell of rotten decaying flesh in my nose, that's not my only problem, I'm getting too old for these late nights and images. My wife has been pushing me to resign. After tonight, I may consider it. Such images, I do not want as a flashback when I am older. One thing is for certain, the visit to Direktorenhaus is off the table, that's annoyed me."

Warren wandered over to the bench where Judith sat next to Doc.

"What have we got then, Doc?"

"Me, a plan to find another job, brought about by what I've seen tonight. It's the second half of your tortured corpse."

"You Judith, what are your thoughts?"

"Deflection required so we can compose our thoughts. I can see people, across the river on the Fischerinsel, sitting outside, enjoying the end of a Berlin summer night. I'm wondering, which is the best restaurant, Doc?"

"There's a good Indian restaurant over there, I went once with my wife, part of the restaurant is an old barge in the river. She's partial to a good curry, it's her English culture."

"That bad, is it, Doc?"

"Warren is damn good at this guessing game, Judith, no wonder he became a detective, you should go for promotion. It's no good, you two getting suited up, especially you, Warren. You have nothing left on your stomach to throw up except bile and blood. Seeing one half of a bloated, greenish-black torso with pond life inside is enough for you two, tonight. It is best if you both wait for the pictures, with the prelim report. At least, there will be no smell of the decay."

"How bad is it?"

"As you say in English, Warren, pretty bad, this is in itself a contradiction. Areas of skin are missing and his face is also disfigured. When a body is placed into the water, the microorganisms in the gut start to break down the cellular structure. Hence, after a short period, the body is full of gas and it surfaces. Cut the body in half, the microorganisms cannot do their work as efficiently, there is nowhere for the gases to be trapped. A half torso reacts differently. When it is immersed, there is no gas build up until the river life starts to eat the inner of the corpse, and then there is a build-up of gas. This process takes longer; also depends on water temperature, anything up to twenty days. The temperature which we have now and looking back, I would estimate that he was thrown in the water approximately two to three weeks ago. Some teeth on the corpse were removed, maybe to make identification harder, the face is disfigured. After what this poor guy went through, it would not surprise me if the teeth were removed when he was alive. This person is going to extreme circumstances to ensure it is not easy to identify him. There's one old scar on his left shoulder."

"Type?"

Doc's patience snapped at the sharp interruption from Warren.

"Stop interrupting, patience! Did no one teach you any manners when you were a child?"

Doc, in one sentence, had rebuked him and made him feel like a pupil, who had broken a school rule. Judith looked at Warren and he knew what she was thinking. It was late, people were exhausted and nerves were on edge, Warren took it on the chin and kept quiet.

"It's a scar from an operation. What this operation was, I have no idea, perhaps, after a more detailed analysis we may have an idea. His muscle structure is more defined than what I have seen on other corpses. Possibly, he visited a gym regularly or worked out. I'll know more after I've performed the post mortem with Astrid but from what I see, our man was a fit person, who met a horrendous ending. Only God knows what he did to deserve this."

"Off the record Doc and just between us three, until the official report is released…"

"No need to finish your sentence, Warren, I've seen enough similarities, you have a serial killer to catch. The hard part, he probably blends into society just like anyone else. Normal job, possibly career-minded, may have a family, girlfriend, boyfriend, who knows."

Warren muttered under his breath, "Sick, warped bastard."

"Warren. Stop right there! This person, as you very well know is mentally deranged but highly functional and intelligence. Don't belittle or underestimate him, you need, both of you to get on his level of thinking. The first body, you both must have heard of death by a thousand cuts, the Chinese method of execution. An executioner could kill someone very quickly by slicing an appropriate part of the body, such as the throat. Some families paid them, so their loved ones would have a quick death. Some had a slow death. The second victim, tongue cut out and the body sliced in four, mediaeval times. Tonight, our victim, after one or two slices of skin removed, would have passed out, unless he was drugged. Infection would have also killed him, maybe it did. The amount of cuts on the body, he would not have survived all that in one go. He was deliberately kept alive. Someone is honing their art of torture, from what I have seen today..."

Judith watched Doc run for the parapet and puke over the edge. It was the second time tonight that she had heard the splat of vomit on water. It was all she could do to stop herself from retching. Judith walked over to him.

"Michael, here's a tissue. Here sit down."

"You were saying?"

Judith looked daggers at Warren and he noticed for the second time tonight that ice-hard piercing stare from her.

"Back off and give him a couple of minutes to compose himself, disappear somewhere and clear your head. Leave me alone with him."

Warren looked visibly chastened by Judith and sloped off, "Are you okay now, Michael?"

"I'm feeling better, except for the metallic taste in my mouth. I need to wipe my beard. It's a long time since someone used my first name at work. Too much Du, Sie and formality in the German language, don't you think? Very old fashioned."

"Cannot disagree, but maybe Warren could do..."

"He's a lost cause, Judith, but damn good at his job, you both work well together; I've watched you both over the years. It's late and we are all now at our physical and mental limits."

"Here's a mint, to take the taste away."

"Thanks, Judith, sometimes all people need is a brief moment of sympathy. It helps to remind them that people care and it's good for the soul. We are all professionals, but we are humans with emotions and limitations. It looks like he has only taken a short stroll. Welcome back, Warren. You need to learn to relax otherwise your body will do it for you. Look for someone with medical knowledge, or who has studied and practised. Whoever did this is no amateur and he kept this person alive for some time. For your information, there was a considerable skin patch removed from his back. The question is: was it removed when he was alive, or after death and why? Your murderer is becoming confident with each body."

"Are you okay now, Doc, sorry for earlier."

"Apology accepted, Warren. I'll leave you two alone; my wife is waiting for me and I have a preliminary finding report to write before I go to bed. She can always tell how bad a case is by the lack of conversation when I arrive home. It's the key for her to talk to me about anything else but work. It is one of our marital survival techniques. I'll touch base with you both later today. The post mortem will be in the afternoon, touch base at about four. We all need to get sleep and tired people make mistakes. I bid you two good night and I suggest you both go home and get some sleep."

Warren and Judith watched Doc trudge in the direction of his BMW.

"He is cranky tonight."

"Whatever that means, it sounds like we all are. I recognise that I don't have the same energy levels anymore."

"This is the third one, Judith, we need to identify him and build a picture of his social life. There is a connection to the previous two. If I was dumping a body in the river, I would go for the road that runs along the edge of the Spree near Bellevue. It's quiet and secluded on that stretch of the Spree."

"Possibility, but let's just keep it like that, there must be other secluded places to dispose of a body. We're tired and you are making an assumption."

"I'm just thinking out loud, there too many thoughts flying around inside my head. I've no doubt, tomorrow, or I should say, later today, I want to see this place in the daylight, before the post mortem."

Warren looked at his watch.

"It's gone two in the morning, Judith, and we both need sleep. If we're lucky we might get four hours, I'll draft out the initial crime scene report tomorrow morning. The forensics team will have to work through the night. Can you drop me off at home?"

"Only, if you talk at me and keep me awake."

Judith could feel her eyes closing as Warren stepped out of the car at Karlshorst; he bid her thank you and good night. Fifteen minutes later, Judith parked the car outside of her flat in Biesdorf. Exhausted, she was pleased that she lived on the second floor, with only one set of stairs to climb. Judith opened the bedroom door, stripped off, dropped her clothes on the floor and crawled into bed. She wrapped her arm around Sarah's waist and snuggled into her back. Sarah pulled her arm in tight, "Hi, I didn't think you would be this late."

There was no reply; Judith was already in the protective land of sleep.

Chapter 2

Warren recognised the clip of his partner's heels walking along the corridor. Judith walked into the office, looked pissed off and slapped the newspaper onto his desk, barely missing his coffee cup. He rescued it for safety.

"Have you seen that? God damn press have more spies on the street then the former Stasi."

"It's not like you to be pissed off so early in the morning. What's up?"

"It was also on the radio this morning."

Warren scanned the first sentence whilst Judith hung her coat up. It was enough, 'Body found in the Spree'.

He stood up and slammed his rescued cup onto the table, the coffee leapt out in protest.

"Those fucking irresponsible editors, only interested in selling papers. You did speak to Ann Marie last night to contain the information?"

He knew his tone had crossed the line with Judith. Before she could cast her stare, as much to say how the hell you can ask such a stupid question in such a manner, Warren was quicker off the mark to apology for the dumb outburst.

"Sorry, Judith, it's the press, they hinder our investigations at times and rattle my cage. Plus, I'm irritable due to lack of sleep."

"We both are."

"Did you get some sleep?"

"About five hours."

"The press has to be managed and controlled, sometimes, to ensure we get the best possible use of them."

"Without hindering freedom of speech? It's a fine line; let's not forget East Germany's past, Warren. Here's a tissue for your desk to mop your coffee up. You don't normally swear."

"It's a reflection of my frustration and the gravity of the situation, which we find ourselves in. Thanks for the tissue. This is now the third murder and the press have provided a platform for a serial killer, without touching base with ourselves, is simply irresponsible. It's always a balance between maintaining press freedom, not jeopardising the investigation and releasing information at the appropriate time in a constructive responsible manner. People will be baying for results and in panic, the word, 'serial' increases peoples and press interest. We're under enough pressure as it is without the public and committees breathing down our necks. It diverts valuable resources. These bastards sometimes think they are the self-opinionated protectors of society, whilst trying to increase their profits. In such cases, they need to work with us."

"They normally do."

"I know you, what did Ann Marie say, you would have phoned her as soon as you saw the paper."

"I did, and like I discussed last night with her, hold off with any release until we had more substantial information. Apparently, there was a freelancer in the area last night, he bypassed her and went straight to her editor, who made the last-minute deadline. There's the disadvantage of modern-day technology, write, click and send around the world."

"It's a shame, the wall is down. We could have arrested that editor and interned the freelancer in Hohenschoenhausern jail to keep each other company."

"Are you finished, Warren?"

"Finished what?"

"Spitting chips out. Is that correct English?"

He looked at Judith; she had just bemused him with another idiom and managed to stop him in full flow.

"Spitting your chips out is the phrase, Judith, also look up soapbox."

"Drink your coffee and calm down. It is what it is, Warren, we cannot change the past, we have to work with it and move forward. It could also work in our favour; at least the public will be more aware. This person is becoming more confident and we may need the public to be more aware."

"The downside is we will probably end up a load of trolls providing false information. The sad thing is that is par for the course, Judith."

"Someone has a definite grudge against men, for whatever reason and is on a mission. I know a few women who wish their ex dead out of frustration but none who would go that far. This is number three; we have now a possible serial killer loose. What the motive is? I think no one on our team has a suggestion based on solid facts, Warren."

"It could be a myriad of themes to suit his abnormal psychological gratification. I'll leave that question for the Psychologists to answer; there, I am out of my depth. Once the lab has digitally recreated his face, we could possibly use the media to help identify him. I mean, at an appropriate time, when we've exhausted all channels of investigation. Can you imagine, you pick the newspaper up, or you're scanning your phone? The last thing I want is for some poor, boyfriend, girlfriend, mother, wife or father to see his face on the front page. That's the last option. We have to be the first to inform the correct people. Now, we need to head off to the locks where the upper torso was found and back in time for initial post mortem results. Can you get in touch with Ann Marie again and prevent any further press damage. They only mentioned the body found near the Bode Museum and they seem to be unaware that the second half of the torso was found. Whoever did this may read the paper this morning and will be wondering why only part of the body was found. It may even irritate them to the point where it has not gone as planned. They've failed to maximise their full glory and who knows it may lead to them making a mistake. I don't want any press release on the fact that the second half of the torso has been found. It gives me the satisfaction of knowing that I have been able to push back at whoever did this. As for social media, do not get me started."

"No problem, I'll get in touch with her to confirm. I mentioned this morning it may be coming her way. What time shall we go to the locks?"

"Shortly before lunch, I've got a review with the seniors now for the next couple of hours. They like their reporting and graphs; it gives them a comforting feeling."

"I'll phone Ann Marie to see what can be done to limit any further damage and I'll set a team meeting for six, which I am sure will piss a few people off."

"Buy those pizzas, which we had last time or something, the troops are easily bribed."

***

The click of the toaster in the kitchen signalled the completion of its morning task and popped up four slices. Anja put the toast, margarine, marmalade and green tea on her country flowered bean bag tray and walked over to her husband.

"What's new in the paper?"

24

Stefan neatly folded the newspaper, placed it perfectly square to the edge of the table and lifted the toast off the tray. Anja sat opposite her husband waiting for an answer as he spread the margarine slowly over his toast. She looked to check the position of his newspaper was correct.

"Apart from the fact, there's still no world peace, they have found a body in the Spree near the Bode museum."

Stefan looked down and carried on spreading the margarine over his toast. "Stop tormenting me, you know we have been waiting for this moment."

"There doesn't seem to be a lot of detail, Anja, either those press guys are becoming stupid, or the police haven't released all the information. They only mention a body, not half a torso."

"I was starting to wonder when it would surface. What did they say?"

"Nothing too detailed, mainly a corpse was pulled out of the river late last night."

Anja looked across at her husband as he passed her the knife. She raised her eyebrows whilst spreading the marmalade over her toast.

"So, only half of the corpse surfaced. It is a shame that it was last night and not during the day. I'm assuming there is no mention of the other half."

"Good assumption, it is within the time period you estimated. They've never mentioned if they found the other half. You're right though, it would have had more effect if it was during the day time."

"Maybe, they're deliberately keeping it quiet, Stefan."

"Or, whoever made the press headline only got half of the story, or information. That's possible."

He looked up and Anja stared across the table into her husband's dark brown eyes. He sat there and looked at her with a blank face; she was unable to read any emotion.

"You really do like to explore the different meaning of a fact. That must be the worst joke, which I've ever heard, half a story."

"But relative, let's leave it for a while, if there is no press release within the next few days, we could drop them some information. I've no doubt that will irritate the police and use up their resources. The rest of the body will surface somewhere, they will find it, or someone will."

"I'm not sure about that, Stefan, to control the police? I'll like the thought, perhaps, when we know more about who is in charge of the case, we can then make it more personal, follow them; find out where they live and who their friends are. I need to think about your suggestion. This is our third, and the police are still no further forward."

Anja noticed her husband look up at the kitchen clock.

"There's something else for you, well for us to think about, you need to make a move or you'll be late for your surgery."

"Damn, Andreas, we would not be in a rush if his corpse had surfaced today. You need to move your car, husband, so that I can go to work."

"Will do, I don't want to be late at the hospital. What're you doing for lunch, Anja? Shall we meet?"

Anja looked at her husband's reflection in the mirror as she put on her mascara, "I'm grabbing some sandwiches at the local bakery on the way in. I've a meeting at midday so there is no chance for an extended lunch break. I'll see you later tonight; hopefully, there will be an update on the news?"

"Your choice, if you don't want lunchtime sex. I thought I would never see the day when you would take the choice of a meeting. Car, Anja, otherwise we 'ill both be late and you have your surgery to open. If you're any later, your patients will be waiting outside. Don't forget we've Filippo's party on Sunday and you haven't bought a new dress yet."

"Shit, I forgot all about that, I'm at the centre tonight; it's my weekly therapy session for abused women and I am at the fitness centre tomorrow morning. I'll have time to have a look on my way to the centre or Saturday afternoon, Stefan. My sister will kill me, if I forget his birthday."

"Not literally, Anja, but it would probably be the less painful option from Melanie."

"I hope that self-centred, self-righteous, arrogant good-looking creep isn't at the party. It's a bad chemical reaction between me and him; Vincenzo is a controller; he puts me on edge. He has no empathy for other people, no respect for women and is full of his self-importance. His last girlfriend had a lucky escape but not after he put her through hell. It's not easy for a woman to leave an abusive relationship and it's not the first time he has treated women like shit."

"I heard that he has another girlfriend, Anja."

"Poor person, I hope that she sees sense quickly. I'll phone Melanie later to see if he's coming, maybe she can persuade Filippo to strike him off the list."

"I have no doubt that he will be there with his new girlfriend. He's a long-term friend of Filippo and he is your sister's husband. We know people like him do not change. Invite him back one day."

"Maybe, Stefan, he creeps me…it would be one less slime ball in the world."

"I've got the point, let's go to work now."

Anja stood in the queue at her local Leckerback bakery and a young couple stood in front of her. The young woman with a stooped posture looked up sideways to her boyfriend. She noticed how the well-groomed young man started to control his girlfriend.

"See look, that's a sandwich with tomato, cheese and lettuce. The other one has an egg; you can have Mayonnaise on it if you want. There's one with salami. You choose, I've told you what's in them."

Anja, found herself staring at the young man as his girlfriend ordered her sandwich and he repeated the order for her. She opened her purse and he took the money out and promptly paid the sales assistant. She could feel her blood boil as the young arrogant arsehole standing before her, lent over, kissed his girlfriend and told her that he loved her. She felt helpless for the young woman who looked exhausted with her self-confidence worn away. She could not help thinking how worried her parents would be for their daughter who was entrenched with such a coercive obnoxious arsehole. She could feel anger building up inside at the frustration of being unable to do anything. She knew what she saw would play on her mind for the rest of the day and hoped one day, life would get rid of him.

Chapter 3

Judith sat outside on the wooden lattice restaurant chairs next to the river walkway. She watched Warren plod along Juedenstrasse. He was slouching, looking down at the ground, he looked tired and mentally beaten down. It was obvious the case was getting to him and not only him.

"Finally, found a parking place, Warren?"

"It's getting worse in this city. I thought that I would have found one in this area without a problem."

"I managed to find one on Rolandufer, the city is growing. Are you okay? You look trodden down, staring at the pavement looking for inspiration. Most people look upwards for help or go to church on a Sunday."

"I'll take as much help as I can get at this minute, Sunday is an option, but right now, I could do with an Espresso to keep me awake. There are too many thoughts flying around inside my head, plus the images of last night kept me awake. The lack of sleep is starting to kick in and that can bring anyone down, it prevents people from thinking clearly. When this case is over, we should both get help, or disappear for a long holiday, preferably where there is no mobile signal."

"Or even before, Warren. A sign of strength is to recognise your weaknesses and limits. We are human and if we push the body too far, it will simply give up without warning."

"Did you manage to speak to Ann Marie?"

"She's done what she can and was in contact with the editors. The one thing she cannot help with is your favourite subject, social media."

"Don't get me started; I'm irritable enough as it is."

"What's the plan?"

"Keep out of the way of the forensics team so they can finish their work. We can pick up and read their report later. I'm not interested in the prelim and I am willing to wait for a final report to ensure all the detail is captured and we do not miss anything. I want to survey the area, obtain a feeling, to where someone could have disposed of the body. What was the reason for this area? Also, see if there is any CCTV, which might help, probably there are none, but it'll put my mind at rest and take it out of the equation."

"Okay. One thing before we go."

Warren looked down at Judith, who was still seated. He knew that tone of voice and felt he was about to get a life lesson.

"I'm listening."

"Have you thought about speaking to someone, go to a doctor, obtain something to help you sleep and regenerate your batteries. Do you remember the last case, which we worked on and when you ordered the pizzas?

"Tired people make mistakes, Warren, and are no good on the team. Your own words 'work-life balance', you beat on about them enough."

"The remedy is that this case moves forward and I feel that we are getting somewhere. I know my limits and you're right what you say. If you feel I have overstepped that limit then tell me, that's your job as my partner, you've already hinted. I will also let you know."

"Deal, but you're close to it, Warren."

"I know, let's walk, talk and change the subject. What're your thoughts about the person who's committing these murders?"

"Mine, keep it in mind I have no training in serial killers. The person is not logical, if he was, he wouldn't have committed these murders. There is a thought process, but not like ours. The window over there, there is a loose brick next to our table. What stops you from throwing it through the window? You would get a great dealing of gratification from the noise, an instant reward, a satisfying feeling."

"The fact you would arrest me."

"And if no one was here? You would still not do it, most people wouldn't. The thought process in the brain prevents most people. Something triggers them, the boundaries; the thought processes break down, for whatever reason. The person who is doing this perceives humans as an object to fulfil their aim. He believes what he is doing is correct, even morally justifiable and will be willing to argue the case. Something has triggered him, in his life, to suppress that piece of reason to kill and now he's found a mission. At what point was the trigger in his life? This is always the question and maybe we will never fully find out or understand. Did the opportunity to murder appear, or did he go out looking?

There're only four types of serial killers, Warren: visionary, thrill-seekers, mission-oriented, the power and control ones; they love the idea of outsmarting the police. Why the torture, which is progressively becoming more brutal, what has triggered that? It's horrific to contemplate that someone who lives a normal day to day life is capable of such actions."

"Place the right person with the correct situation at a point in history and humans are capable of horrendous actions. Some, after their actions were capable of going home to their families. You have to only read books on the concentration camps. I've no reason to challenge your thinking, your thoughts are similar and you've confirmed mine. He falls under power and control at this moment and he's outsmarting us and that pisses me right off. I believe he'll become braver and he will contact us but what the hell is driving him on this mission? A man, who brutally kills other men, has happened in the past, but it's a rarity. It's approximately two years and we're still not much further forward, Judith. Three mutilated bodies, there's a connection somewhere and hopefully, this surfaces with the third corpse. It looks like CCTV will be of no use. I've only seen CCTV on the walls of the Direktorenhaus pointing downwards to the windows, none in Kloster or Rolandufer Strasse. The only other ones I've seen is the camera pointing down towards the lock gates."

"Did you notice any?"

"Same as you and I'm not surprised, Warren, it is Berlin, but we had to check and hope. Let's sit down; over there on those tables, next to the water edge, it gives us a good view of the locks. It's serene here with a beautiful view of the Fischerinsel, blue sky and not a breath of wind; it's hard to believe what happened last night."

"I'm hoping this body provides a link, Judith."

"You are not the only one."

"No one reported a lost person for the first body and we were unable to identify who he was. The second one, we managed to find his girlfriend via his DNA on the database, he was a small-time drug pusher who lived in Koepenick. The level he pushed drugs at, wouldn't have attracted the level of violence, which he received. A few of his so-called friends got nervous and stopped pushing for a while, which was a positive. When we interviewed his girlfriend, the amount of grief she showed was less than what you would expect from a loving relationship. Her father was pleased to see the back of him and he wanted us to congratulate the killer when we found him. He was on the list of suspects for a short time. What sort of love keeps a beaten woman in a relationship?"

"How long have you got, Warren? It's a complicated subject and it is not love. Hopefully, we can identify this new victim, the case starts to break and then you can get some sleep."

"It might stop the nightmares. Last night, I felt as if I was on the outside looking in. I could hear and see all, unaware I was asleep, a sort of surreal nightmare. The type where you wake up; lie still in the solitude of the darkness, wondering if it was real and you still question it the next day."

"As we said earlier, let's look out for each other. Change of subject, look at those boats in the lock."

"Which one? The party boat belting out the music."

"It doesn't matter. Look at the water level, the boats are being lowered down to the next level of the river. The water level at the Bode museum is lower than here. There's no way the body could have drifted from the direction of Bellevue. How long have you lived in Berlin, Warren, and you didn't know the flow direction of the river. It blows your original assumption of where the body may have been dumped."

Warren stared across the table at Judith and remained silent as he turned around to double-check and avoid her smirk at his lack of local knowledge.

"You're right, I was wrong, bad assumption, tiredness, enjoy the moment, they are rare, and it was late last night. I suppose you will claim the fact that you are from Dresden and it exempts you of this knowledge."

"I will savour this moment."

"So what are you saying, Judith? The body could have been put into the river here or close by? What about the other half, no one would dump a body in that area; there are simply too many people. Granted this road is next to the river, the same as the Bode museum, but it's the height of the tourist season. There are always people, couples, buskers sitting on the bridge, someone would have seen something. I cannot believe that half a body floated past the Nikolaiviertel all the way to the Bode museum, a major tourist area. Maybe, it did go through the lock and ended up there. It is also possible, it went via the Spreekanal and not these locks; the distance is not far."

"We live in a city that probably has more rivers and lakes than Venice, Warren. Most of them are interconnected. These rivers connect from Wannsee to Erkner."

"Where's this conversation going, Judith?"

"What if the body was dumped from a boat and not a car? Look at the distance from this wall to the river, there's a pathway below, Warren. The murderer would have had to be super fit to throw half a corpse into the river from here. I'm sure he would not have carried it to the water's edge. The last two corpses were found in the lakes east from here and were difficult to find. This corpse wasn't, it was placed in this area deliberately to be found, possibly a few weeks ago for maximum effect. You've gone quiet, Warren."

"It's a possibility, bloody hell, there're a million boats in this city, not literally, but a damn lot. I'll throw a curve ball back to you, what if the both parts of the body were thrown into the water at separate areas. It's a possibility that one half was disposed of in this area and the other further upstream for maximum effect."

"Possible or it could have floated partially submerged downstream, via the Spreekanal. I cannot see anyone taking a boat through the locks with a body in it."

"I want to know who this guy is, Judith, and his face to be digitally recreated. Then, I want every gym in Berlin visited, when necessary every boatyard, workshop, marina and shops that sell boat accessories. Overtime is not limited for the next eight weeks. The budget can go to hell and I am sure the seniors will have no objection. Their public and political necks are on the line. Doc estimated the body was probably in the water two to three weeks ago. Pull the CCTV from the lock over the last four weeks, that's if they keep it that long and obtain a list of all the boats that went through. I appreciate the bodies could have been disposed of in another manner, but it is a starting point. This guy is not going to stop and has a mission, what it is, is still the question. He's starting to play with us and that thought is starting to really piss me off, Judith. We need to also head upstream."

"Why?"

"We need a fixed point to start from, three provides a pattern. Spilt Berlin into four quadrants, all the corpses have been found in one quadrant. This river runs past Treptower Park, then Oberschoenweide and down to Köpenick, where it splits into two and connects the other lakes. The first one was found at Rummelsburger and the second in Langer See. That's my only thought and we have to start from somewhere."

32

"I think we've seen enough here, Warren, and the logic makes sense. We need to head back; we have the autopsy, which I am not looking forward too."

Chapter 4

Warren and Judith walked over to the lab and they could see Astrid was fully concentrated on her screen. She did not notice them as he turned the music down on her speaker.

"Afternoon, that's my music, Warren."

"Have you got no headphones, Astrid? Your taste hasn't changed over the years. You still like your East German rock music."

"I am not a fan of sticking something in my ears. It helps me to concentrate when I'm summarising my initial findings and it deflects what I have just seen. Have you any plans for tonight, Warren? I'm cooking; I've whisky and beer, your choice. After spending the last few hours looking at a tortured, partially skinned, decaying corpse, I could do with some company."

Judith looked curiously at the both of them and had often wondered about their friendship.

"Okay, you're on. What time? I'll bring the wine and I'll take the last tram home."

"See, if you can find Portada red wine, I shared a bottle with a friend last week, I recommend it."

"Where did you buy it?"

"You are the detective, now you have another case to solve by 8.00 tonight, or whenever your team meeting finishes. I've a guest bed, if you want."

Warren deliberately deflected the question and the curious look from Judith.

"What have we got, Astrid? Does this corpse talk?"

"Oh, yes! It is amazing how much information you can obtain from a dead person, Judith. The question is how much of it is useful? Also, what is not of interest now but might be useful later for that unasked question at the start of the investigation."

The sound of the excitement in her voice surprised them both. It was as if she had received a surprise present.

"I can show you if you want, or we can review the pictures on the screen."

"I've seen the corpse once, so we know what to expect. Besides, photos do not convey the reality, plus the smell is still in my nose."

"I heard you threw up last night, Warren, no surprise. I hope the smell of food and wine tonight will numb the smell of death. It can linger for a long time. All the years in this job, it is the one thing I have never accepted, but tolerated, the pungent smell of decaying flesh. There is nothing worse than going on a date after a horrendous autopsy. How do you clarify to the good-looking guy opposite, that all you can smell is death? Turn off the music Warren, it is not your taste and let's go through. I'll send you the link in an email with the prelim report and photos, so you can share them later with the team."

Astrid took the corner of the white cover and pulled it back. The two mutilated bloated, purple and black halves lay before their eyes. The remnants of the body looked reminiscent of pieces of decayed meat laid out by a butcher. She noticed him stagger in shock and placed her hand on his shoulder, "Are you okay?"

He smiled back at his long-term friend. He could feel himself emotionally switch off, there was a job to do and his emotions had to be put to one side.

"Christ, the smell, gone are the days when you could smoke to hide the stench. I'm fine; I need that glass of wine now though. This may sound stupid, cause of death?"

"No such thing as a stupid question, it is just a lack of knowledge. Unknown, I doubt that we will find one specific cause. This guy was tortured whilst he was alive and was kept alive long enough for some of the wounds to heal. He suffered, Warren. Anyone of the procedures, which he underwent, could have killed him."

"Which wounds have healed?"

"Not fully healed, the areas, which were skinned, as you can see on the thighs have partially healed. The other areas, on his back, where he was skinned have not healed as much. This indicates a different period. This is number three; I am convinced now, that whoever is committing these crimes has medical knowledge. These marks around his ankles, your other victims had similar marks."

Although, Warren could clearly see the marks, Astrid felt the need to point as if he was a student in her classroom. This was her world, her science, so he played along with the role. It made him smile inside as he entered, yet again, the professional cold world of his friend.

"It's obvious he was restrained to something, possibly a chair. The marks are narrow and they have cut into the flesh around the front of the ankles, also around the wrists. Either he was restrained tightly or, from the constant movement they rubbed through his flesh."

"Maybe he struggled against his bindings, type?"

"Two types are indicated in the report."

He looked bemused at Astrid and looked for an answer.

"I thought that would surprise you. First, tie wraps would be my educated guess. The wounds here, around the ankle, are narrow and deep, he was bound tight. They are easy and functional to use and match the width, but without material evidence, it cannot be conclusive."

"I can accept that, it's not the first time criminals or the police have used tie wraps. Next?"

"You can see here on his wrists, there's a similar pattern, except these are deeper. It indicates his arms were possibly restrained tighter. The skin tissue underneath his wrists looks like it peeled off, not skinned like other parts of his body. It indicates, to me, he was restrained in the chair for several days. You look speechless."

"Good observation, you mentioned two types."

"Rope, polypropylene, favoured by boat users, Judith. We are in Berlin, but it is also used by other sports enthusiasts. I enlarged the restraint areas of the ankles and found a couple of threads in the wound. Since I cannot find secondary binding marks, I assume the rope was used shortly before or after his death, for whatever reason. I have only found threads on the ankles."

"I hope it wasn't when they severed the body; that would mean he may have been alive to the last moment."

"My same thought, Judith, why to restrain a dead person?"

"Can you cover the corpse, Astrid, to give him some respect, I cannot take much more. Can we switch the projector on?"

"No problem, Judith. Warren?"

"The same for me."

The projector only served to magnify the gruesome wounds and decaying flesh. Warren flinched, "Christ, I'm not sure what is worse; the magnified pictures or the reality?"

36

Astrid carried on.

"His head was also restrained. We can assume the restraint was made of an acid-resistant material, possibly plastic. The area underneath wasn't burnt."

"What do you mean burnt?"

"Let me finish, Warren. There are also marks on either side of his mouth, not clean-cut as you would expect with a knife. Possibly a thin wire? Perhaps with a gag in his mouth? That would stop him from screaming outwards, all the energy would go inwards."

"We have known each other for years, Astrid, how do you keep so clinical?"

"No option, you must switch off, Warren. What part of, interrupt, did you not understand?"

Astrid carried on; her voice was now ice-cold, a different person to whom he knew outside of work.

"There are no acid burns on the body, which in my opinion indicates his body was protected, the act was deliberately done to disfigure his face."

"Perhaps protected?"

Astrid took a deep breath at being interrupted once more.

"This is where it becomes sick and warped."

"It already is, Astrid, no wonder Doc was so shaken when he came out of the tent and provided us with the option not to view the torso last night."

Astrid ignored him and moved to the next slide, which showed an enlargement of the eyes. Warren fought the retching and struggled to hold it back.

"As you can see, sorry, Warren, I need a glass of water."

"We'll join you, Astrid."

All three stood in silence staring into the lab sink; their backs to the horrific projection on the wall, Astrid broke the ice.

"Whoever did this ensured his eyes were open at the time. Instinct is to close the eyes, throw a bucket of water in the face of someone and they will close their eyes."

"Whoever did this is off the scale."

"Agreed Warren, but there will always be psychopaths in the world. The burn disfigurement is fairly precise; look at the edge around the neck, the area was masked off, with something. Plus, there are no burn marks around the eyes and the eyes are not burnt out. The acid wasn't thrown in his face, I would say it was, this sounds the wrong word, but it's the only appropriate one that I can think of.

His face was painted with acid, his eyes pinned back to witness the act. The skin had started to heel and that indicates he was alive when it was done, the eyes were deliberately kept open during this act."

"How do you know that?"

"Each eyelid has two holes and also above the eyebrows. This is my professional judgement and is written in the report."

"Without showing us the rest of the details, Astrid, is there anything we can use?"

"There is, Judith; I will avoid the details of the pond-life found inside the body, which will need a more detailed analysis. What I am doing here is to provide a summary of the major findings. To sever a body in two would leave one hell of a blood splatter pattern and take a lot of effort. Try it, take a piece of meat and hack it in two, it is impossible to do in one go and it takes a lot of effort."

"Where are you going with this, Astrid?"

"The slit in his neck and the rope fibres around his ankles, Judith."

Astrid looked at Warren. She had just confirmed the link and the fact they now had a serial killer on their hands. Warren remained silent and walked over to look out of the window to collect his thoughts. Astrid carried on in the background.

"The blood was drained, same as the first victim. The rope marks around his ankles were tight enough to leave the threads, which I found. My judgement, he was strung up, his neck slit; the blood was drained out, then lowered and severed. No one deserves this type of ending."

"Depending on what he did, some people might say he deserved it. We have to look at history, what humans do against other humans, Astrid. Is it possible to confirm if he was alive when he was strung up?"

"If he was alive, the pressure from the heart and gravity would have left a hell of a splatter pattern when the jugular was sliced. My thoughts are he was killed before. I will skip the torture wounds and the partially skinned areas on the torso and thighs. They were healing and that indicates the victim was alive and in captivity for several weeks. When you look at his build, it would suggest he was a regular visitor to the fitness studio, or he kept fit at home."

"What about fingerprints?"

"The tips were removed with a corrosive substance, Judith, probably the acid, which they used on his face. His fingernails on his left hand are shorter than his right, probably he played a musical instrument, guitar? Try pressing the strings on the frets with long nails. Just a logical assumption, that makes him right-handed."

"Dental work, Astrid?"

"His teeth are in good condition, except for the three that were removed but like fingerprints, dental records need to be matched. The cut marks through the body were clean and sharp but several cuts were required to separate the torso. This would suggest it was done with something like a butcher cleaver. Look at the zoomed-up picture of the vertebrae, you can clearly see the cut marks of the blade, yet another fingerprint. Find me the knife, Warren, and it can be matched to the blade marks on the vertebrae. This is the first concrete mistake, which the attacker has made. If you can also find evidence of his skin at the scene, we can DNA match this body and hopefully, the last two. As for organic material, I've taken some samples from the intestines. I expect this to be nothing more than river bed material."

"When will you be able to have a digital reconstruction of his face? I want to trawl his picture around all the fitness centres. We need to build a profile of his life and see what the connections are to the other two corpses."

"We do not have the technology here and it will take a few days for a detailed reconstruction, Warren. It is also late Friday afternoon and the weekend is upon us."

"The problem here is? I assume they all have phones and are contactable."

"How do you tolerate him at times, Judith? He should have waited for me to finish and you should know me better. If there is a problem, I bring a solution to the table. I have already been in contact with colleagues. They will digitally scan the skull tomorrow and then recreate his face on the computer. They cannot guarantee a hundred percent likeness, but it will be close. Initial results will be tomorrow, Sunday latest."

Warren looked straight into Astrid's eyes.

"Thank you, I can read you like a book, we've known each other for a long time, what're you thinking, Astrid?"

"As I said, he made a mistake tonight cutting through the bone. Three teeth pulled out, the third victim. Two ways you can look at this, he got clumsy or he left you a clue and wants to start to play with you. With this corpse, he certainly hasn't achieved omne trium perfectum."

"The perfect set of three."

Warren looked at Judith who shrugged her shoulders.

"We learnt Latin at school; I've had to wait all these years to find a use for it."

Warren looked back at Astrid.

"Control and power and he is on a mission, two signatures of a psychopath. The question is? What is his mission and why target men? I've no doubt you will find other clues. The only commonality, which we have, is that all three bodies were recovered in East Berlin."

"Would you drive halfway across Berlin with a body in your car boot, Warren?"

"Judith suggested that the body may have been dumped from a boat. There're plenty of waterways in Berlin and it's not an unfeasible proposition. If every doctor, dentist, fitness centre and boat owner required must be visited, then so be it, Astrid. The team is big enough, but it will take time."

"That's quite a job you have now."

"Get me that digital recreation, Astrid and tonight, no talking about work, I need to clear my head and let all this information calm down. I've no doubt the subject will crop up, we're our worst own enemy. What's on the menu or is it a takeaway?"

"I'm cooking, it'll be nothing fancy, cooking is my way to de-stress, maintain my sanity and a work-life balance. Bring two bottles of red. The guest bed is still on offer, I have a spare toothbrush and razor if needed."

Judith looked at her pale-faced partner as they walked back to the office.

"Are you okay? You look washed out."

"Who wouldn't after those details that we have seen. Will you do one thing for me?"

Judith noticed the soften tone of his voice.

"You know I will."

"Arrange the availability of a psychologist for the team. What we are seeing and dealing with is off the radar of a normal investigation. The support structure needs to be put in place to help people, including us; we are not immune to these effects, Judith. I know this team; some will see it as a weakness. It has to come over to them as a positive approach to move the case forward. Some will reject, I have no place for macho alpha males or females. Anyone who is not interested is off the team, including us. One more item, let's move the meeting until eleven tomorrow morning. I do not want the team going home tonight, to their wives, boyfriends, girlfriends and children with those pictures fresh in their minds. I know it is a murder case but one night will not make any difference to this case. What will make a difference is if everyone has a good night's sleep and are fresh, tomorrow morning."

"Then don't drink too much wine tonight, Warren."

Chapter 5

Warren pressed the round stainless grey steel button on the bell board. Astrid's energetic voice came over the intercom.

"Evening, I hope you have brought more than one bottle of wine."

"Two bottles, red Portada as ordered."

"Perfect, you're allowed in now."

The door lock clicked open and he walked up to the second floor, Astrid was waiting for him at the door.

"It's a long time since we have spent time together."

"I'm looking forward to this night, it's a good idea. A small piece of normality in the crazy world we find ourselves in. Tonight is perfect timing, I'm getting grief from Judith for looking burnt out and I'm under orders not to drink too much wine."

"Judith is only watching out for her partner. You are right about tonight; it is a piece of normality."

"You look relaxed."

"These, they're my knock around the house clothes, white tee shirt and leggings. The glasses are in the cupboard over there."

"White's not the best colour to cook in, Astrid."

"I know, but it's a comfortable shirt."

Warren looked down at her duck slippers, which she was wearing and momentarily shook his head in amazement.

"What are you shaking your head at?"

"Your slippers?"

"They are a present from my sister, don't you criticise. There are spare house slippers over there for you, plain black."

"So, what's cooking tonight?"

"Barbeque spare ribs from Aldi. You're right; a white tee shirt is not the best to colour to wear. I'll change it. I threw my work clothes in the bin rather than try and wash away the smell of decaying death."

Astrid stripped and Warren watched her disappear into the bedroom.

"I don't hear the sound of glasses or a cork."

The sound of a cork being pulled out of the bottle rang around the kitchen as Astrid came in.

"That is one of the best sounds, which I love to hear, it means the start of a relaxing night."

"Or the start of a hangover, Astrid. That colour tee shirt is more suitable for spare ribs."

"No hangover, there's work tomorrow and someone will have more questions."

"Who's that?"

Astrid walked along the narrow kitchen, Warren stood in a corner to keep out of her way. She looked at him and slowly stroked the side of his face with her fingertips.

"A moody, grumpy, ageing, tired looking English detective; who seems to have lost his humour and needs time with an old friend to remember, there is a life outside the force."

"You're staring, Astrid."

"I noticed it yesterday, your sapphire blue eyes, once so full of warmth and life, look cold, dead. This case has got to you."

"Firstly, no work talk, it was promised, secondly, there's nothing better than the direct honesty of a Berlin woman."

"What's the point of not being able, to tell the truth to a close friend? Let's pour the first wine."

Astrid watched the red wine swirl around the glass and waited until Warren had filled both glasses.

"That's the first bottle nearly empty, Astrid, they should make smaller glasses."

"Err, no, it saves having to top the glass up a second time. Prost."

"Prost Astrid, to old times. You do know we will end up talking about work at some time tonight."

"Yip, but at least it's in a relaxed atmosphere, away from the chaos of work."

"Let's keep the discussion as short as possible, Astrid."

"Okay, I have no problem with that, but I do have a problem that the table is not set, knives and forks are in the draw over there. When you're finished can you prepare the salad?"

Warren set the table along with another bottle of wine and crossed over to the window to look out across the garden.

"The garden hasn't changed much, from what I remember."

"I bet you still remember the first time you came here, Gabi brought you around, she was your contact in the East and I was her support. We were pleased when the wall came down; we had no desire to be arrested by the Stasi. It was a risk though that we were both willing to take. At that point in time, I never thought we would both end up working for the police."

"Long time ago, Astrid, have you heard from her?"

"No, not since she managed to help you put Andre in jail. We know her; she has put that part of her life behind, justice for the death of her father. It was the last thread that kept her bonded to Berlin. She has probably started a new life, Warren."

"Possible, maybe she will surface."

"You trusted her with your life."

"And you, that sort of deep relationship you get with friends is rare but time moves on and relationships change."

They both looked at each other and a moment of silence fell as they reflected on their past relationship.

"Salad, Warren, it's not much longer before the meat is ready."

He picked up the knife, which sliced easily through the cucumber. Astrid noticed him look at the knife.

"What's up?"

"I'm wondering just how easy, or hard it is to slice a body in half. Sorry?"

"No need, it's not as easy as you think. Have you ever watched a butcher with his meat cleaver? There are also the vertebrae to breakthrough. If you want, I can rig a simulation if you want to get a feel?"

"I'll pass on that one but I'll bear it in mind, if I want to understand the force used, or any blood spatter patterns."

The oven beeped to signal the ribs were ready and broke the conversation.

"Two options, you can sit and I'll serve or you can help?"

"Why ask the question when there is only one answer Astrid. They smell damn good."

"Go and top the glasses up, I'll bring the food in."

Warren's mind wandered as the murder case ran through his mind, he didn't notice Astrid as she brought the food in.

"You look miles away."

"Thinking about the case, Astrid."

"Okay, here's the deal. You are my guest tonight, my rules. Whilst we polish the ribs off and drink the first bottle, we can talk about the case. Once we start the second bottle there is to be no work talk, two bottles will cloud our judgement. It is healthy to switch off from work."

"I'm not sure if alcohol is the best way to switch off. What do you think, Astrid?"

"It will stop, it's a case of time, several reasons: he may die, burn out, kill himself, is caught or leaves the area. The only problem with burning out and leaving the area is that he may start again."

"Only one option for me, we catch him. I want that bastard behind bars somewhere secure. What the hell flips a person to do this?"

"What do you mean, Warren?"

"Whoever has done this probably holds down a full-time job, he's your next-door neighbour, a guy you go for a drink with to the pub, probably loves his dog and has a boring hobby to de-stress. Yet somewhere, the wiring has burnt out via a short circuit and provided him with a distorted view of what is right in the world. Killing people, I can understand the reasons, in the right circumstances, I've been there, and it still affects me to this day. This is a whole new level for me and the team."

"Warren, look at me, listen to your voice, take care, this is getting to you, you need to keep some distance and remember that you're not just a detective but also a person, a human being with limits. This case has got to us all, but we have to give our soul a distance. It's a long time since you mentioned the death of that soldier; it was self-defence, a different time, different politics. I still remember that time when you needed my help. I know now why you said yes tonight, you needed a confidant to open up and you knew I needed a close friend."

"Not a confidant, a close friend, Astrid. We've known each other for a long time, even before I joined the police after the wall came down. We trust each other."

"This guy is smart, intelligent and educated, Warren and he will push us to limits, which we didn't know we had. To do what he does and keep the person alive, requires knowledge of drugs and medical training. The longer he remains free, the more his confidence will grow and with that, he will take more risks. He has already made his first few mistakes, albeit maybe planned, with the last victim. The cuts in the spine, that is like leaving a fingerprint, the last two bodies; he never cut a bone. The procedures, which he used, require medical knowledge, second mistake, there will be others. We will find out who this guy is and a connection to the last two murders. You've gone silent."

"I know I've never worked on a case this big before with so must focal attention. I've dealt with other murder cases where you can almost understand the reasons but this…even the size of the team is a new scale for me, Astrid."

"How's Judith coping?"

"A lot better than me, she has a stronger personality, or she's better at suppressing things."

"Trained in the GDR, not like you guys from The West."

"You're biased."

"Got it in one. Keep an eye on her; we all have our limits, even ex GDR detectives who had to deal with the Stasi and KGB. More wine? The guest bed is still an offer and this is now the start of the second bottle and work has now finished."

"The last regular tram leaves in two hours, we have enough time."

The morning sun streamed through Astrid's bedroom window as she got up to go to the toilet. The door to her guest room was ajar and she looked at the undisturbed bed. She cursed briefly inside, 'Damn the wine, his blue eyes and sense of humour.' Astrid smiled inwardly at the night of passion as she continued along the hallway.

Chapter 6

Judith looked at Warren and shook her head as he plodded into the office and mumbled good morning.

"What language was that; I'll take German, English or Russian? Get some caffeine inside you and then try good morning again. Or how about, good morning Judith, how was your night and then I'll ask you, how was yours? Out on the tiles last night? As you say in England. You have black circles around your eyes and looks as if you were up most of the night. How many bottles disappeared?"

Warren looked at her and knew he would dig a hole for himself if he retaliated. He placed the cup on the corner of his desk and sat down in front of his computer. He stared over the top of his computer directly at her and wondered if she knew anything, or was she probing. He knew that smile and look as she stared back waiting for a reply.

"Sorry Judith, good morning."

"Here are some paracetamols for your head."

"Okay, how was your night last night, Judith?"

"I went with my new girlfriend to the Waldbühne; there was a Schlager band playing."

"You're in a new relationship, brilliant, I'm happy for you. Did you get a second date after taking her there?"

"I see that you have still no German culture, even after all these years in Germany."

"I can live with that. On a more serious note, I'm happy for you, hope it works out. What's her name?"

"Sarah, you know what she called."

"This is what, your third girlfriend in how many months?"

"The second and last one didn't work out because she had to leave the city for work."

"Escaped would have been a more apt description," Warren ducked as a crumpled paper ball flew over the top of his screen.

"So, where did you stay last night? I saw you walking in with Astrid this morning, when I drove along the street."

He knew that she had him. He hated it, but he loved her feminine curiosity, how she could drive the truth out of him with one question. His first instinct was right; she was probing; now he was pinned in a corner by a skilled interrogator.

"I've known Astrid for a long time, Judith, we cooked last night. I stopped over at her flat last night after sharing two bottles of wine."

"Guest bed, I hope."

"Where else do you think, Judith, or are you just after station gossip."

"No, but you should both change your body language when you walk together."

"Here's your paper ball back. Sometimes, I hate your feminine curiosity, have you got nothing to do? Sharpen a pencil, investigate a murder or something?"

"Yes, we both do, open your email, there's an initial picture of the deceased's face. The team worked through the night to send a first impression. They still need to complete their refinements, but it gives us the first image and in time for the team debrief."

"I thought we would not have received that for a few more days. What is your first impression, Judith?"

"He wouldn't turn my head in a club. In fact…he's not what I would class as a man. He looks like the type who would be more interested in himself than his partner, but some women go for that, I never understand why? When we see a person who we like, our sub-conscious has decided that within less than a second. This guy, for me, indicates distance, not the sort of man I would take home to meet my parents."

"He doesn't creep me but he… I don't know he doesn't look like the type to give empathy. It's a digital recreation so there is not a lot of emotion in the picture. At least, it will be good enough as an initial picture for the meeting. We'll wait for the refinements before sending the team out. When will they arrive, Judith?"

"Max two days."

"For me, that is today and tomorrow, no doubt they will send it last thing tomorrow. Get in touch with the lab, Judith; I want that completed picture so we can get it out to the team, tomorrow afternoon at the latest. We can then start to tick off the fitness centres one by one. When we have found a name, then we follow it up with the doctors and also dentists. Slowly, we will build a profile of his life and find a commonality between the three victims. This murderer is on a mission and we need to understand what it is."

"What time's the team meeting?"

"Go for eleven and put a short meeting in the calendar for tomorrow afternoon to distribute the picture. Are you happy to lead the meeting?"

"No problem for me, Warren. Any particular reason why?"

"Simple, that group have never had a female lead before. I am after a close-knit team and I want to watch and observe their response. There is one interesting ageing character forced on me. To be polite, his attitude to diversity and respect for women requires recalibration. He is a bad influence on younger members of the team who are generally more accepting. If he does not tow the rope in the meeting; you can decide to do with him what you like. I'll support your decision to the seniors, even if you decide to keep him."

"Are you using me as a stooge?"

"No. If I was, I would be ordering you to do it and using you as a reason to get him off the team. I am asking you, the decision is yours. I'll lead the meeting if you wish."

"I know who you are talking about; there are a few female officers who have had enough of him."

"Here's their chance to put him down. He will be side-lined after this, as a dinosaur who didn't adapt."

"Okay, you're on, Warren. I'll lead, with one proviso, I'll lead other meetings and we share that workload."

"Deal, I've no problem with that."

The only room left for the meeting was the white-walled room with plain cloth chairs and tan brown Formica tables. It was still on the list to be renovated; Judith looked around and felt transported back to her GDR days. They both stood at the front and faced the team who were wondering and nervous of about what was to come.

"Are you ready?"

Judith nodded her acknowledgement to Warren, the team looked bemused as he moved and stood to one side.

"To date, we've had three murders over the last two years, each one progressively more brutal than the last."

Judith pointed to the pictures of the three victims on the screen.

"Due to the commonality between them, we are treating these now as serial murder. Each corpse was found in a particular quadrant of Berlin and each corpse has restrain marks. Why men? The reason is still unknown, but we have a serial killer of men on the loose. The murderer's mission is also unknown. A male serial murderer is not common but not unheard of and we know he's becoming braver and more brutal. The first two bodies were discovered in a remote location, this one, as some of you know was found in the middle of the city. Half of the corpse was found in the river near the Bode Museum, the other half at Mühlendamm locks. It's almost as if he is starting to taunt the police and placing the body for maximum effect. I'm going to spare you the pain of sitting through all the details and enlargements on the screen. When you return to your desks, you will all have a link to the prelim report and historical data on the other cases. I want each one of you to read the files, on all three cases and look at the photos, this way we are all on the same hymn sheet. Communication is the key; some of you are new to the team, if you see anything, read anything that raises a question discuss it with your colleagues. Disseminate, question and discuss as much information as possible, there will another meeting tomorrow."

Judith perused the silent audience and the generation divide.

"Before I move on to the third victim, there is one additional item I am raising, this applies to all members; coping mechanisms. Some of the younger members in this room may believe you are immune. The same applies to, let us say, the more experienced colleagues who have developed individual mechanisms. Either way, we're all vulnerable; we all have our limits and a combination of work, stress, coupled with personal stress outside of work can take you down. You're no good if you burn out; it is not fair on the victim, your relationships and your team members. Each of you will receive an email with the contact details of a psychologist. Please, if needed, use this person, do not be a hero. If you have any doubt, use this professional service. It's not a sign of weakness; it's a sign of strength. Before we move on, just to warn you, the pictures you will see of our third victim are gruesome."

Judith indexed the first picture, the acid burnt face appeared on the screen and silence fell around the room.

"As you can see, his head was restrained and you can see the marks on the edges of the mouth. According to Astrid, the acid was carefully, possibly brushed onto his face. There are no burn marks on the upper torso or shoulders. Also, there are no burn marks around the eyes, even though his eyes were pinned back, thus ensuring he saw everything. The facial skin had started to partially heal, which indicates…he was alive after this event. Since it had only partially healed, we can assume death followed within a short timeframe."

Judith clicked the button and the next slide showed enlarged pictures of the restrained areas around the ankles and wrists.

"The wrists and ankles look like they were bound with tie wraps. In addition, there are secondary marks on the ankles where rope fibre was found."

"Why two bonding marks, Judith?"

"It's an obvious question, Karl, with a sickening twist. You are all aware that the body was hacked in two."

Warren looked scanned the room, never before had there been such silence. It was as if the team was waiting for a climactic ending or unable to absorb the macabre details. Judith scrolled down to the next picture.

"As you can see, there is a slit in his neck. The assumption is, he was hung upside down and the blood drained from his body. We do have a fingerprint and can be seen from this slide. The cut marks on the vertebrae can be matched to the implement, find the implement. You are all very quiet or in shock. Karl?"

"I think we are all trying to comprehend the grisly details and the fact a human being has carried out this hideous act, Judith."

"The next slide will show how we believe the victim looked. It is an initial composition; the detailed picture will arrive tomorrow."

Judith clicked the mouse and the recreated picture of the victim's face appeared on the wall.

A question was fired in the direction of Warren, ignoring Judith.

"How realistic is the picture and how do we come into the equation? What is your plan to split the team, section areas and correlate the information into a central database, etc?"

"Ask Judith, Kurt. I'm a bystander in this meeting, Judith's leading it."

"That's easy, Kurt, first, the hairstyle is an artist's impression based on the latest fashions. He was healthy, non-smoker, good muscle tone, which indicates he possibly visited a gym. The rest I am told is as realistic as the software allows, we will receive that more refined picture tomorrow. Future questions, please direct to me."

"So he lived a healthy life and died a horrendous death. His fitness and health didn't do him much good then. Did it?"

Judith looked at the ageing detective who had never managed to move with the times. Silence fell around the room and Judith looked at Warren who shrugged his shoulders, raised his eyebrows as much to say; it's your meeting to control. Judith looked at the team and maintained the silence to control the room, and then spoke in a calm voice.

"All, let's get this straight; it's my meeting, our investigation. The victim somewhere has a family, we all have families, and perhaps he had children, girlfriend, boyfriend, wife or husband."

"We all have different tastes, don't we?"

"You are perfectly correct, Kurt. The world is a colourful place and no more so than Berlin. When I have to communicate with people who overstep their professional boundary and show no dignity or respect to others, I'm pleased that I have a girlfriend. I do not tolerate your derisive remark towards the victim in my meeting, even if you class it as a deflective, off the cuff remark to release tension. Your statement overstepped the boundaries of respect and dignity, Kurt. You're not welcome in my meeting, leave the room, you're off the team. If you want to discuss this later, you know where my office is. I've a meeting to conduct."

"Only Warren has the authority to remove a member of the team, not you."

Kurt looked silently across to Warren for support; his silence was short-lived.

"Judith's meeting, Kurt; her rules, her decision, she has already stated, we work as a team. You have shown yourself not to be a team player."

He had not expected such a rebuke for an off the cuff remark and lack of support from a male colleague. Without even looking at the rest of the team, Kurt stormed out of the room. He knew his career was over. Judith carried on the meeting.

"The autopsy indicated no previous illnesses, except for his appendix, which was removed, when? We have no idea. Dental indicates two fillings, one root canal work and a crown. Apart from that, he had healthy teeth, except for the three, which were extracted; perhaps it is a sign to mark the corpse as a third victim? We need to put a name to this person, find his history and find a link to the other victims. This we will achieve. To date, no one in the area has reported a new missing person. This is where your lot come in; the photo, get out there and visit every fitness centre in Berlin and especially this quadrant. Karl, you can lead up the teams. Since the bodies were found in this area of Berlin, this is where we will start first and work outwards towards the perimeter. Whoever did this will probably kill again and up the stakes."

Judith paused and looked around the room, there was shocked silence.

"Never before have I had so few questions."

Marleen, a younger member of the team who was sitting at the back quietly, spoke up.

"How long was the body in the water? It would take longer for the two halves to surface than one corpse. It's also temperature dependant."

"It's estimated the body was put in the water, two to three weeks ago. It's not known how long our victim suffered, I've gone back two months, and the missing persons' list requires to be followed up by the team."

"What type of person are we looking for?"

"That person could be your best friend. Elaborate your question; I can almost see your brain thinking."

"You mentioned he was kept alive. Someone would need medical knowledge?"

Judith caught Warren looking at Marleen, who was unaware he was watching her.

"We have no evidence of that, but it is under consideration, let the facts develop the case and bear that in mind. The person may have the knowledge, but it does not mean he is medically qualified."

"Sorry for not clarifying the question more specific."

"Understood, not a problem, Marleen. All of you remember, there is no such thing as a stupid question. Read the information, digest it, talk among yourselves and question each other. Communication, as I said before is the key. Okay, you have a job to do, go back to your desks and read the files. Also, do not forget the offer of the Psychologist. Karl, provide me and Warren, your plan to visit all the fitness centres by midday tomorrow. Meeting ended."

Warren waited until the room was empty and looked across at Judith.

"What are you smirking at?"

"First time someone has knocked that chip off his shoulder and he deserved it, he was bang out of order. Someone with his experience should have known better, but he has never adapted with a change in attitudes and modern-day policing."

"Knock what off his shoulder?"

"Sorry, English expression of when you put someone down who deserves it and he did. We don't need such self-centred arseholes on this investigation. It's being a long time coming for him, a dinosaur that never moved with the times. You have the respect of the team for booting him unceremoniously out of the room, Judith. Such an attitude is not tolerated by the younger generation and a few of them will be pleased to see him go."

"I've no doubt he will complain, Warren, and with his experience, he probably has a few contacts."

"He will, and had, Judith, I was asked to take him on my team, no one else wanted to work with him. I reluctantly agreed because I owed someone a favour. He will be side-lined now; his days of involvement with major cases are over for him. Catch up with Karl, Judith, and his plan to visit the fitness centres. Also, Marleen, watch her, she is keen and has a lateral thinking approach. Her autism has advantages and she's a useful member to the team. She has an eye for detail and also analysing information. She may not be able to communicate questions accurately or explain situations very clearly, but she came highly recommended. If you have any detailed analysis you want doing, give it to her and leave her alone, when she's finished it will land on your desk. Don't wait for her to explain, that will not happen, invite her to your forum and ask her to show you. She has a routine, Judith; she is the only one on the team that can refuse overtime. I need to expand the diversity of the team, it's come from the top down and it's a good thing. That dino, Kurt, had to go. He showed himself up today for what he is, non-accepting of change. The younger, more diverse generations are coming through and we need to work with them. Speaking of dinos, I've got a bloody report to write for the seniors and also a damn budget review."

Chapter 7

Stefan looked at his wife checking her red cotton summer dress in the mirror. He could tell from her facial expression that she was not happy.

"What are you thinking, Anja? You're checking your outfit, but you are miles away."

"Vincenzo, he's coming, he's a complete shithole and a wanker. Filippo, will not change his mind, I spoke to my sister. If he's not careful, Filippo will pay a price for that relationship. Melanie has him already on a short lead."

"What's she planning?"

"She will leave him if he pushes it any further. Melanie is starting to feel a lack of support from him as her husband, especially the way Vincenzo behaves and disrespects my sister. I don't like to see my sister upset by an overbearing, testosterone-filled wanker of the male species."

"So, you do not like him as well."

"Got it in one, how's my lipstick? I bought it to match the dress, but I am not too sure."

"It's fine. Well, with you and your sister at the party, I hope he behaves himself. I would hate to come between you two."

"I simply do not like men who demonstrate hostility, mistrust towards women and their entrenched prejudices. And neither does my sister."

Anja ran her hands over the side of her dress to smooth out the creases. Stefan looked as she admired her figure in the mirror. Anja turned around and faced her husband for the compliment.

"Still not a bad figure for someone in their mid-forties?"

"That's the best compliment you can think of. What shoes?"

"Sandals, Anja."

"You answered too quickly."

"I know, it does not matter what I say, you will try on three pair before we leave."

"Can you get the meat out of the fridge while I sort out my shoes? It's a shame that we could not spit roast Vincenzo on the BBQ instead."

Stefan looked at his wife; he knew that she was not joking. For the first time, he began to think where her limit was and where was his limit with her. For a moment he felt a sense of insecurity in their relationship.

Vincenzo, one metre ninety tall and full of narcissist confidence, stood upright before the panelled oak front door to Melanie and Filippo's house. His mobile beeped the sound of a text message and without respect for his host's property flicked his cigarette onto the porch and stamped it out as he read the message. He knew if he could keep the communication going with his ex-girlfriend that she would come back, she and the other one had before.

The door opened and Melanie stood before a tanned Vincenzo with threaded eyebrows and a goatee beard. She thought about how to kill her husband after the party for inviting the self-absorbed slime-ball.

"Vincenzo, not so good to see you, it's been a while, unfortunately, not long enough and you have just put my husband's life at risk. However, Filippo will be pleased to see you. Sometimes, I will never understand him, even after all our years of marriage."

She noticed him look at her cleavage as he spoke.

"Sorry, I'm late, I'm sure you do things that Filippo does not understand and he accepts you for what you are."

"You can look me in the face if you want? My tits don't have a mouth."

"If you do not want them looked at then don't put them on show."

"You've never had much respect for woman, in fact, none. You are alone, I thought you would have brought your girlfriend, or did she manage to have a lucky escape."

"We separated last week; she wanted to go on holiday with a couple of girlfriends, her loss. It's not the first time, she'll come back; they always do."

Apart from wanting to kick Vincenzo in the balls with her stilettos, Melanie wondered how she could bring her husband back to life so she could kill him a second time. More than once, she had asked Filippo to break the relationship but their business history had bonded them together. She had warned him that if Vincenzo started trouble tonight, he would pay a heavy price and the threshold had been crossed.

"Come in, you know where the beer is, grab yourself one. The BBQ is around the back; go straight though, you might find someone to talk to who does not know you."

"Where's Filippo?"

"I have no idea."

"Bratwurst and a beer, it sounds good to me, Melanie. It's always a pleasure."

Melanie entered the sitting room; Filippo was busy selecting a bottle of whisky from his mahogany, glass front cabinet. He knew from the stern look on her face and the clomping of her heels over the wooden floor that he was in trouble.

"That creep of a wanker has just arrived, alone. I'll be in the garden, Filippo, talking to my sister, just so you know where I am when you want to talk, I asked you to un-invite him. When you have found a good reason why he is here, you know where I am."

Melanie did not even wait for a reply and strode out of the room leaving her husband with a sinking feeling in his stomach. Conflict was not his way and he hated tension in the house, especially with Melanie and he tried to avoid it when possible. The last thing he wanted today was to be caught between both sisters. He knew he was in trouble for inviting Vincenzo, one sister he could cope with; he had married her, the both of them together, especially Anja, who took no bull from any man. He suddenly found himself between a rock and a hard place, if he did not go to the garden, the two would hunt him out, like a pack of Hyenas. He hoped his wife might calm down after a couple of drinks with her sister; he knew inside it was only hope and the reality would land in front of him. He had crossed the line with his wife and the long-term friendship with Vincenzo must end. Melanie saw Vincenzo boring her sister and Stefan; she had to admit, he carried himself well. Despite that, she never liked men who all always took longer to get ready than a woman. The balance for her was simply wrong, he was too well-groomed and his attitude to women stunk. Filippo had mentioned more than once that the police had been called to his flat, only for no charges to be brought against him for violence to his partner. She totally blanked Vincenzo when she walked over and stood with her back to him.

"Heh, big sister, I see you've got stuck with wanker of the year. Let's walk; the two boys can talk, men talk. Well, one of them can, the other one will just talk about how good he is."

Stefan was suddenly left alone staring at Vincenzo after having his wife kidnapped by her sister.

"That's just damn bad manners by those two to disappear like that; they have no respect for men."

"I'm sorry, what do you mean by, those two?"

"Your wife and her sister, she has a nice cleavage though, also not a bad arse."

"Those two as you put it, have a name and one is my wife. You're also a guest of Filippo and you want to discuss his wife's cleavage and arse. Tell you what Vincenzo, I'm off to get another beer and bratwurst, you're an arsehole. I can have a more intelligent conversation with the bottle opener. You really think people are there to be used for your pleasure."

Vincenzo shrugged his shoulders as Stefan went to the BBQ to collect his bratwurst and beer. Vincenzo looked around to see who he could engage in conversation with. He saw Christian and Maria by the edge of the swimming pool and headed off in their direction.

"Melanie, why do you allow that low life in your house?"

"I don't, it's Filippo, Anja; they grew up together in the same part of Italy. They went to the same school and looked out for each other like brothers, especially when they started their import, export companies. He even supported Vincenzo when he was charged with tax evasion, Filippo had no choice the companies were interlinked. That is the downside of our marriage but why should I let Vincenzo destroy something that myself and Filippo have built up."

"You never mentioned the tax investigation."

"We all have our secrets, big sister, even you will have some."

"Some secrets are best not known, Melanie."

"He has a reputation of violence towards women, Anja. When I opened the door today, he told me how his girlfriend had dumped him, but she would come running back. He is so cocksure of himself. I could kill Vincenzo and Filippo; he's on a final warning tonight. The police were at Vincenzo's house a few weeks ago but his girlfriend wouldn't press charges. He even stared at my tits when he started to tell the story. I feel sorry for her; unfortunately, some women go back, for whatever reason."

"The reasons are complicated, believe me, Melanie. I know what I hear at the centre."

"You are still doing the volunteer work?"

"Still doing it, I was there last night, how much longer I carry on is the question. Sorry, I interrupted you."

"At the end of the day, Anja, I see him for a very short period in my life and one day, he will do the world a favour and die and I hope it's painful."

"True, Melanie, and hopefully, the quicker the better. If he looks at your tits again, he'll be on the floor and you know that I'm capable of doing that."

"I'll stand on him and screw my stiletto into his balls."

"Speaking of heels, where did you get those leopard skin heels from? They're gorgeous and sexy."

"Online, I'll send you the link, sister. Here, you can try them…what the hell is the noise over there?"

Anja and Melanie left the patio and went around the side of the house. They could see Vincenzo lying on the ground, the drinks table knocked over and glasses floating in the swimming pool. Two female guests were holding Maria back and Christian stood in front of his wife trying to calm her down.

"Now's the chance to screw my heel into his balls, Anja. I didn't think the opportunity would come so quick. I'll bet you a free night out that Vincenzo did not realise that Maria is ex-police and she does boxing as a hobby. He's really pissed her off."

Vincenzo, in shock, clambered to his feet, pulled a handkerchief out of his pocket to wipe the blood from his head and nose.

"Leave it, Melanie, look, Filippo is on his way, stay here and let them sort it out."

"If he doesn't, he's in deeper trouble with me later and he knows he has already stepped over the limit."

"What's happened, Christian, Maria?"

"That arsehole touched my wife; he put his arm around Maria's waist assuming he could do that."

"I can speak for myself, Christian. That guy is a creep, Filippo; he should not be let loose where women are. We were all talking and he came within my personal space and put his arm firmly around my waist, without my permission. Why some men think they can touch women and think that we must swoon to their attention leaves me speechless. He deserved what he got and should realise that not all women are weak and vulnerable. Somehow, he's too stupid to learn a lesson."

Vincenzo carried on wiping the blood.

"Fuck you, bitch."

"You have proved my point, too stupid to learn, you really are ignorant and ill-mannered. Do you want me to put you on your back again, your choice?"

"Christian, Maria, I apologise, for his behaviour. The fact I invited him makes me partially responsible for what has happened. The reason why I apologise for him is because his ego and lack of respect will not. In his eyes, he has done no wrong. I should have adhered to the guidance of my wife."

Melanie and Anja looked at each other.

"I told you he was on a final warning; I'm going to savour and milk this moment for now and for later. The fact his voice is calm means Filippo is as mad as hell." Melanie joined her husband's side for the moment of glory, placed her hand on his shoulder and smirked at Vincenzo.

"I hope you both accept my apology. Maria, you are right, he is an arsehole and I made a bad judgement by inviting him today."

Filippo turned and stared Vincenzo straight in the eyes.

"You have disgraced this house and my guests. For a long time, because of our history, I've tolerated you and your attitude to women. You simply cannot insult our guests, in our home. It was uncalled for to put your arm around her waist. You have overstepped the boundaries of respect for me, my wife, our guests and respect for women. Please leave our house."

Vincenzo, broader than Filippo squared up to him, stared straight into his eyes and pointed at Maria.

"She attacked me and you throw me out?"

"Very observant, it looks like you are not as stupid as Maria thought. I and my wife own this house and I've requested you to leave and you're still here. Which part of leave did you not understand Vincenzo and not through the house. Leave now, because if you don't, I'm sure there are enough women here to escort you out. This long-term friendship is over."

Melanie could not resist blowing Vincenzo a kiss as he started to walk.

"Bye, Vincenzo."

Melanie spun around and headed back over to her sister.

"That's been a long time coming, Anja."

"What do you mean, Melanie?"

"Filippo was simply warned. I've tolerated a lot over the years with that wanker, as you get older, your values change. I told him if Vincenzo upsets anyone today and he did not eject him, as well as breaking off the so-called friendship, he would be minus a wife."

"Nice to see, you finally have your husband under control. It took a while."

"I need to spend time alone with him later, Anja. He will be upset, today he has brought a long-term friendship to an end and that will hurt him. What the hell was that noise from the front? It sounds like glass breaking."

Both sisters opened the front door in time to see him kicking a wing mirror off Filippo's BMW. The rear window was also smashed. Vincenzo stood and looked at the two women and walked the length of the car whilst keying the doors.

"Fuck you two bitches."

"That's it."

Anja grabbed her sister and prevented her from storming over to Vincenzo.

"Leave it; he's looking for an excuse to hit you. Its paint and a mirror, you both have more than enough money for the repair. Don't worry, life will catch up with him and teach him a lesson, which he will regret and forget."

Filippo arrived at the front of the house in time to see Vincenzo finishing keying his car and stood in front of his house. Vincenzo looked at him waiting for his revenge. Filippo stared in silence at him, not reacting to the verbal abuse. He turned around and walked up the steps of his house and closed the door.

"It's a car, Melanie, it's fixable and insured. I am not going to give him a reason to carry on this argument. If we did, he would stop in our lives for longer. In fact, I will not even phone the police, if I do that, it will allow him to have further contact. I'll just pay for the repair so he is out of our life as quickly as possible. We control this situation, not him."

Melanie knew that look in her husband's eyes and the soft tone of his voice. Despite what had happened Filippo had remained calm. She knew he was right and the car would be easily fixed and it was the better option. Filippo turned to Anja and despite living in Berlin for over thirty years he still spoke German with an Italian accent.

"Most of the guests will stay a while longer, out of respect and then slowly drift off. Stop as long as you like Anja, you know where the key is for the wine cupboard."

Anja stood next to her smaller sister and smiled.

"I already have one, Filippo, Melanie had one cut, just in case you lost one, for emergencies only, you understand."

61

Filippo looked at the sisters standing before him, shrugged his shoulders, raised his hands, muttered something about two sisters that were too much to handle and headed off to the garden.

"It would be a brave man to stand between us, Anja."

"I'll catch you later sister, we will head off home. We have had enough excitement for one day. Filippo will also need some support from you and probably one of his whiskies. I'll come around sometime later next week for wine; it's a while since we have spent some time together."

"Bring your swimming costume; this weather will not last all year, Anja."

"Look after Filippo, sister, he's a good man and loves you. I'll see you later, I'm off to find my other half now and tell him he is ready for home."

Chapter 8

The Berlin blood red, evening sun was setting as Anja and Stefan drove home in the direction of Erkner, silence filled the car. She looked at her husband who was deep in thought and she knew he was mulling over what had happened. The events of the day had only firmed her opinion of Vincenzo. Stefan pulled the sunblind down to reduce the glare from the sun.

"We've been driving for ten minutes and you've said nothing, total silence, that's not like you to be so quiet after a party. What's wrong?"

"I am enjoying the sunset and trying to switch Vincenzo out of my mind. Look how red it is, it looks like Berlin is on fire. The power of nature can be so humbling at times. We forget that we are just beings, part of this nature. We feel sometimes the civilisation, which we have created is above nature, it can isolate people into a false sense of security. Then you see such a magnificence view and it reminds me that we are a small part of the equation and Mother Nature is more powerful and controlling. It can be kind, gentle, caring and then teach you a hard lesson. Nothing can exist without the other, all events are interlinked."

"It's called Biophilia; I did a course once at the hospital on how people recover more quickly when exposed to nature. It's too deep a subject for tonight and with such a beautiful view. The sunsets are spectacular here. Do you remember when we went to the Drachenberg? We took a picnic, a bottle of wine and a blanket to watch the sunset. It must have been one of our most sobering moments, the quiet power of nature."

"We weren't the only ones there; it was after two in the morning when we left."

"So, what are you really thinking, Stefan? I can hear your brain ticking. We've been together that long now that we can read each other like a book. You're thinking about the events of today."

"Vincenzo, he is a complete low life, Anja. Not only has he no respect for women but he also insulted your sister and her husband. How the hell someone in life grows up with such a super overbearing, macho, testosterone-filled attitude, I'll never understand. He's the sort of guy who gets men a bad name. I'm pleased Filippo threw him out; he was very calm and diplomatic in how he handled the situation."

"It was that or Melanie would have thrown Filippo out."

"It was impressive when Maria thumped him and put him on his back. I only saw it from a distance. I'm not sure who was in more shock, Vincenzo or the people watching. It certainly would have dinted his macho pride being belittled by a woman."

"Some women are capable of handling themselves; he should have asked her what she did for a profession and a hobby before he started to fondle her waist. He would have had second thoughts if he realised she was an ex-policewoman, boxing was her hobby and she used to do riot training. Filippo will avoid conflict whenever possible. He had no option; evict Vincenzo or conflict with Melanie. She had virtually threatened him with divorce if Vincenzo stepped out of line and he did not react. Melanie had enough from that slime ball over the years. The snide comments, the way he would look at her, accidently brush past her. No woman should be made to feel that uncomfortable, not only in her own house but anywhere. If Filippo had not thrown him out, I think some of the other men or women would have done it."

"It takes a lot to push your placid sister into a corner."

"What do you mean?"

"Threatening, Filippo with divorce."

"There've been a few people over the years, Stefan, including me, who have suffered thinking that my sister is an easy pushover. They mistake her compassionate kind-hearted side as a weakness. Passive-aggressive, but it takes a lot of pushing to get her to the aggressive side. I certainly would not like to be the defence lawyer in court going up against her."

"At least, Filippo did the honourable thing and flung him out, Anja. I overheard Vincenzo talking earlier that he has resigned from his job. He was bragging that he's going into early retirement."

"He's only in his mid-forties?"

"If you remember, Anja, his parents died and left him quite a lot of money, plus with his banking background, he made money also on investments. He was making his mouth go that he was going to travel the world and he needs to plan his journey."

"No doubt it will be: Asia, Vietnam, India or China, it seems to be in fashion. Hopefully, he meets a hungry python on his journey and it crushes every last breath of air from him."

"Hopefully, the snake would have better taste, but it's a good idea, Anja."

Anja looked in silence at the tree-lined road. He could read her thoughts. Every time there was a problem with her sister she would reflect on her mother. Since she died, there was no mother to turn to for guidance. He knew it was best to leave her deep in thought for a few minutes. Stefan broke the ice as they drove through Köpenick.

"So, what are your thoughts, Anja?"

"Mine, the same as yours, but I'm uncomfortable with the idea, Vincenzo is too close to family. It would have to be by chance communication, no telephone calls, nothing that can be traced. An accidental meeting, we know where he lives, so maybe you, I might just...let's say bump into him and then invite him over for a meal and a threesome."

"It will be on a single journey ticket. Afterwards, we can remove his suitcases, flight tickets; it all has to be timing, the same day that you bump into him. If it's too early, then he will probably put dates into his phone, something on social media. It has to be spontaneous. The timing would have to be perfect and if it isn't, then we will have to pass on the opportunity. When he is leaving?"

"That, Stefan, I can find out via my sister next week. Vincenzo has probably bragged to Filippo or Melanie and she tells me nearly everything. Let's change the subject; sickos like Vincenzo take up too much time and too much negative energy," He noticed the smug grin and the illuminated look in her sapphire blue eyes.

Anja unbuckled her seat belt and ignored the warning beep as they drove along the country road. She slid her hand between his legs, looked at him and pulled his zip down.

"Sex now, or later when we get home?"

Stefan smiled at his wife and enjoyed the thought of receiving a blow job.

"Later, Anja, I cannot concentrate on both things, especially at this speed and both sides of the road are lined with trees."

"Your choice, it did not stop you last week when we were doing 160km/h along the autobahn. It sounds like a visit to our playroom when we get home; you can use the new cat of nine tails whip, which I bought the other day. I need to try it out before using it on Vincenzo. It has the narrow leather cats, so it stings more, I might even attach metal studs to it. Men are so vulnerable in the right hands. It's a shame, it will be a threesome, which he'll not enjoy, and not live to tell the tale, but he will see it to the end."

"You really have no empathy for people like him."

"Nor guilt, I certainly will not be empathizing with his pain and suffering. Men, the likes of him rob women of part of their lives. They destroy relationships and families and if there are children involved, it can destroy their future. And for what? To fulfil a macho need of control, they are not true men. Some women are lucky and escape but it takes them a long time to rebuild their lives and trust, they lose part of their life. The bastard deserves it all Stefan, it is his own fault. They are the abusers and rapists, we never ask them to commit their crimes. I never thought so soon that we would find another victim; they come to us. I found a book on the flea market last week; there are some interesting chapters on Chinese and middle age torture. The advantage is that we both have the medical knowledge to prolong suffering. The book may be of use. When he's gone, the city will be a safer place. Just one thing, after this, let's disappear, we're both highly qualified Drs; maybe do some charity work in Africa. If we carry on, we will end up making mistakes. I'm not interested in spending my life in prison because of men who have no respect for women."

Anja looked out of the window at the hypnotic effect of the trees and reflected on her mother. She knew why she wanted to go to Africa. The question was when to tell Stefan the reason why.

"You've drifted, Anja."

"Sorry, my mind was wandering."

"You certainly live up to your Russian name, Anja, bringing goodness to the world. Africa sounds good, working for a charity, putting something back into society, helping people who need it. You're right, it's the law of averages, we will make a mistake and Vincenzo is too close to home. We need to move on, before we become too comfortable and confident."

"I'm not interested in comfortable, let's get home and quick, I'm horny as hell. I need to be fucked and hard from behind or against the bedroom wall. I'll phone my sister later this week to find out when Vincenzo is leaving the country."

Chapter 9

"Morning, Judith, how was your evening, what time did you get home?"

"Shortly before ten, and then I went straight into bed followed by a terrible night's sleep. My bloody next-door neighbour had a visitor, she was loud and I'll leave the rest to your imagination."

"I'll pass on that one. Get yourself some caffeine."

"Not a bad idea."

"I thought you looked tired."

"What do you mean?"

"You must have been damn desperate for sleep. You still have an earplug stuck in your right ear."

Judith raised her hand and pulled the yellow plug out of her ear and looked at it.

"Shit, I thought something was not right this morning and old age was starting to creep in."

"Taking the plug out will not stop old age. Hopefully, you can concentrate on the rest of the day without falling asleep."

"Are there any updates from the team, Warren?"

"I managed to persuade a small number of people to work additional overtime, on the digital recreation. It's on the P drive; the main difference is that it now looks more like a photograph. I'll email it out to Karl to pass onto his team."

Judith leaned back, put her arms behind her head and twisted her neck. Warren heard the loud crack and cringed.

"That's better, it's all cramped up from last night, and I have this dull tired headache. There is one thing I did learn from Karl; each fitness centre has approx. two to three thousand members to make it pay depends on the size. Thirty fitness centres and there will be more, that is over ninety thousand members. As you said, we have split Berlin into quadrants and working from the centre outwards, one quadrant at a time, the one you recommended. The list will be completed today and the first centres will be visited today. It will take time, diligence and patience."

"In other words, Judith; plain, boring, detective work. There is nothing else we can do; hopefully, it turns up a solid lead. Although, we have a reasonable size team, manpower is not unlimited. Hopefully, we get a lead; I'm not interested in having another body turn up."

"No one is, Warren, but I feel the clock is ticking."

"I went through the report last night at home, alone, in peace."

"It's not exactly the best bedtime reading, Warren, unless you want nightmares."

"All the wounds were measured and accurately recorded, length and depth. The incision cuts are, roughly, all the same length; I'm assuming those were done by one person. The areas where he was skinned, each one was individually thought out, planned and the victim was kept alive for their maximum pleasure. There is a pattern, the skin, which had partially healed was from smaller areas, the shoulders, the forearms. Most of the incision cuts had also healed. The areas where they had not fully healed or had not healed were from the larger areas, thighs, chest and back. Removed after death, or shortly before, there is no conclusion, for what reason? I cannot imagine."

"Trophy?"

"I feel sick at that thought, Judith. What brings you to that quick conclusion?"

"It wouldn't be the first time that people's skin was used for trophies. Read your history books. In the last war, people's skin was used as lampshades."

"I don't like to entertain that thought in my mind. The last two victims also had areas of skin removed, except, we recovered their corpse, whole. Why the hell would they slice a person in two?"

"It was probably to spare him and them the last moments of a painful death. That's why they drained the blood out via the jugular."

"You've lost me, Judith."

"When you lose about twenty per cent of your blood, your body starts to experience hypovolemic shock. Blood pressure drops, heart rate increases to compensate, couple all of that with the pain of being cut in two. They could have given him drugs to relieve the pain so he could see his last few moments. I believe cutting a live human being in two was a step too far for whoever killed our victim. Our victim was strung up like a pig on slaughter, blood drained, the incision was small, and then hacked in two to delay the decomposition cycle. It's also possible that he was killed shortly beforehand and then strung up."

"What the hell or who are we dealing with, I've gone cold."

"Someone with a chronic mental disorder, violent social tendencies, highly intelligent, logical thinking process…"

"Psychopath."

"That's the summary, Warren."

After two years, they knew they were not much further forward and the stakes had risen. A third body and a psychopathic, serial murderer was on the loose. He felt his frustration and anger gnawing at him, feelings, which he normally had under control.

"Are you okay, Warren? You seem to have drifted."

"The thought of the fact that we now have a serial killer, raises the stakes, the pressure and the complexity. Mixed feelings, Judith; anger, hatred, frustration, the case is not moving forward quickly enough. Throw in the thrill of the challenge to catch and stop them before they find a fourth and couple that with mental and physical exhaustion. It's quite an unhealthy cocktail, which we find ourselves in."

"You mentioned, 'they', why Warren? Let's expand our thought process."

"I was just thinking laterally, no hard facts or evidence. It's been playing on my mind for a couple of days. It's an assumption and I know, we should not assume and let the facts build the case. Our latest victim, Judith is of a reasonable build, approximately 105kg. It would probably take two people to transport this body, especially, when he was dead and then turned upside down to drain his blood. One person could do it, but two people…it seems more logical. The last two victims did not have the same build."

"Your assumption, I have no argument against it, Warren, makes sense, but we need facts and hard evidence."

"Let's not dismiss the idea that two people may be involved. We need to explore all avenues and keep an open mind and no prejudice, which, unfortunately, can sometimes drive decisions. I believe the murderer or murderers have made their first mistakes. The wound on the vertebrae, that is like leaving a fingerprint. The marks of the cutting implement are left on the bone and can be matched up. All three bodies were discovered in the water, also within one quadrant, enough for us to think about a pattern and the fact two people may be involved. Each victim was restrained and kept alive, whilst tortured, each one is progressively worse."

"People with medical knowledge, Doc mentioned this, Warren, maybe qualified, well-read, it would not be the first time that medical personnel have flipped out."

"They would need access to drugs, Judith and also know how to use them. Missing persons?"

"I have checked the list over the last two months. There are several but none fit the facial recreation. It's possible our guy is a loner in life, adopted, no brothers, sisters, not from this area, no close friends. Perhaps, that was why he was singled out."

"Possible, but he is in the system, somewhere, Judith. It's impossible to go through life and not surface somewhere and not talk to someone. It is also Germany; you need to register for everything here except going to the toilet."

"There are a lot of people in the world who have no one to talk too, Warren or want minimum interaction with people, for whatever reason."

"That I know, Judith."

He looked across at Judith who was staring at him waiting for the apology to the sharp interjection.

"I'm not finished."

"Apology, what were you going to say?"

"Perhaps, vulnerability is one of the criteria for these predators. Everyone has a weak point, Warren, their Achilles heel. Someone got close enough to lure them in. None of the victims were strangled, killed on the spot. These men let their guard down, almost as if they were invited to their death. Who sent the invite is a question, male or female?"

"That could depend on their sexuality. We have only identified the second body and he was in a relationship. Albeit he was the abuser, we suspected his girlfriend for a short while. She felt no remorse and was relieved that he was out of her life. Possibly, your theory is correct, Judith. It certainly opens up another avenue of investigation. I'm going to throw this one on the table, keeping an open mind. Do we have a female on the rampage? I don't think we should close that possibility out."

"Then two people, the last corpse weighed 105kg. There are not many men who can carry that weight and even fewer women."

"There are a lot of unanswered questions, Judith and we have to keep digging for facts. Push Karl for an update on the fitness centre visits, and provide an update daily. I want to know what corner of Berlin, the victim lived in and his personal life. It is going to take time, weeks but patience and a detailed approach will pay off."

Chapter 10

Anja knocked on the solid oak front door of her sister's house and paused. She wondered how much longer she would see her knowing her life and Stefan's had to change. A spasm of guilt filled her stomach knowing that she could not tell her sister the truth. The betrayal of trust was necessary to protect her sister and to her it was justifiable.

There was no answer, so Anja opened the door and walked in. Silence filled the house, which meant one thing; they were in the garden. She noticed an open bottle of Rioja red wine on the kitchen table and poured herself a large glass before walking out to the swimming pool. Melanie and Filippo were sound asleep, stretched out like two lazy cats on the sun loungers. She looked down at her sister and gently kicked the sun lounger to wake her up.

"Anyone could break into your house, the front door is open, sister."

Melanie rubbed her eyes and stood up to cuddle her sister.

"The sun is not good for your skin, Melanie; you need to cream to stop the wrinkles from spreading."

"Too late for that, I crossed that line a few years ago. You are always worrying about me, Anja. I see you have found the wine. Did you bring your bikini? It's hot and I'm ready for a dip to cool off, there will not be many weeks left of this weather. Strip off here and change, Filippo is sound asleep. It's a long time since we have swum together."

"It used to be regular when our mother took us to the competitions. The sweet shop afterwards was always my favourite part of the night."

"It was the main reason why you came. Have you still got your medals, Melanie?"

"They are in the cupboard, upstairs, too good a childhood memory to throw away, Anja. Let's put the wine glasses at the edge of the pool, there's some shade over there. It will save having to get out if we want a drink."

Anja and Melanie deliberately bombed like two teenagers into the pool ensuring Filippo got soaked and woke up. He lifted his straw hat off his face, looked across at them as they gracefully swam the length of the pool like two ballerinas in the water. He knew he was isolated; the two sisters were together, Filippo, bid his hello to Anja, stood up and retreated to the kitchen to grab a cool beer. He looked out of the kitchen window as they climbed out of the pool and dried themselves off.

"That's better, Melanie, I'm sure the days are becoming hotter in Berlin, it is three months now and still very little rain. It will rain sometime; summer is coming to an end. Let's lie down and bask, I'm sure Filippo will not mind me pinching his lounger. It looks like he has done a runner and found some solitude. How's he doing?"

"What do you mean, Anja?"

"After the night, he threw Vincenzo out, he lost a long-term friend and it must have hurt him."

"Remarkably well, Anja, or he's keeping it to himself, I think the friendship was coming to an end, it was only a question of when and that day, Vincenzo provided the reason. If he was not such a slime ball, I would thank him."

"You never could tolerate him, could you?"

"He could lie in a ditch and die for all I care about him. Since it happened, we haven't spoken much about the subject. Perhaps, he was looking for a reason, which Vincenzo provided."

"What Vincenzo did that day, Melanie, was bang out of order, but not out of character. I will never understand why some men think women are their property to do with what they want."

"It takes all sorts to make a world sister, and there are plenty of weird men on this planet. Fortunately, men like that have no place in my life, we were lucky to meet who we did. His last girlfriend, I heard, had to call the police; he had physically hit her. She refused to press charges but left him the week before the party. Apparently, he found her via social media, one of her, so-called friends. He turned up at the door, threatened her and then knocked her to the ground. She also found that her car had been tampered with, brake pipes cut. The shit police put it down to a domestic and mentioned there was no proof that he had actually tampered with her brakes. It was only her suspicion."

"I'm convinced the bloody police look for reasons not to investigate and they have the nerve to write on the cars, 'We are there for you', I lost my faith in the police years ago."

"You're not alone there, Anja, after what we went through with our mother in Africa and then your attack in your early twenties. No one was prosecuted."

"It took a long time for me to trust a man again and Stefan was very patient, Melanie."

"You both work well together and really suit each other. Does he still press flowers for a hobby? I must admit, Anja; I find it a strange hobby."

"Everyone to their own, sister, it's his thing. It helps him to de-stress from work. It is his private world where he can be alone with his passion. I'm sure even you have secrets, it is part of a healthy relationship."

"My relationship with Filippo is healthy."

"Lots of secrets then? Tell me a few."

"No."

"Ah, bedroom secrets"

"Change the subject, Anja."

"What's your holiday plan for this year, Melanie, somewhere exotic?"

"Asia, Indian, somewhere in that region, for four weeks, not sure when yet, maybe Filippo has an idea, here he comes."

"Hi Anja, how are you keeping?"

"Good to see you surface, Filippo."

"I thought it was best to keep out of the way. When you two are together, I may as well be a wallflower."

"We were just talking about your secrets, but Melanie kept stump and changed the subject to holidays. I hear you might be off on a trip to Asia or India. Make sure you do not run into Vincenzo, I heard him talking that he may be off to explore Asia."

"That relationship is over, long overdue; I should have listened to your sister a long time ago. Anyhow, there's no chance to bump into him, despite the small world we live in today. We will probably not go until September and he is travelling sometime in November, he told me the date, but I forgot. Why don't you and Stefan come along for a holiday? Join us, the four of us, it should be fun. When was the last time you had a holiday with your sister?"

"Other plans, Filippo, we are thinking about Africa."

For a second Anja froze, if she could, she would have swallowed the word, Africa, back. Her sister looked at her in disbelief. Sitting relaxed after a swim, glass of wine and in the secure company, she had let her guard down. Melanie jumped in on the conversation.

"Not there, Anja, anywhere but there, we spent enough time there as kids. Go somewhere different, explore."

Anja had convinced Stefan about Africa, it was part of her plan, which he was unaware and she would worry about those details later. They were both right, with time, mistakes would be made and she had just made one. She wondered if they had made any others without realising what could be pieced together. For the first time, she felt a ripple of apprehension in her stomach. Melanie waved her empty glass at her husband who instinctively stood up and headed off to the kitchen to collect the wine bottle.

"Are you okay sister, why go back there? We left it a long time ago, is Stefan aware of the history?"

"I'm fine, Melanie; except for the fact that my glass is empty. He has never been there and he does not know our history. It's a large continent and why should we avoid it just because of the past. Why should he know what happened in Africa? There's no need. It is our family history and our mother's history. It was just an idea, Stefan mentioned it and how could I refuse. I will plant another seed in his mind."

"Phone him, Anja. Why don't we all go out for a meal tonight, sit outside, watch the sunset go down, relax and let the world go by. I love that English phrase, there is nothing to compare in our language. The nights are starting to close in and the opportunity will become scarce, Anja."

"It sounds a good idea but he is working late today and I have promised to cook for him."

"You really are happy with him, Anja; I'm so pleased to see it. The move back to Germany finally destroyed our family, a series of events that started in Africa; cost our mother her life, later nearly yours and our father his sanity. I worried about you after that attack when we moved back. I thought that you would never love again, finally, you found someone not just to love, but someone you can trust and rely on."

"There are still times when that cupboard door opens, but I have learnt over time how to put the memories back in and close the door."

"You two look deep in conversation, here's the wine bottle."

Melanie stroked the arm of her husband and looked at her sister.

"He's so well-trained, it took a few years."

Filippo looked down at his wife and smiled and looked across to Anja.

"It's from the years of beatings and being handcuffed to the kitchen."

"If Stefan refuses Filippo, I whip him until he goes to the kitchen. We both have our methods to train our men, they secretly enjoy it."

Filippo looked across to his wife and smiled.

"Again, I feel vulnerable when you two are together. I would like to change the subject before Melanie gets any new ideas. Since, you cannot make it this year on holiday, I propose a toast, to next year; hopefully, you can both make it."

Anja felt a heavy sinking feeling in her stomach as she raised her glass, but she had the information she wanted. Her sister was sitting next to her and she knew there would be no holiday together. Melanie was correct; she had her secret, one she hoped she would never find out.

Chapter 11

"Morning, Warren, you should have come into work earlier."

He looked at Judith bemused by the statement, it was 7.30.

"What brought you in so early, Judith?"

"I could not sleep, the case was running through my mind and it was pointless, just lying there looking at the ceiling. Plus, it is the worst day of the week; Monday, may as well get it over and done with. Do you know how many fitness centres there are in Berlin and outside? Never mind, it's irrelevant now."

"The last two weeks did not bear any fruit; I have heard we were starting to look at centres on the outskirts of Berlin. Spit it out, Judith, I know that look in your eyes; you look like a child on Christmas Eve. You have information that I don't have."

"We've found the possible name of our victim; he's called Andreas Steinbauer and lives in Erkner. We have the address. The info came in late last night and I picked it up this morning. You are on the copy as well when you log on."

"Mosquito country."

The puzzled look on Judith's face demanded an explanation.

"The last time when I was there, I stopped off for a Kebab and ended up eating it in the car before I was eaten alive. Speaking about cars, whose are we taking? The centre will already be open for the early birds."

"Mine, it's more comfortable and it will get us there. You really need to buy a new car, Warren; your Fiesta is dying on its wheels."

"I am planning one for the turn of the year. Your car, good choice, it has air-con, the seats are more comfortable, plus, I cannot be arsed to drive so I'm pleased you volunteered."

Judith waited for the red lights to change in Friedrichshagen to turn left onto Fuerstenwalder Damm and momentarily, people watched.

"We see the world from a different side, Warren. Look at the people going about their daily business and perhaps going for a coffee and cake next to the lake, who knows? Meanwhile, we're investigating a vicious serial killer, how the hell did we end up in this job."

"Let's kill the subject, it's a question I've asked many times and still not found an answer. Often I've thought, how can I change my life and I have still come up with no answer. The job is like a drug, it stresses the body and it is unhealthy, but we need a health fix to offset the stress. On the way back, I'll buy you a coffee and cake to put a moment of normality back into our lives, Judith."

"You're on."

Warren turned to Judith as they drove along Fuerstenwalder Allee and passed Müggelsee.

"You're about to speak, I know your body language, plus you've been quiet too long and that is unusual for you."

"The Müggelsee and the Dämeritsee."

"What about them?"

"They're all connected and Erkner is on the edge of Dämeritsee."

"Your local knowledge is improving, how long have you lived here?"

"While I remember, the Brandenburg police are informed; I forgot to mention that earlier. We did that when we started to look at fitness centres on the edge of Berlin."

"The waterways flow through the middle of Berlin. Picking this quadrant was an educated guess, Judith. We had to start somewhere and now the third victim has a link in this quadrant."

Fifteen minutes later, Judith and Warren stood inside the lift to the fitness centre.

"You were right about those damn mosquitoes; I've already been bit, Warren."

"I hate the damn things, Judith, one bite and the area swells up, bloody allergy. They have no purpose on this planet as far as I'm concerned."

The manageress saw them both walking across the foyer and walked over to greet them. "Morning, welcome. I take it you're from the police. The twilight manageress phoned late last night to say she had a visit regarding identification of a person."

Judith at one-eighty tall looked directly at the athletic woman who stood before them.

"Correct, but what made you think that we are from the police?"

"You both have no kit, you have a serious look on your face, the stressed, beaten-down look and you're also slouching. Regular fitness helps to reduce stress, improves work-life balance and posture. I'm Frau Meyer and you are?"

"I'm Kommissarin Hellwig and this is Hauptkommissar Fischer, we're both from the Mordkommission, is there anywhere where we can talk in private?"

Tina looked blank at both of them and stood speechless. Judith and Warren looked at each other realizing she was unaware of the news to come.

"Sorry, sure, yes. The Mordkommission, that was not mentioned, the message was that the police were looking for a missing person. Let's go to my office, it's over there, we can have privacy."

Tina turned to her colleague, "Christian, please ensure we are not disturbed until we are finished."

"Please sit here, these seats are more comfortable. Your colleague, last night was vague. He showed the manageress a picture and she confirmed his name in the database. Apart from that, he did not impart much more information."

Warren showed her the recreated picture.

"Yip, that's him, what happened to him? If you are allowed to tell me."

"Thank you for confirming his identity. He was tortured and then killed. The two halves of his body surfaced in the middle of Berlin."

"I remember reading that story; I never thought I would be sitting in front of two police officers."

"How can you remember him? I mean you have more than one member."

Silence fell in the room as Tina looked at the two of them knowing she had nothing good to say.

"Truthfully."

"Lying is not an option in front of the police and especially in a murder investigation."

Judith looked at Warren, she could tell from the blank expression on his face that he was not in the mood to be pissed around.

"The guy was an arsehole, complete and utter wanker."

"Everyone is an arsehole to someone in this world. Particulars?"

"He loved himself, the sort of guy who couldn't understand if a woman did not have sex with him. He would talk about how successful he was and how much money he had. He had mastered the art of inability, or an unwillingness to hear anyone's point of view unless it was to his advantage. He would be-little women, had an over-inflated attitude and also tried to peddle soft drugs. We found that out by accident, someone tipped us off. A few of the women also complained about him and his inappropriate behaviour. We were going to suspend him, but he disappeared; now I know why."

Judith deliberately interrupted and felt a less irritable questioning technique would be more appropriate.

"You meet more than a few when you're a woman. Such people, I don't stop anymore for the conversation, they are not worth the oxygen."

Warren looked across at Judith; he knew he would not like the man on the receiving end of that conversation. He also realised his partner had taken over the questioning. Judith carried on.

"Are drugs a problem here or is this an isolated case?"

"Look around, people are here for fitness, meeting friends socially, getting out of the house and the odd drink at the bar. Drugs, if they are used are on a very small scale here and if used, are used outside. Using drugs for them would be like polluting their body."

"What do you know about him, personal details?"

"He was in his illusory sycophantic world. He let it slip at The May Dance this year that his parents had died when he was in his twenties. He did mention where he was born and to be honest, it went in one ear and out the other. It was a dance party, not the place for a sob story."

"Brothers, sisters?"

"None that I am aware of."

"Girlfriends, boyfriends, friends?"

"One that I was aware of, he brought her to the party. About one seventy, dyed long red hair, would put her in the mid-thirties, I have no idea what her name is. You can also speak to the female members here, one of them threatened to lay him out for his attitude."

"Sounds like my sort of woman, independent and not afraid to take on men. What made her flip out that night?"

"Your deceased had tried a few times to bring up the topic of a threesome with some of the members. A few of the woman were already pissed off with him; he rubbed women up the wrong way. The final straw was when he caught his girlfriend texting; he took the phone off her and read it in front of the group. Luisa, one of the women he approached earlier launched into him. She wasn't alone, the rest of the group were behind her and it takes a brave or stupid man to take on a group of women and especially Luisa. She teaches self-defence and he was asked to leave for his safety. She will be starting her shift shortly, you can talk to her."

He knew Judith was now in full flow, he sat back and people watched through the glass-walled office. He realised how fit he used to be when he was in the army; Tina was right with her observation.

"We would like a full list of addresses of every member in the last two years and also when they visited the gym. When will you be able to provide the information?"

"It's not a problem, I'll have someone compile the address list today and I'll send you the information, it may be later tonight or early morning. Either way, you will have it by tomorrow. The frequency profile will take another few days; we run the software only once a week. You will be surprised how many people join in January, sign a contract for one year and then tailor off never to be seen again. I'll separate those for you from the regular attendees. You will also receive the time of entry and length of stay. Before you ask, if someone else can use a card, each card has a photo ID and it is checked on entry."

"That's fine."

"Just a second, there's Luisa, starting her shift. I'll grab her."

Tina stood up and went outside to talk to her. Less than thirty seconds had passed, when they reappeared.

"Hi, Tina mentioned about Andreas."

"We're investigating his murder."

"One less wanker on the streets, at least it saved us from doing it."

Warren jumped in and Judith noticed the flat tone in his voice.

"The guy was tortured and then hacked in two and his body dumped was in the Spree."

Tina kept quiet knowing Luisa would not take kindly to the tone of his voice.

"You should have left him there, food for the fish and rats and saved the taxpayer some money. A change to the tone of your voice would be appreciated. Because you're a policeman, it doesn't give you the right to talk to me in that manner."

Warren knew it served no purpose to retaliate and Judith looked at him as much to say, keep your mouth shut and let me talk.

"What happened later?"

"Not a lot, he left with his girlfriend, unfortunately, some girls go for the bad men. The last time I saw her was sometime in June, early June, just by chance. She had a black eye and I noticed marks around her neck. I invited her for a coffee, just around the corner from here, I had the feeling she wanted to talk, but she refused the invitation. She mentioned her brother had been in touch several times and she was planning to leave Andreas."

"Do you think he was aware that she was planning to leave?"

"She looked frightened enough, but I have no idea and didn't ask. She did mention that he was planning to leave for a holiday with friends and he had sent her out to get some toiletries. I think it was his way of belittling her, showing her injuries in public. Whether she went back to her brother's house after our chance meeting, I've no idea. All I do know is that he stopped coming to the gym, now we know why."

"What did you tell her?"

"She was lucky that she had family support and a way out. Stopping with Andreas would be the hard way through life. Unfortunately, not all women have someone to back them up in a crisis. We will have to stop future payments now."

"So his bank account is still active. Can you provide the details of his bank?"

"No problem."

"Do you know the name of her brother, also the family name?"

"His first name, no, but she did mention that he works in the villa next to the old brewery near the Spree tunnel. Her name is Sabina Karsch."

"Thanks for your time, both of you, it was helpful."

"I've no love for men who use violence against women. A relationship is based on trust, respect and love, not violence. I hope you find his killer so people will stop worrying. The press is good at whipping things up."

Judith looked direct into Luisa's eyes.

"I take it your thoughts apply to the female sex as well. It works both ways, there are some men who are in a violent relationship and beaten up by their partner. Violence in any relationship is not acceptable. We will send someone to collect the list. Here are my contact details, call me when it is ready."

Warren and Judith sat in her grey Golf and looked out of the window. He broke the ice.

"What are your thoughts, Judith? Have you calmed down?"

"I have a problem with people who are not open-minded and look at the debate from one side. I'm hungry, there's a kebab shop over there and I need a

Doner Kebab with garlic sauce. After my stomach has been fed then we can talk, are you game?"

"Sounds good to me and also it seems you have already decided for me."

Warren watched Judith stomp off in the direction of the Imbiss. It was a long time since he had seen her riled.

The pair of them perched their elbows on the white round metal table and bit into the kebab. Warren watched Judith lose the battle with the sauce and handed her a serviette to wipe her mouth.

"So, let's talk, your thoughts now that your stomach is being fed." Judith glanced across the table at him.

"It's not open for discussion, but some attitudes piss me off, very quickly. Andreas, was not popular at the gym and she's right about the fish food. Unfortunately, we are bound by the law to investigate a case that is removing vermin from the street. And yes, I know, hopefully, those rules never change. Despite my profession, I'm allowed my own opinion and allowed to blow off with a colleague, friend who I can trust. As you once said, it's good for your health, better out than bottled in."

"It is bottled up, not in. I'll keep quiet while you are in full flow."

"The person who is doing this is on a mission. The first victim was violent towards women and the third one. I bet one year's wages, the second involved violence against women too. If there is, hopefully not, the same trend will follow, if there is a fourth. All the bodies were found in this corner of Berlin, the lake, the rivers are all connected. If it was me, the next body I would dump somewhere else, somewhere away from Berlin or on the other side. Unless, he grows in confidence and keeps to his territory."

"You keep using the word, he, Judith."

"Men tend to be the more aggressive of the species. I know, as we discussed earlier, we should keep a more open mind."

"Whoever is doing this Judith has lost their humanity. I dread to think if there is another corpse and the suffering that person will have to go through before they die. Death would be welcome. We need to go to the villa where Sabina's brother works and then visit him."

"Before or after I finish my kebab?"

"After, another two minutes will not make much difference."

"Point taken. It looks like we have a long day before us. I'll cancel my date for tonight, Warren, but you owe me and Sarah a bottle of red wine."

"Sarah?"

"Depending on the process, you can have two. How is it going with you two?"

"It seems to be working and my daughter likes her. No point in having a new partner if your child does not get along with them."

"Or vice versa. So where did you two meet?"

"Taking an interest now, are we? Or just being polite to keep me happy."

"I am taking an interest so I don't open up any more holes."

"Dating App, I'm getting too old to wait and meet someone the old-fashioned way."

Judith scrunched up the remains of her kebab in the paper and threw it into the nearby bin.

"I'll start to get some background info for you while you enjoy finishing your kebab in peace. It might save you buying a bottle of wine. I'll start the ball rolling."

"Here, you need this serviette; some of the garlic sauce has dripped onto your skirt. Skip the sauce next time."

"No chance."

Judith returned in fifteen minutes with information. He knew by the stern look on her face as she walked up to him that she was not happy.

"What's up?"

"He was known to the police. On more than one occasion, they had paid him a visit for disturbing the peace. One occasion, when they turned up, there was a fetish party in full flow."

"Not illegal, Judith."

"Not until it turned into a punch up, then the police were called."

"At least, there would not be a shortage of handcuffs. I would not be surprised if our victim was at the centre of attention, Judith. Hopefully, they took the addressees of the attendees."

"They did but how many do you think were valid. I don't think you take your ID card to such a party."

"I take your point, Judith. How the hell can you overstep the mark at such a party, everyone is open-minded and respectful. How else could such a party work? Berlin is famous for the hedonistic scene. We can pull out more details about the party when we return to the station. Perhaps, his girlfriend can shed some light."

"Another time, his girlfriend was in the hospital with broken ribs, she refused to press charges. The police had been to the house on several occasions; the last visit was seven weeks ago. A neighbour had called the police; he had heard screaming but nothing was followed up."

"I know this guy died a horrible death, Warren, but really, I've no sympathy for him."

"Neither do I, Judith, but as you said, we have to follow the law and no mass murderer has the right to decide what is right or wrong. Let's visit where her brother works, if he's not there we can obtain the address and visit them. Then we can interview them both together. At least we now have a timeline for when he was alive."

"We need to show some sensitivity here, Warren. She's been through a traumatic time in her life and she will be wondering where her future is going. Then, we turn up investigating the murder of her ex. She will need her brother for support and it looks like he is the only one that she trusts. Also, you can be, let's say not the world's best diplomat at times. I tend to balance you out."

"I know you do and I can tell from the look in your eyes when I have overstepped the mark. She may even be relieved that he can no longer harm her, Judith. We need to ensure they were not involved. I very much doubt it, but we need to eliminate them from our enquiries, as we say. For the first time, in a long while, I feel that we are moving forward. Let's head off to the villa and find her brother."

Chapter 12

Judith and Warren pulled up outside Sabina's brother's house. The earthy smell of autumn was in the air and the trees were showing their multi-coloured red and golden leaves. A middle-age balding broad man sporting a ponytail was splitting wood to add to the winter store. He noticed them as they both walked towards the gate.

"Afternoon, you look very official. What can I do to help you?"

"Police business."

Judith took out her warrant card and introduced her and Warren.

"We're investigating a missing person and we're looking for Sabina and Axel Karsch? Your workplace told us where you lived and that he was on holiday. Could you turn that machine off, please?"

"Sure, sorry, she's home, I'm her brother, Andre. Let me guess, it's about Andreas, has someone killed him by any chance? Please tell me yes. After what he did to my sister, I would like to thank him, it will save me putting his head through this log splitting machine. Come in, she's in the kitchen preparing food. I can tell from the deadpan look in your faces, it is him and he is dead."

"Before we go in, we're from the Mordkommission and we're investigating his death. So, you will be overjoyed with the news."

A moment of silence fell between the three of them, Axel spoke up.

"Overjoyed is an overstatement but life has a strange way of delivering the good news. I hope it was a slow painful death. This day is getting better. Spare me the details; the fact that he is dead is good enough for me. Please, let's go in the house."

"Before we go in, no mention of this to your sister, we will ask her to identify the photo and then inform her of the news."

Judith and Warren stood before a woman in her late thirties with a limp posture and long red hair. Judith decided to speak first.

"Hello Sabina, we are both from the Mordkommission and we are investigating a missing man called Andreas Steinbauer. We understand that you were in a relationship with him. Can you confirm the face on this picture?" Judith passed the photograph to Sabina who stared in silence and then looked up directly at Judith.

"It's my ex, the bastard who destroyed my life."

"No, he didn't sister; if it was destroyed, we wouldn't be building a future. The past is closed and we both look to the doors that open, together. Time will ease the wounds and memories will fade. He's lost."

"You don't need to worry about him anymore Sabina, he is dead, murdered. Can you tell us, when did you leave him and when was the last time you saw him?"

Sabina stared emotionless at Judith, in disbelief, at the news she had heard.

"That, I wasn't expecting. There is no overwhelming sadness, I am relieved if anything, the anxiety of him turning up has gone and he is out of my life, finally. Sorry, you caught me off guard with that. I left him in, middle of June, the exact day, I am sorry, but that time is all a blur. I should have listened to my brother two years ago, but I thought I could change him. I wasted two years of my life."

Judith looked empathetically at Sabina and felt sorrow for what she had gone through.

"It is only wasted if you do not learn from it."

"He was a controller; isolated my sister from her family. He used to constantly criticise her and one day he beat her. She ended up in hospital; broken ribs and what did the police do? They did nothing, she was afraid to prosecute him and they took the easy route. He thought he broke her until one day something inside her snapped and she walked out on him."

Judith looked at Sabina who was sitting next to her brother.

"What snapped inside you to leave him?"

"When I moved in with Andreas, it was good, the full use of the house, his car and I started to feel beholding to him. Step by step, he gradually isolated my freedom and my family. A few times, I knew Axel was at the door, but I was not allowed to answer or I had to make an excuse why he could not come in. He would criticise me, the way I looked, dressed, walked, joke about me in front of so-called friends. Eventually, he took the mobile phone off me that he gave to me. I wasn't allowed to go out with friends, or if I did, on the odd occasion, he would always turn up to play taxi driver home. It saps your strength and eventually, you lose the will to fight. Until one day, when he went too far with the beatings and I ended up in the hospital, black eye and marks around my neck. I've shed blood in every room in his flat. After I was discharged, I went out feeling as if the world was revolving around me. I could hear my father inside my head. All he ever wanted for me was to be independent of a man, lead my own life. It was as if he was there, watching what was going on. I carried on walking in the surreal world. Andreas told me to bring some toiletries home, so he could go on holiday. I bumped into a woman from the fitness centre, somehow she had remembered me. She had the feeling I wanted to talk and invited me for a coffee for whatever reason; I declined, perhaps panic. In fact, the whole day was surreal. I ended up going into a cafe; I sat next to the window, holding my cup and people watched. A woman with long blond hair, it's all I remember asking if I was alright and sat opposite. We…I talked, she listened and she did not say much, but she was very empathic. I don't even know to this day how I decided to leave him. Perhaps, it was time or something the woman said or made me realise, I had to move forward. I knew that I had somewhere safe to go to, some women have nowhere and I turned up here. I was sitting in the porch when Axel came in from work. I never went back to the house, even for my clothes. The clothes, which I arrived in, were all I had."

"Did you not think that it was strange that such a controlling person didn't try to get in touch?" Sabina looked at Warren, her eyes and face looked distressed as she carried on.

"He tried initially and after a short while it suddenly stopped, two or three weeks, if I remember. We were relieved and surprised that he gave up so easily. He is and was a controller, power seeker, now we know the reason why he stopped. He did turn up once at our house, a few days after I left him."

"What do you say to him?"

"Axel spoke to him."

"Simple, I told him that I would put him in hospital, but he did not seem to understand the message. He just stood there, cold, calm, and emotionless, even when he was threatened. There was no adrenaline flow, fight or flight; his eyes were dead, like shark eyes focusing on a prey. It's the first time that I have been frightened. That was when we stopped the internet, etcetera and we both got a simple pay as you go phone. Only two people know these numbers, me and my sister. When you find the murder's address, let me know, I would like to thank him."

"The victim was tortured, Axel."

"And, if you are looking for sympathy, you need to go elsewhere. Perhaps, when he appears at court we can then pass on our thanks."

Judith noticed Warren's body language change at the understandable aggression from the brother and opted to stand back to allow him to blow out.

"You hated this guy."

"Yes, I simply do not like men who control and especially abuse women."

"Enough to kill him."

"Enough to enjoy the fact that he's dead and out of our life. Murder him no; life has more to offer and what would it do for me and Sabina? No doubt after this conversation you'll want to eliminate me, us from your enquiry. That's the phrase you use and one reason why you are here. When was he killed?"

"We're estimating the middle of August."

"The answer is easy; we decided to disappear for the three weeks in August to getaway. We went to Rostock, do you want hotel and restaurant receipts."

"It would help, that way we have the evidence of where you were at that time. Do you both live together? I mean do you have your place, Sabina."

"Yes, we live together. She lost her job because of that wanker. He took her independence away. My sister became afraid to leave the house unless it was on his orders."

"Axel please stop venting your frustration at the police." Judith looked at Sabina and she felt sorrow for her going through such an ordeal.

"Now, you know why he did not get in touch. You have the chance to build something new, look for the door that will open and try not to look at the ones in the past that are shut. I know it is easier said than done, but I'm speaking from experience. If we find anything in his flat that is personal to you, do you want it back?"

"No, anything that is there is a memory, which I do not want. You can burn all my clothes."

"What did he do for a living, where did he work?"

"He never had permanent employment for years, just like most of the people he knew. Job shopping here and there, temporary contracts just to make ends meet. He used to blame me for the lack of income. My job as an administrator was the only real source of steady money until he took that away."

"Can you tell us who his friends were and where they live?"

Sabina looked up at Judith.

"Some I have met, where they live, I've no idea, try the bar next to the lake, tomorrow, about six. Ask for Friedrich Rhode. He's about your height, shoulder-length brown hair. They would meet up once a week for beers. None of those guys could have done what happened to Andreas. They are not sick and twisted enough, they peddle a few drugs, rob the odd house, that's their way of living."

"The woman who you drunk a coffee with, I know you said the day was a blur. Could you describe anything else about her?"

"Not really, I did not even ask her name, and she did not ask mine. I was spaced out, she had blond hair, long, and that's all that I really remember. Sorry. It was a chance meeting, but one that changed my life, for the better."

"Sabina, Axel, you have been really helpful. We may be back later with more questions, it depends on how the case progresses. Look after yourself Sabina; it seems that you have a caring brother."

Judith stood up at looked across to Sabina's brother.

"If there is anything else that you can think of that may help this case then contact us."

"I wouldn't waste the cost of a telephone call to find the killer, that person…"

Warren interrupted.

"Try and think about that offer. If we find that you have withheld information appertaining to the investigation of a murder, I will arrest you. Who then will help you sister? Think about the bigger picture."

"Noted, and if you have no further questions, I invited you into my house, it's time to leave."

Warren and Judith headed back to her car in silence.

"Did you have to be so hard at the end, Warren? He's a brother who is helping his sister to rebuild a life. They have had their justice today. Memories are still raw."

"He deserved it. Like I said, his bigger picture is to help rebuild his sister's life. We have a serial killer on the loose and withholding information, or even threatening is not an option. They may have had justice today, but they have no choice but to help with the enquiry. Are you free tomorrow night for a beer, Judith?"

"That's a sudden change of subject. I would prefer not to be but I'll join you. These middle age boys with thinning hair, I have to see."

"Why do women sometimes go for the bad ones, Judith, I'll never understand."

"Neither do I. She is lucky and made the easy decision, albeit a hard decision. Stopping in such a relationship would be the hard route through life. At least her father had planted a seed before she lost her way."

"There's someone out there Judith, outside of his close friends, who knew him, Sabina and his attitude towards women is enough to result in his death."

"Someone, who is intelligent enough to do what they did but not associated with him, Warren."

"What do you mean?"

"People tend to move around in semi-fixed social circle. People with a PhD very rarely go out for a social drink with the local drug dealer or a brothel owner. An extreme example, I know, but it is to highlight an example. People associate at levels of intelligence and interests, which they have in common. That's where I'm coming from. It's someone who knew him but on the outside and then did their homework to find out what he was really like as a person. We need his complete internet, phone, social and banking history. Forensics has already started to turn his flat upside down. We will visit them tomorrow afternoon to see what they have found and then we've that bar to visit afterwards."

Chapter 13

Warren and Judith crossed over the crime scene tape to Andreas's second floor flat. Judith noticed Astrid in the kitchen and walked over to leave Warren to his own devices.

"Has the team found anything, Astrid?"

"Hi, Judith, several different life forms growing in the bin and the kitchen sink. It's obvious, no one has cleaned for several weeks, there's a fine layer of dust everywhere. The team probably could read fingerprints straight off the surface."

"If my partner ever complains about my flat being dirty, I'll send her a photo of this place as a comparison."

"How're you and Sarah getting on?"

"It's working up to now, it is still early days. Have the team found anything significant yet, Astrid?"

"Not at this moment, Judith, some women's clothes, shoes and bags in a wardrobe. I don't think he's the type to be a transvestite, his flat would have been more organised and feminine."

"They belong to his ex-girlfriend, Astrid, we managed to track her down and we have also spoken to her. She mentioned that she had left him several weeks ago. She had nothing except the clothes on her back. Something inside her made sense and she moved in with her brother. We visited them yesterday and she does not require anything from the flat. The clothes can eventually be destroyed."

"She's a brave woman, Judith, good for her to get out. Not all women are so fortunate. That took a lot of guts. We found a cane with blood on it in the hallway; also we have found patches of blood on the hallway and bedroom rugs. We will need a DNA sample from her to confirm if…I think the reasons are obvious?"

"We'll contemplate if it is really necessary, she has been through enough and would it really add any value to the investigation? She has already told us that she shed blood in each room from the beatings. We are unable to prosecute the dead."

"Point taken, pity, there is no afterlife to prosecute lowlife. I see he is harassing Gunther."

Judith turned around to see a slim built police officer at the computer who looked like he still needed permission from his mother to go out.

"I think you'd better go and rescue him, Judith, Warren can be overpowering with young officers."

"He's not that young, Astrid."

"He is to us."

Judith walked over and stood behind Warren.

Gunther looked over his shoulder at the new member of his audience and shrugged his shoulders, "I didn't realise computers worked faster when two people stand behind the operator."

"It's bad enough with Warren, literally breathing down my neck."

"What have you found, Gunther?"

"I've found a few things, Judith, email traffic with his friends but that dropped off last week of July, it also ties up with his phone records. There are porn sites, downloads, extreme BDSM, swinger clubs, knives, gun sites and how to purify drugs on his internet history. There's nothing really out of the ordinary, for me, I've seen this type of stuff on other cases. You would be surprised how many people are looking at these sites, Judith. That is the downside of this technology; it has opened up the world to the taste of everyone. One time people would have struggled to find this information, now a fifteen-year-old, with a mobile at the bus stop can access these sites. Society is changing and I'm not sure if it is for the better."

Warren looked down at Gunther.

"Which were the most frequent sites visited and also can you list the most frequent email traffic and phone numbers?"

"Not a problem, this guy was careless and did not believe in good housekeeping, it is reflected in the state of his flat."

"Give me a shout when you're finished, Gunther, or send them to my computer so that I can review them."

Warren turned to Judith.

"Sabina left her abuser middle of June, Warren. We found his body at the end of August. Doc estimated two weeks in the water, the email traffic stopped middle of July. The body was tortured, some areas had healed, assume two, three weeks in captivity and that takes us to approx. middle to end of July. We know he tried to get in touch with Sabina after she left and then it suddenly stopped end of June start of July. It is safe to say our victim disappeared middle of July and spent three to four weeks in captivity."

"I agree, where are you driving this to, Judith?"

"Sabina does not look strong enough to carry a bag of shopping, let alone half a corpse. Also, unless she is a trained actor, her response to the demise of her ex seemed natural. Plus, they can also prove they were on holiday at the estimated time of the killing. If she was still living with him at the time of the murder, she would be a prime suspect."

"But they may have been involved in the abduction, Judith."

"Slim theory and we will not rule it out at this time. Someone must have known the couple, or Sabina, Warren, in what capacity, I've no idea. The assailant was aware that she had left Andreas and was close enough to get to him. How he was entrapped is the open question. At this moment, we cannot rule them out but they are low down on the list of suspects."

Judith and Warren were interrupted by Gunther, who shouted them over.

"There is something else?"

Judith and Warren looked down at Gunther.

"It looks like someone has been in the flat. I never noticed it until the sun shone through. The dressing table, over there, the dust, it looks like when, whoever was here; the corner was wiped, for whatever reason. It is very faint, but you can see it. Someone had rubbed their hand or something over the corner. It feels as if that person is fastidious about cleanliness and was disgusted with the level of uncleanliness. Like a white glove barrack-room inspection. My mother was obsessive with cleanliness and would often rub her hand or fingertips on furniture to check to dust. Whoever did it is left-handed; the arc of the rub goes from left to right. Also, that person had his keys and came here after the fact, Warren."

"But why not take the computer, Gunther?"

"Possibly they just wanted to survey the lair of their prey. It's outside of my skill set and one for the shrinks."

"Gunther has a point."

"I've no reason to challenge it, Judith. Good observation, Gunther and well spotted, that is the sort of detail that can make a case. If someone has come back and that person wiped the corner, it says something about their character."

"Is there anything from the neighbours, Warren?"

"No, they've been questioned Judith, but it's the sort of block of flats, where people, let's say keep themselves to themselves."

"I'm going to throw a wildcard to set up a train of thought, lateral thinking. His girlfriend is gone, a lonely man fed up with masturbating in front of a computer screen. No one to play his games goes looking for or offered an adventure. Someone loured him away after his girlfriend left and knew the relationship. It still goes back to how close was this person."

"Where're you going with this, a woman does not have to be close to lure a man away, could also be a man. If a woman is involved that would be out of the ordinary."

"I am certain now that we should look for two people, a man and a woman. I know we played with this idea before and I believe; cannot prove it, but I feel that it was a woman who came back to the flat. The woman is more dominant."

A momentary silence fell between the two of them as he tried to contemplate what she had just said.

"You've gone quiet."

"I know. I am trying to come to terms with the idea, Judith that two people with psychopathic, emotional instability disorders met and formed a relationship. Remove any one point in history that prevents them from meeting and we probably would not be here now."

"It has happened in the past, Warren."

"I know, but it's now on our table. Let's go outside and get some fresh air, Judith."

Warren and Judith walked along the corridor; there was no one, only the sound of a television could be heard from the odd room. He wasn't surprised that no one knew the flat had been empty for weeks. The fresh air filled his lungs as he opened the outside door and took a deep breath.

"Autumn is setting in Judith; you can smell the coolness of the air. The temperature will just go down now, the rivers and lakes will eventually freeze over. After all these years, I still despise the Berlin winter. Change of subject, I'm starting to rant. Why did someone come back to the flat, what were they, he, she looking for, Judith and why a woman?"

"Both males and females can have OCD, but women tend to lean towards contamination and cleaning. All I am saying is the odds are higher, that it is a woman who wiped the corner. Perhaps they were perusing, savouring a moment of glory. I don't think anyone will ever know what makes a serial murderer fully tick. There's no proof, Warren but I think it was a woman who came back, possibly with a partner, wiped her hand across the furniture disgusted at the mess. She or her partner is fastidious regarding cleanliness and detail."

"A female involved with the serial killing of men. I'm open to ideas, Judith. If it is a couple, then I would be looking for a partnership, not two close friends living separately. Friends cannot keep close secrets. This sort of relationship requires a deep bond of trust. Two people who can, on the outside, function normally in society as a couple, and that makes it all the harder."

"We should speak with Sabina again, Warren. We need to understand how he ticked; sex is a powerful emotion."

An hour later, Sabina opened the door to Warren and Judith.

"I never expected you two to be back so soon, my brother is out, come in; we can talk in the kitchen while I make you a coffee."

Warren and Judith leaned with their backs to the marble worktops and perused the kitchen. It was a world apart from where they had just come from, clean, neat and organised. They both looked at each other as much to say how the hell did she end up in the other relationship?

Sabina brought the coffee over and looked at Judith to invite the first question.

"Your kitchen, who keeps it so organised?"

"That's me, it keeps me occupied?"

"Andreas's flat."

"The pigsty, I gave up trying to keep it clean."

"Did you go back there at any time after you left, Sabina?"

"It was a one-way street for me, the decision was made and it had taken too long to make it. If I went back, it would have betrayed the trust of my brother. The simple answer is no."

"There's another question, related to the case. We are trying to understand more of his character. When did the violence start?"

Judith looked across the room to Warren who knew to keep quiet.

Sabina's hazel brown eyes stared directly at Judith.

"Andreas was the hero, looked after me, he made me feel worth something and would do anything for me. Then bit by bit, without realising it, step by fucking step he took my independence away. He got inside my head and ground me down. The violent outbursts came when he felt he was not in control. These started after about six months into the relationship. He would blame it on his, so-called childhood upbringing. You see it was not his fault that he hit me. I was just there, in his way and I caused his outbursts. The violence was my fault, according to him."

"How bad was it, Sabina?"

"Black eye, broken arm, bruises I lost count. The relationship became more extreme to the point where it broke me. I stopped seeing it as a relationship that I could fix."

"Your boyfriend was into BSDM, we found evidence on his computer and also contacts to a swinger group."

"Towards the end, the sex games became more extreme, the swinger parties, and well…one thing led to another. One night a couple came around and he overstepped the mark of respect. There is a lot of respect in BDSM circles for each other's partner, that is one thing I learnt and he didn't. He forgot the golden rule of no, which means no. The couple left and he blamed me."

"Do you know who they are?"

"The names, I cannot remember, it was about seven months ago and possible their names were fictitious."

"How did it all start?"

"Internet, Judith, web sites, emails, the names of people; we were never sure if they were real or alias, no one ever talked about their profession. There was simply no personal information exchanged. Anonymity was the key. Within a short period, no one invited him any longer and I would be the focal point for his anger. He became more violent and something inside me snapped. In a strange twist of fate, I learnt respect from the people in that circle and the woman I met in the cafe. A door opened for me that I knew my brother always had open, I was lucky."

Warren looked across the room at Sabina.

"Woman, you mentioned her yesterday. Can you remember anything else?"

"Not really, it was a role of fate; I have no idea what her name is. Like I said yesterday, he beat me up and I had to go to the hospital. That pushed me over the border and when I came out the whole world felt as if it was revolving around me. The woman sat down next to me, long blond hair, tied up in a bun, why she sat next to me, I have no idea. Maybe she could see that I needed to talk. Before I knew, it she had dragged my entire history out of me, a good listener."

"Had you seen her before?"

Sabina turned to face Warren.

"No, even though my coffee cup was nearly empty, she still sat opposite me."

"Maybe she recognised a survivor."

"Or she recognised a victim who was ready to become a survivor. I never went back and my brother found me on his step. I left the cafe before she had finished her coffee. In fact, I cannot even remember her drinking it. The whole day was a blur."

"To confirm; after you left him that you never went back to the flat? Not even to collect any clothes."

"No. You have searched his flat and probably found my clothes. Burn them all, I want nothing from the flat. Why are you pressing me for further confirmation?"

"We believe someone had, after he was abducted."

"How do you know?"

"We cannot say. Is there anyone that you can think of that your ex may have pissed off?"

"No, not too that level of murder."

"The woman, can you describe her a bit more?"

"Blond hair, as I said, she had an expensive bag, and her perfume was White linen. That's all I can remember."

"We will find out who done this and the other two murders. We believe they're linked."

"The abuse went on for too long and maybe I'll never be fully over my past. I've a lot to thank my brother for and also the woman in the cafe. I slept last night knowing he'll not come back into my life. I know you have to find the person who did this, but for me, I'm not that bothered. I have my justice and my future."

"Sabina, he cannot hurt you now, but as your father said look to the doors that will open. One of them is already open, your brother. I have met a few people who do not have that support or an escape route. You are lucky."

Warren saw Judith point to his watch, he knew they had to leave and head off to the lakeside pub to interview Andreas's friends.

"We'll head off now, but we will need you to make a formal statement sometime but thank you for your help. Every little piece of information we can obtain is helpful."

"I'm not planning to run anywhere, there's no need now. I no longer have to worry if he is going to be there when I open the front door or go to the shops."

Chapter 14

Warren and Judith parked on the gravel single track potholed road leading down to the lake edge. The wooden Swiss style pub with the beer garden was off the tourist track. They both noticed a group of middle-aged men enjoying one of the last warm autumn evenings.

"What do you think, Warren? There are no other male groups here and very few people sit inside when the weather is this good."

"You know, sometimes you get the feeling when you see a group, you can sense the atmosphere by the way they sit. Look at the two, one leaning back, arms folded, the guy opposite leaning over on the table. The rest of the group are sitting back in their chairs, which are a safe distance from the table allowing them easy access to get out. It almost looks like something is about to kick off. I've a suggestion, Judith, there's a free table over there; you sit there and watch my back. If there's any trouble, feel free to step in and help me."

"I thought you brought me here for a relaxing drink. I'll go first and reserve the seats."

Warren waited a minute and then walked over to the table where the men were sitting.

"Evening, I'm looking for Friedrich Rhode, a friend of Andreas."

"And who are you then?"

"Police, I'm investigating his murder."

A moment of silence reigned as the five men looked up at him.

"At least, I'll not have to speak to him again." "And which one are you, Friedrich Rhode?"

"That's your fucking problem to guess who I am. You're the detective or are you incapable of doing your job."

"I am very capable. We can discuss it here, or at the station; I only have room for one in my car. There's also the second option, I can request additional

100

transport for you all. How long did you know him and what was your relationship to him?"

"Fuck all to do with you, Bulle."

"Friedrich sit down, Andreas is not worth the hassle."

"At least, I have one name now and he has confirmed that you knew Andreas."

Friedrich walked around to Warren and squared up to him, eye to eye. He felt someone grab his collar and belt, and before he could react Judith's knee was in the base of his back and Friedrich's face was pressed into the gravel.

"You're coming back to the station, insulting an officer, threatening behaviour, obstructing enquires and whatever else I can dream up."

Warren, as well as the group and a few guests, looked on speechless at what they had just seen. Judith cuffed him and pulled him up to his feet.

"I take there's room in the back of your car, Warren. We can phone uniform and arrange to have him formally picked up."

"When the hell did you learn that."

"Training in the DDR, plus I kept it up until I moved to Berlin."

Warren looked at the slim partially balding middle-aged man.

"What the hell was all that about, a so-called friend, whatever, I don't care. For your information, he was tortured, and then cut in half and his body was dumped in The Spree. Would you like to help with enquires to find the murderer or shall we arrest you now for obstruction of police enquiries? Before I go any further, we're interested in catching a serial killer; we're not interested in any petty crimes you lot get up to. It's your lucky day, there is a bigger picture."

"I suppose Andreas's bitch, Sabina, told you where to find us. He shared her around a few times, not a bad screw, especially, one in front and one from behind."

Judith twisted the cuffs and looked directly into his eyes.

"That's not polite, no respect for women, neither did two of our corpses and I assume the third one. I hope you don't get on the wrong side of the killer or you may find yourself tortured and hacked in two after your skin was peeled off."

Friedrich stared back at Judith, he could tell from the calm tone of her voice and her passive mannerism that he had crossed well over the border with her.

"Talk now or later, either way, you will talk. If not now, the police will ensure they occupy most of your time and your friends. You will become very unpopular with your ageing boy band of friends."

"We lost contact with him months ago and never bothered to find out where he was. We have a small drugs ring, soft drugs, peddle a few stolen goods, but that's our limit. He overstepped the mark and wanted to pedal harder stuff. We found out that he had beaten Sabina up, pretty badly enough to put her in the hospital. The last thing that any of us want is a long stretch in prison for hard drugs or associate with someone who beats women that badly. It is about five months since we last saw him and before you ask no one can fully verify that."

"Good to hear that you have your boundaries when he beat her up. It looks like we know enough about your activities to arrest you. Pity, we don't have the time and resources to investigate what these boys get up to Warren. As we said, higher priorities are calling. Can you think of anyone who would want to kill him…in such a vicious way?"

"Who he associated with, outside of our group, we've no idea."

"So, you speak for the rest of the group."

"Ask them yourself, it's obvious that you can talk. The only other place he went to was the fitness centre."

"What about relations, brothers, sister, parents?"

"Sister lives in Australia, Perth. He never mentioned his parents; maybe they had disowned him, no idea."

"Any contact with her?"

"Not that I am aware of, he only mentioned her a few times."

"Mobile phone?"

"Pay as you go and before you ask, save your energy, you can have the number. Do you want anything else from me?"

"Not yet, but we may in the future, here's your ID card back."

Warren looked at Judith as they walked along the yellow gravel path back to the car.

"What do you think, Judith?"

"Within the bigger picture, a fairly harmless group of middle-aged men, who have not left their teenage years behind. They seem to have at least some standards, not very high ones. They have no wish to pedal hard drugs and end up in jail. They also did not like it when they heard Sabina was beaten up. We have their details and we can do a background check. I don't expect to find anything more than small-time offences, certainly nothing relating to the level of our investigation. I'll run the check to confirm. What shall we do now, Warren?"

"Home, you have Sarah waiting for you. This job can destroy relationships, Judith and you have just started one. It's been a long day; let's see if the flat search brings any additional information tomorrow. We need also to visit the cafe where Sabina met the woman who changed her life."

"I'll go in the morning before coming into work."

Chapter 15

Warren was reading through the initial forensic report on Andreas's flat when Judith plodded into the office. She dumped her backpack bag onto the chair.

"You look weary."

"Ever had a teenage daughter?"

"What do you mean?"

"Berlin night clubs, my daughter finally came home at five this morning, without sending a text message. The generation that can text the world and let them read on Facebook what they have eaten for breakfast, suddenly, they forget the number until they need a mother to pay for a taxi."

"Tired or mad as hell?"

"Tired and irritable from lack of sleep. The mad as hell part went out of the window when I phoned the taxi company and gave her, the wrong number by one digit. She ended up getting through to a sex line."

"Explain that one to your daughter why you have a number for a sex line. Anyhow, I thought you were having a romantic night for two with Sarah?"

"We did, but Sarah left before midnight. She is on the early shift today at the care home."

"So, that's why you phoned a sex line and I thought it was a man thing."

"Enjoy the moment. It's not often you get the chance for me to dig a hole. What're you reading?"

"Grab yourself some caffeine."

Judith sat down in silence, both hands clasping her mug and stared at Warren. He wondered how long she would stay awake.

"Your cup is empty."

"I know, I'm trying to summon some energy. Last night is catching up."

"I'll pour the coffee, don't move."

"I wasn't planning to. I went to the cafe as planned, it turned up nothing. The owner didn't recognise a picture of Sabina and as for a blond woman; it was take your pick. Frustrating because we both know someone was there. What's on your desk?"

"It's the draft report on Andreas's flat, Judith. We've got: internet, email history, an old appointment card, shopping, clothes, shoe receipts, an appointment for a doctor. We're waiting for the mobile phone records, which he took off Sabina and also his number, which was gratefully provided by his so-called friend yesterday."

"What type of search did the team perform?"

"Each room was squared off and then followed with a fresh eyes approach. Why?"

"Just curious, nothing more, making conversation. I'll get in contact with the doctor to find out why he was there."

"Not worth the effort, Judith. Doctors, as we know don't even have to inform employers if the employee is not fit for work and they may be in charge of people's lives. We'll have to subpoena the information."

"I can ask and he can say no if he does not wish to help a serial murder investigation. Besides, I could do with some fresh air, I need to keep moving."

"Go for it. How's the team progressing with investigating the gym membership list and when Andreas visited the gym?"

"I received an email from Marleen this morning, on my phone. I popped around to see her before I came here so she could explain. It looked like a load of dots on a graph to me."

"I told you she was good at analysing a large amount of detailed data. Marleen has a lot of respect from other parts of the station."

"Here you are, I've just opened the email on my computer. From the two thousand seven hundred plus members, Marleen has cross-referenced the list to the date, times and when other members were there. I'll show you, come over here."

Warren knelt on the floor next to Judith and looked at the cross-referenced graph, of dates, length of time spent at the gym and a varying-coloured dots number of dots in a graph.

"Okay, Judith, I can figure this out in time, but it'll be quicker for you to explain the graph key."

"These dots here are the outliers where there is a limited overlap of time and contact regularly with members. These, within the standard distribution curve, indicate a greater overlap of data, peak time. This group in the centre have the highest possibility of contact with other people. It's not certain, it's just the laws of possibility and a chance to structure who we may interview first. You can clearly see the groups of people who he may have come into contact with."

"It's a start, the chance to take some people out of the investigation. This is going to take time and manpower, Judith, but there's no option. Split the team as you see fit, at the end of the day, it's the same amount of work and overtime."

"All door to door."

"I know, old-fashioned footslog, also cross-reference who was at the gym Xmas party."

"Marleen is one step ahead; she has already prepared it."

"We need to narrow that list down, understand who knew him and what their relationship was with him. I expect to see names crop up more than once and then on a more regular basis. There's one thing for certain, all three bodies were found in this one quadrant of Berlin and one now leads us to this corner. I cannot believe our killer met all the victims in the fitness centre but there may be a link to the past."

"I don't think our killer would be that stupid, to select three people from one centre, Warren."

"How this links into the other two murders; we need to find out. I am interested to see who he had contact with at the centre. Someone knew him and his violent history with woman, how close they were to him is an open question."

"I'm going to throw an open thought for you, Warren. We are talking about linking to the past, how about connecting the past to the present."

"Is that not the half empty, half full glass scenario?"

"Sort of, the link is already there, just unforeseen with the future. I'm just trying to look from a different angle."

"Keep that thought then, Judith and dig up what information you need. Keep me up to speed though. Start with case one and go through it in detail, fresh eyes. I cannot help feel that there will be a fourth. Whoever is involved now has a taste for torture and the slaughter of human beings."

Chapter 16

Stefan had left early for work; Anja turned over and tucked the duvet under her stomach. She lay in bed looking out of the window at the trees, swaying as leaves floated to the ground. Today was Friday, a day off work and the start of a well-earned long weekend. Stefan would not be back until after five and she started to wonder how to fill the day. Anja drifted back off to sleep and it was nearly ten when she woke. The sun streamed through the window and the sky was a sapphire blue, Anja had no interest in going to the fitness centre and she knew there would not be many more warm days left to sit outside. The thought of a gentle walk through Koepenick appealed to her. A cup of coffee, cake and reading a book was about as much stress as she wanted today. Restaurant Krokodil sprung into her mind, the thought of people watching on the promenade as well as the boats going by appealed to her. The decision was made where to spend her lazy day and Anja headed off in the direction of her shower room.

Despite the November chill in the wind, the sun brought enough warmth to sit outside. Anja found a patch of sunshine and sat in the reclining chair with a blanket over her legs. She watched the tourists walk by and the boats go up and down on the river. *Heaven, what a way to relax,* she thought. She decided to have a low-calorie count day to compensate for not going to the fitness centre. The thought was short-lived as the slice of chocolate cake and cappuccino arrived. She surveyed the rich darkness of the thick slice as the waitress placed it on the table. Anja looked up as she was about to devour her first mouthful. She could not believe it; Vincenzo was strolling along the promenade. She knew it was a chance and today could be unfortunate for him. He caught her eye, waved and strolled over to Anja.

"Vincenzo. What a small world? Sit down and join me for a coffee, if you have time."

"I have time for you; it's your sister that scares me. It's a while since we have seen each other. The last time was the party and before that was at the fitness centre. Do you still go there?"

"Please sit, the centre, not so often these days. A few times this year, Xmas party last year and that's about it. The novelty wore off, good intentions and all that. So, what brings you to Koepenick today, off work on a holiday?"

"I resigned a few weeks ago and yesterday was my last day at work."

"It sounds like you have some sort of plan for the future."

"I've saved enough money in the bank, plus my inheritance will last more than a few years. So, I plan to travel and enjoy my life. I am flying to Hong Kong tomorrow, afternoon flight and then onto China, after that it all depends on my mood, and who I meet on the way. I may even apply for a one-year work visa in Australia, there's no hurry."

"Sounds like an adventure, that's something I will never have the chance to do until in later life. Three weeks maximum, I'm too tied up with the practice. Do you plan to visit relations on your world journey, mother, father, sister?"

"I'm an only child and my parents died several years ago. To be honest, it's also fuck all to do with my, so-called friends, especially Filippo, I hope he suffers in the abyss of hell. I'm simply disappearing out of Germany and will return if and when I'm ready. You are the only one who knows the details."

"Sorry to hear about your parents."

"No need, we never got along, Anja."

"So, what are you doing today, a last-minute wander to kill time? Are you taking a girlfriend with you?"

"I am travelling alone, my bags are packed, the flat and fridge are empty, there's no point in buying any food; it turned out to be a blessing that she never came back. Why would I want to take any baggage with me? It would only spoil my fun." 'Baggage', 'it', Anja cringed inwardly at the use of those words. A woman to him was a dispensable item to be used and no longer human. She looked at him with empathetic eyes and touched his shoulder to show sympathy.

"Sorry to hear that you're no longer together. You are right though, why take some when you will have more fun alone. It sounds like an adventure of a lifetime to travel, go where you want and talk to who you want without any ties. No baggage, good decision."

"It's her loss, Anja, not mine."

"What happened at the party that night? I only saw one side of the story."

"Some people are too sensitive, I passed a comment, a compliment and her husband took offence to it. The woman cannot remember what she was called, seemed to take also an offence." Anja turned onto her side to deliberately face Vincenzo to signal a deeper personal interest. She could not stand the slime ball sitting next to her, but it was time to reel him in. The opportunity, which had presented itself, was too good to miss.

"It happens; unfortunately, some men and women are too sensitive. Some men also see women as their property and the need to defend their male status by controlling women. You drew the short straw with Maria; I agree with you, she overreacted that day."

"Is that her name, her husband should bring her under control."

"Some men are too controlling and some not, it should be a balance between two people, Vincenzo. That balance can be fun if applied correctly between consenting adults. Some women like control; some men like to be controlled by a woman, or both can switch. It all depends on their relationship and of course, the situation they may find themselves in. Stefan, my husband, switches; despite our marriage, we are both independent and that works for us. We do not see each other as property but a relationship based on equality and respect."

Vincenzo looked silently at her, unsure if he was reading correctly between the lines.

Anja felt a flow of excitement through her body, she simply could not believe her luck and the opportunity was too good to miss. She had her prey in her clutches.

"Would you like to walk, I'm tired of sitting and people watching. The joints need to be freed up."

"Sure, but I'm surprised you speak to me after what happened at your sister's house."

"She has her life and I've mine, Vincenzo. Personally, I'm not too keen on Filippo, but it's her choice. Let's walk along the river, a couple of more months and it will start to freeze over. We're coming to the end of the good weather."

Anja linked Vincenzo's left arm as they walked and snuggled close to him. Vincenzo willingly accepted the close attention from her.

"Another reason to leave the city, Anja, is to escape the Berlin winter, it can be harsh at times. Let's walk to Freiheit Fünfzehn and sit down next to the ship. It's around the corner."

Anja could feel Vincenzo wanted to control the rest of the day. There was a bigger picture for her and in the scope of her plan; it was a necessary detail to go along with.

"Okay, if that's what you want, I'll go along with that, but I need to be home by five."

"Why five."

"Stefan comes home at five."

"Sounds like you play the role of the obedient wife."

"Me, never, but he likes to think it. Maybe, sometimes, I play the obedient role but only when it suits me. Sometimes, I play the disobedient wife."

Anja looked straight into Vincenzo's piercing sapphire blue eyes.

"You seem to be a person who likes to dominate women, obedience and domination what a perfect combination. Tell me, I have a suggestion; do you have any plans for tonight? You said that you have no food at home, why not come over to our house and I will cook you a meal, have a few drinks and let's see how the night slowly develops. It is your last night in Germany."

A moment of silence fell between the two of them as Vincenzo absorbed what was on offer.

"Okay, it sounds like it could be an interesting night, a farewell party before I leave. What time should I come over?"

"Let's say seven, it gives me time to prepare the food and also decide…what I will wear. So change of plan, let's skip Freiheit Fünfzehn, I need to head off to buy some food and start preparing for tonight. We'll see each other later then? Actually in about four hours."

"Promised, I'll be there."

"Okay then, leave your car, Stefan will bring you home."

"The car is gone, sold it a few weeks ago, so it will be public transport. In fact, it is not worth me going home, I'll travel direct from here. See you later, Anja." Anja headed off in the direction of her car. The intense distaste for Vincenzo flowed through her body as she walked along the promenade. She felt contaminated by him but like a good actor, she would subdue her true feelings for a short period later tonight. First, she had to make a short call from a public telephone box.

"Stefan, don't answer, I bumped into Vincenzo today and I invited him for an evening meal. I assumed that you would have no objections. Can you ensure to bring some Propofol?"

Stefan hung up as his colleague looked across the table at him.

"What was that about?"

"I've no idea; someone muttered something and then hung up, probably some weirdo."

Chapter 17

Stefan swirled the Cognac in his glass, looked at his watch and wondered how long it would be before his wife would appear. It would only be another hour before Vincenzo would arrive and the food was prepared. He heard the clip of heels at the top of the landing and looked up. Anja, attired in black stockings and lace-up corset, step by step slowly and seductively descended the stairs.

"There's no need to tell you how great you look, you know."

"You can always tell me again, I'll never get bored of that. You men are so easy, a bit of nylon, shoes, corset, makeup and you go all limp. What whip shall I use tonight? These thinner strands hurt more. I may even use the ones with studs, just for Vincenzo."

Anja stroked the whip and pulled the cats slowly through her hand.

"Let's see how the controller likes to be controlled tonight and lose his freedom."

"I'll leave that choice to you, Anja; pity, there's no time for a quickie."

"That's not your choice tonight; you're not in control of the sex. Anyhow, it's time to put on a dress, something very innocent to serve the meal, afterwards. Did you remember the Propofol, Stefan?"

"I still had some from last time."

The doorbell rang just after seven and Vincenzo, complete with his threaded eyebrows, goatee beard and a perfect tan, stood before Stefan.

"Hi, Vincenzo, pleased you turned up, come in, please, let me take your coat. The weather is starting to change outside."

"How could I decline the offer, it was good of your wife to offer. Your house is not too easy to find by bus."

"Ah, you came by bus."

"I sold my car, did Anja not mention it?"

"No, she didn't, it makes no difference, I'll take you home, or perhaps you may stop, we have a guest bed. Let's see how the night develops. Anja, Vincenzo is here."

"Two seconds, I will just put my oven gloves down."

Vincenzo saw Anja strut across the floor and already he felt his hormones level increase.

"Hi, pleased you came; we would have been disappointed if you failed to turn up. What would you like to drink?"

"Whisky, Anja, no ice, smoky or peaty, if you have one. You are looking very sexy tonight."

Stefan could not help think what an arsehole. Two seconds into their house and Vincenzo calls his wife sexy.

"Thank you, this was the intention of tonight; a few drinks, some food and later, let's see what happens."

She could feel herself cringe as he placed a hand on her back and felt the corset strings. She gently brushed it to one side and looked him in the eyes.

"Later, yes, it's a corset, just to confirm your thoughts. We've plenty of time, let's say you will miss your last bus home, it leaves very early. Why don't you boys sit down, have a drink and a chat, while I finish the food?"

"That sounds good to me."

"So, Vincenzo, Anja mentioned you are off on a world tour, alone."

"That's right, woman free but not for long, I'll find someone on route for a bit of fun. My last ex had no respect for men and that was her problem. She wanted independence and didn't realise her status in our relationship. I am content that she is gone, no baggage for this trip. In any relationship, the man has to be the dominate one, in charge. A relationship cannot work without rigid sexist roles. When a woman enters a relationship, she has to understand these roles. Understand what I mean? It's all about control."

"So, you're a controller."

"Unless, it comes to sex, then role reversal is okay."

"A switcher, eh! Well, you may be in for a treat tonight if that's what you're interested in."

Anja walked into the room and sat close to Vincenzo.

"So, what have you boys been talking about?"

"Vincenzo is a switcher; he likes to control women in a relationship, but he enjoys also the submissive side of sex."

113

"Then he's in for a treat tonight. The meat is in the oven, it should take about another two hours. I had set the timer earlier, but I forgot to switch the oven on. Since we have spare time why not start now. We could show him our downstairs playroom, Stefan. I'm sure we will all be hungry later. Vincenzo, are you interested? It's your leaving party."

Anja took Vincenzo by the hand and led him past the dining room to a door in the hallway. He noticed the table was only set for two, Anja saw him look.

"I haven't finished setting the table yet, Vincenzo."

Stefan followed the two downstairs and closed the door behind them. Vincenzo looked in amazement as he entered their playroom. He noticed a swing suspended from the ceiling, an examination chair and a St Andrew Cross.

"Man, you have one hell of a playroom here."

"It is one of the advantages of buying an old World War Two bunker and converting it to a house. The walls are nearly two metres thick in some parts and no one can hear any noise."

"You must have a lot of fun."

"Definitely, you can scream as loud as you wish."

"What's that book over there, Stefan?"

"It belongs to me, Vincenzo, it's special, it helps me to de-stress from everyday life. I press flowers for a hobby; the cover is manufactured from a very special material, well, special to me. I would prefer if you do not touch."

Anja observed the two as she slipped off her A-line dress. Vincenzo turned around to see Anja standing in her underwear and red high heels. In her right hand, she held a cat of nine tails whip.

"Strip if you want to play, now."

The tone of her voice was firm and Vincenzo instantly knew he was in a submissive role. Anja saw her husband walk over to his favourite stool so he could sit and watch as Anja circled her prey. The switching between dominant and passive was a role play they both enjoyed.

"Which part of the strip did you not understand, Vincenzo. Now, if you want to play, or are you so dumb, you do not understand the command."

The dominant commanding tone of her voice had increased. Vincenzo obeyed and threw his clothes to one side and faced Anja waiting for his next order.

Anja draped the whip over the back of Vincenzo and spoke softly into his ear. Unknown to him, Vincenzo would come to fear that soft firm caring tone coupled with the smell of White Linen.

"Is that how you live at home? So untidy, throwing your clothes on the floor. I'm not your maid or your mother, pick them up, fold them neatly and place them on the table where my husband is. Respect our house, you are a guest here, do not forget."

Vincenzo, naked, obeyed like a schoolchild, picked up his clothes and neatly folded them onto the table where Stefan was sitting.

"I like order, neatness and control. Stefan, are his clothes lined up square to the edge of the table?"

"Not quite, Anja, I'll rearrange them."

"It looks like he needs to be punished. Over there, arse against the cross, legs spread and arms up, punishment for not been orderly."

Vincenzo obeyed, spread his arms and legs. Anja tightened the leather straps around his wrists. She ran her tongue across the tip of his hard penis as she knelt in front of him to fasten the leg straps. She stood before him and Vincenzo noticed she had picked up a ball gag for his mouth.

"What's that for?"

She slapped him hard across his face.

"You don't control and ask questions here, Vincenzo, open your mouth, like a good little boy. The ball gag will stop you from screaming and make your orgasm more intense as your feelings implode inside you. The small holes still allow you to breathe."

Vincenzo obeyed and Anja pulled the leather strap as tight as she could. Vincenzo let out a muffled protest as his mouth was forced wide open. Anja looked down at Vincenzo's now semi-erect penis and wrapped her whip around the stem. She stared him straight in the eye.

"See, how powerful women can be, you have gone all limp. Are you afraid of me? Obviously, you only like submissive women and are not capable of handling a dominant woman. What a wimp, such a controlling man useless in the hands of a dominant woman. Within half an hour, you have lost control, see how powerful I am. There you are, meek, mild, helpless, unable to move, pathetic specimen of a man. You're not such a women abuser, after all, you are easy prey. I hate men with a vengeance who abuse women; you are even an insult to an alpha male." She grasped his penis and balls tightly in her fist. Vincenzo let out another muffled protest as he wondered what was about to happen. Anja moved closer to Vincenzo to whisper in his ear.

"You can understand now, when I said the gag would intensify your screams. You have not really screamed yet, but you will."

Anja slammed her fist into Vincenzo's scrotum; he swallowed his scream as the pain and the sickly feeling rose up to his stomach. She watched his rib cage heaving up and down. The contorted pain in his face said it all as she twisted his scrotum in her hand.

"It works, the gag intensifies everything. Enjoy your pain, there is more to be derived. I have to see my husband now, you can watch." Anja walked over to her husband and wrapped her lips around his penis. Vincenzo could only watch and suffer his pain as her head bobbed up and down. The expression on Stefan's face showed that he had cum in her mouth. Anja stood up, straightened her hair, turned around and looked at Vincenzo. She walked over to him as she wiped the sperm from her lips and rubbed her fingers over his lips. Vincenzo noticed that she had a blindfold in her hand.

"Your turn to have your senses heightened."

Vincenzo unable to move and now blindfolded waited for the unexpected. He could feel his heart rate and breathing rate increase as fear started to seep in. Vincenzo screamed inwards as he felt the metal studs on the whip tear the flesh open on his chest. He felt the warmth of blood flowing down his body.

"I'll attend to your wounds later, but first let's see if you can tell the difference between a man and a woman, pity, it is still limp. Still, it gives us something to work with. Let's see what I can do to turn you on, even if you cannot see."

He heard the sound of her heels walk towards him, there was silence as she stood before him. Vincenzo's body flinched as she rubbed her finger along one of the open wounds. He screamed inwardly and panted with the burning pain as she pressed her nail into the ripped flesh. He felt a firm hand around his penis.

"Maybe, I should cut this off for what you have done to women, one ball at a time and stuff them in your mouth. Maybe not, I'm not too sure yet."

Vincenzo twisted and turned as he tried to free himself, helpless, fully at the whim of his captures. Unable to see, unable to scream, outwardly, heart-pounding, and his thoughts ran riot at what might happen. The whip struck his chest again, the pain raced through his body.

"That's enough Vincenzo…for today. We do not want you to suffer too much on your first date. Besides, I have no more spare time, the meat will be ready shortly and I'm hungry."

"Stefan, why not give this little submissive man a blow job, a treat for his own self-inflicted suffering. After all, he wanted to play the role of submissive. Who knows, he might even get aroused."

Anja watched her husband kneel in front of Vincenzo who felt the hot breath on his penis, he felt sick at the thought. Every sense in his body was going crazy as he tried to make some sense of his situation. Suddenly, he felt a sharp stabbing pain in his right thigh and slipped into unconsciousness. Stefan stood up looked at Anja.

"Not so much of a man now, is he."

"They never are."

"We can put him in the cell later, Anja, I'm hungry. He will be out for a few hours."

"I need to get out of this outfit, it's getting uncomfortable."

"It looks damn good though."

"You try wearing it for a few hours, besides; it's not practicable to finish cooking our meal. And before you ask, I have put your Cognac on the table. Yes, you can fuck me later but let us eat first. Can you attend to his wounds, Stefan, while I finish the meal? The last thing we need is an infection to set in."

"Sure, no problem, it will not take long. I am pleased you did not damage the skin on his back, Anja."

The smell of the slow-cooked pulled pork drifted through the house. Anja walked into the kitchen in a long loose-fitting spaghetti strap dress. Stefan was already in the kitchen putting the plates out.

"You look more relaxed now."

Anja spun around with a smirk on her face as the bottom of her dress swirled.

"It is less sexy but more appropriate for a meal. I've left the ventilation hatch open to the cellar for when he comes too. The smell of the food should drift down. Poor soul, he's probably starving."

"Where did you get that idea from?"

"Remember when we went to Skye."

Stefan noticed she had her mischievous twinkle in her sapphire blue eyes.

"The castle, which we visited. The dungeon was between the dining room and the way to the kitchen. They made a slot in the dungeon, so the smell of the food would drift into the cell where the prisoner was starving to death."

Stefan looked at his wife as she slowly teased the pork out. He had no reply and again he felt himself wondering about his wife's limits.

"The pork looks very tender, Anja."

There was hardly a word spoken between the two as they savoured the meal. The glasses of Cognac were left untouched to celebrate the end of a good meal. Stefan finished and placed his knife and fork across each other on his plate and looked at Anja.

"I can hear you thinking. You have that zoned out expressionless look on your face."

"You're right. I think I need to play some music whilst I'm thinking a few things through. Holst, Planet Suite?"

"Start with Mars, Bringer of War; it's my favourite. You were right, Stefan."

"About what?"

"Your new stereo, there is a difference between a digital and valve stereo system. I tried it the other day."

"Come sit down with me, Anja."

"What's bothering you? We hardly spoke a word at the table."

"Revenge, uncontrolled Anja knows no bounds. This is number four and I've no doubt there will be others, which will come our way. You're on a mission and each time we've explored and justified the boundaries, but we need to know our limits. Unless, we know them, then we will spend the rest of our lives in jail. Something, I believe we are not interested in if it happened then your mission is at an end,"

"Where're you going with this, Stefan?"

"This is our last, hear me out. Unless, we stop or take a break, we will make mistakes. With all the last bodies, we knew them all, that is a connection back to us that the police have not found. Let's take this in a different direction and taunt the police. Drop them a letter, a tape, perhaps, send them another one just after we have dumped Vincenzo but tell them that they will have to wait for the winter thaw. No more killings, Anja, we move to control and play."

"Control and play, sounds fine to me, Stefan. I quite like the idea of tormenting the police. Send the letter from a different part of Germany, or a country. Commuting is so easy for criminals these days, thanks to the Schengen agreement. Do not use our printer; it's traceable via the mark the laser leaves on the paper."

"I'll use the one, which I bought from the flea market, Anja. There's no traceability."

"The music is so clear, precise, organised and under the control of the conductor. Listen, Stefan, you can hear every piece of the orchestra. It is sheer perfection, crystal clear, perfection."

He looked across to his wife. She was deeply engrossed in the fine details of the music searching to isolate the different instruments. He knew, it was time to leave her alone and enjoy his Cognac.

The effects of a long day, good food and Cognac were starting to set in. He felt tired and tomorrow he would have to face a business conference in Dresden. There was one more job to do before heading off to bed. The effects of the drug on Vincenzo would be wearing off and he needed to chain him standing up in the one metre by one-metre cell.

Stefan stood before a delirious Vincenzo and shackled his wrists to the pulley. Vincenzo, semi-conscious felt the weight of his body suspended in mid-air.

"Do you know what I do for a hobby?"

Vincenzo could hear the footsteps walking around him.

"Flower pressing, it's so relaxing, I collect rare flowers, the book is on the table that you saw earlier. It's full, time for a new book and I will need a new cover. I am pleased Anja left your back untouched. Luckily, for you, I have a new lampshade."

Vincenzo felt a needle in his thigh and he drifted back into unconsciousness. Stefan pulled the limp body into the cell with the overhead pulley and locked the watertight door behind him. Stefan felt contaminated, unclean after handling Vincenzo and he could see dried blood under his nail. Tired and exhausted he stepped out of the shower, Anja stood before him. He knew that look in her eyes; sleep had become an option, which was now postponed.

Chapter 18

Vincenzo gradually entered the conscious world. Unable to see, his arms shackled above his head, mouth taped closed, he could smell the damp, musty, humid air. Alone, the darkness, the solitude and sensory deprivation started to play with his mind as he entered full consciousness. Panic and fear started to set it. His heart rate increased. No clothes were sticking to him as he felt the sweat trickle over his naked body. He realised he was naked, the floor, he could feel the concrete floor, but it was enough for his feet to take his weight. His heart pounded as he struggled to breathe through his nose. Muddled thoughts started to clear as the drug wore off. Bit by bit, his senses became more alive and terror replaced the muddled panic thoughts as adrenaline flowed through his body. Vincenzo started to tremble and moved his right leg to one side. Unable to scream, he swallowed the feeling inside as he felt the blood run down his leg. He instantly jerked to the other side only for his other leg to be cut. Terrified, trembling with fear, he heard the sound of metal sliding. The few seconds of silence was an eternity, he hoped that someone was there. The light stung his eyes as the peephole slide moved back. A calm spoken feminine voice enveloped his claustrophobic confines. He recognised the soft smell of the perfume.

"You see, why anyone should have respect for you is beyond me, it leaves me totally speechless. Then again they probably never did, but they were too afraid to tell you. Not a nice position to put women in. Oh, before I forget, your arms are bound above your head, but you know that. It's for your safety; the cell, which you find yourself in, is one-metre by one-metre. The walls are covered with extremely rough concrete, move left, right or back, you will cut yourself. I got the idea from a museum I visited once. Be careful not to damage the skin on your back. By the way, in case you have not noticed, your chest wounds have been attended to. We do not want you to run the risk of infection. The only reason your mouth is bound is to stop you from screaming, it adds to my enjoyment. Plus, it's just, well; I don't like the noise of a grown man screaming like a terrified little boy. I will remove the tape eventually, just like my other victims, after they died. Damn, I let that slip, you now know your future, not many people know their future and today, you should feel honoured. This is your fault, no one to blame but you. How does it feel that you always blame other people for your actions, 'you made me do that', is always a good phrase, never own the problem or take responsibility. There's only one person to blame for where you are now, figure it out, you are intelligent enough. If only you learned dignity and respect, such a simple thing."

Vincenzo felt the warmth of urine running down his leg; the acidic odour filled his nose.

"You've pissed yourself; you really have no respect for people around you, still learned nothing. You need a shower, you smell like a pig."

There was silence, he hoped for at least some more sensory input from his capture. The silence continued for what felt like an eternity. Again, the sound of the gentle spoken voice caressed his ears.

"What is the greatest? Pain or the fear of pain, or not knowing how you will die? You have no control over these things. I do. Control, that's something you know about, what it feels like to not be in control. You opted for the submissive role. No need to worry, as I said before, I will remove the tape."

Vincenzo felt a brief moment of relief at this possible small reward.

"When I cut your tongue out, or perhaps, rip it out. Difficult decision."

Vincenzo's body swallowed the scream of fear inwards at the thought of his future. The adrenaline flowed as his mind raced unable to find an answer. He twisted his body trying to free the shackles which attached his arms above. Again he brushed the jagged concrete walls and screamed as more blood ran down his legs.

"Your mind is already racing, the power of the language of control. You just don't know if I will cut your tongue out. Living in fear and under the control of one person, I think you now realise, it's not a pleasant experience."

Vincenzo heard the crack of a valve opening followed by the welcome relief of cool water flowing over his head. The temperature in the cell dropped and the air freshened, much to his relief. Vincenzo never heard the metallic sound of the spy hole closing, only the sound of water flowing over his head echoed in his ears. He could feel the cold water rising over his ankles and gradually over his waist. Left alone with his fear and darkness he felt the water rise. Trapped, unable to move in any direction his most dreaded fear, drowning was now a reality. The oxygen would run out and his lungs would burn and scream for air only to be replaced with water. The gag reflex would expel the water only for his lungs to refill and cut off the oxygen. He tilted his head back to gain a few more seconds of life as the water circled his shoulders. The wrist cuffs dug deep into his skin as he struggled to pull himself upwards. He realised there was no ceiling or was it a high ceiling, all he knew was that he had bought a few more moments of life. The muscles in his arms burned as they filled with lactic acid, his time was limited and he took a deep breath hoping when he surfaced, there would still be a pocket of air. Vincenzo surfaced, unsure of the water level, his lungs were screaming for air as the involuntary muscles took over the breathing. Air-filled his lungs and the light blinded him as he heard once more the grating sound of metal. The soft voice spoke again.

"Fearing for your life, did you really think I would kill you so quickly and easy? We needed you clean. I don't like to work on dirty bodies."

Vincenzo felt the water level lower over his naked body. Exhaustion had set in; Vincenzo mumbled.

"We need to get you out, attend those wounds and provide you nourishment. Stefan, can you inject him? Then we can winch him out like a pig in a slaughterhouse. I'll attend to his wounds to prevent infection; we need to prolong his life."

Vincenzo's wounded naked body drifted back into the conscious world as he woke up on a hard wooden bed. He squinted to keep out the bright light in the corner and noticed his wounds were bandaged. The cell was larger, he had room to walk around and he wondered how long he had been here. His mouth was dry; he could not remember the last time he had drunk. Vincenzo returned to the bed and curled up into the foetal position; he laid his head on the wooden slats and tried to shelter the bright light from his eyes. Deprived of the sensory aspect of night or day, he wondered what time it was and in fact what day. It was a simple question, a simple need to know, no answer, no human touch, no human interaction, Vincenzo felt withdrawn, alone in his mind. The grating sound of metal echoed around his cell and a tray was pushed through a small doorway in the corner. Slowly, he crawled off the bed and noticed food and water on the tray as it came into focus. He hobbled across the floor and picked up the tray, chicken, salad, rice, bread and two litres of water. Vincenzo sat on his bed with his back to the wall. The basic human need had set in, safety; this corner had now become his safe space. He was protected from behind and could see anyone coming through the door. The loss of freedom, pain, disappointment, misery, loneliness, ridicule, rejection and the fear of death, were now his unwelcome companion. He looked at the offerings on the tray and stared, it was a welcome moment of civilisation, a brief view of the outside world.

The grating sound of metal echoed again around the cell, this time from the door. He heard footsteps walking. His mind raced as to who it was, Anja or Stefan, or were both out there. He looked to the inspection slot in the door. It was Anja, he recognised her perfume and Vincenzo had no doubt, she was surveying her prey. The slot slammed shut and then he found himself in total darkness, unable to see his hand in front of his face or his food.

"Anyone who says they are not afraid of the darkness is a liar. Enjoy your inner lack of sensory input dissolving into your mind. The pain-relieving drugs, which we give you, will wear off in about one hour."

Vincenzo heard her footsteps drift into the distance, total darkness and silence filled his cell. He fumbled for his food and stuffed it into his mouth, a brief sigh of relief flowed through his body. He knew this moment of normality would be short-lived. The burning pain would slowly start and soon spread like fire through his body. Vincenzo crawled into his safe corner, curled up again into a foetal position and waited for the pain to worsen. He realised they wanted him alive, but he had to suffer, it was their rules, for their sick pleasure. He knew it was a small grace that they would eventually give him painkillers, but he wondered how long they would let him writhe in pain.

Chapter 19

Stefan curled up on his oxblood red Chesterfield seat and stared out of the patio doors to watch the sunset. This was his safety zone, his place where he could relax. The glass of Cognac nestled comfortably in the palm of his hand as he let the world go by and his mind drifted with the beauty of nature. His solitude was short-lived as Anja walked into the sitting room.

"Anja, can you bring the Cognac bottle please; I'm unable to get rid of the musty taste of the cell in my throat. It's either that or I am heading for an infection."

"Until you are certain, no kissing."

"Let's open the patio doors, Anja. I enjoy living here; the silence combined with nature envelopes you like a blanket. The fresh smell of the water from the lake is a stark contrast to the dry air of Berlin. The wildlife and living so close to nature each day, there is no way that I could live inside a city again."

"Even Vincenzo has not disturbed the peace, Stefan. I hope he enjoyed his meal. The painkillers should be starting to wear off."

"How long will you let him suffer tonight, Anja?"

"Two, three hours, I don't what him dying of shock, I would feel cheated. I'll give him some Morphine later; I'm too busy enjoying the evening."

Stefan looked at the burning autumnal red Berlin sun, sinking behind the trees; winter would soon raise its head, the nights were already dark and cold. Anja curled up on the sheep-skin rug, snuggled into her husband and wrapped her arms around his legs. He wondered how his wife could be as cold the night air and have a caring heart. Anja slowly caressed his thigh and a warm feeling of relaxation flowed through his body.

"What now? How shall we move forward? How long do you plan to keep him as your torture toy, Anja?"

"You've never asked that question before? Why now? We've always let it run the course until we decided the time is right to dispose of the body."

"That I know, but winter will arrive shortly, for me it is bad timing. Vincenzo surfaced too early; it's another six weeks before the lake will start to freeze."

"We could play with him another two, three weeks. We can then let him slowly die and freeze his body."

Anja stopped caressing and rubbed her finger along his thigh as she looked away. He knew that body language and that an idea had sprung into her mind. "Spit it out, Anja, an idea has crossed your mind. We've been married too long; I can almost hear your brain thinking."

"We do not kill him, well, not directly. Playing with the mind can be greater than physical suffering, combine the two? Psychological and physical torture?"

"Where's this going?"

"I read a magazine article today, medieval torture. Open his wounds up, cover his body in a sweet substance, encapsulate him and then let the ants do the rest. Then place a mask over his head with a tube so he can breathe and pour the ants into the mask. It was an acceptable practice, a few hundred years ago."

"The practice is still acceptable today, for you. I would still like to wait until the lake freezes over rather than freeze the body. Can you move over, Anja, I need another drink."

"I brought you your bottle."

"I know, but I remembered that I have another bottle, which is nearly finished. This bottle is new."

Stefan walked over to the table and poured another Cognac. He looked at the bottle, deliberately, to avoid eye contact with Anja and wondered what her limits were. He knew he would support her, he was too deeply involved, but he knew she had exceeded his limits.

"We could freeze the body, Anja; the only problem is that it will rupture the cellular structure and forensics will spot this. We would need to prevent anaerobic and aerobic decomposition. We could reduce the temperature of the body to near freezing and place it in a vacuum. The absence of air, humidity, surrounding organic matter would slow the decomposition. The ants, which you have introduced, would also die, thus preventing decomposition. In summary, it becomes a complicated technical nightmare. I suggest, we keep him alive and wait for the cold snap. The timing was wrong with Vincenzo, but we can work with it. A few more weeks and then do what you want."

"What about the letter to the police? When will you send it?"

"I will send it after my business trip, the end of this week. I will deviate from my route and send it from somewhere remote. I think we should give Vincenzo the morphine and antibiotics now. We need to prolong his life a few more weeks and stop the physical torture. Perhaps, try psychological torture, the light, leave it on and deprive him of sleep, just a thought until we bring it to an end."

That was a phrase she had never heard from her husband before and she felt as if he was taking control. Anja looked at her husband, she felt for the first time, doubt, lack of trust. She was unsure why she had this feeling with Stefan, but it was there. She knew now was the wrong time to challenge, this could wait until the body was disposed of. Or was he right? Either way, she felt doubt and for the first time, she inwardly questioned herself.

"You're right, Stefan, painkillers and antibiotics. We're both skilled enough to keep him alive for a few extra weeks. We'll wait until the temperature drops then dispose of him, but I will not be robbed of my enjoyment."

"No one is robbing you, Anja; your pleasure is only briefly delayed."

"The letter, send a photo of him from the shoulders down. Let the police know, they have failed again to protect, it will up the stress on their team. Print the letter now and seal it in an envelope, at least, I know it is then ready to be sent. We stop the killing and play with the police. I've listened to what you said, earlier. We will make mistakes, perhaps, we have and three bodies were enough to identify a pattern, this is number four. I will not spend the rest of my life in prison."

Stefan hesitated at the words spoken by his wife. A moment of contentment flowed through his body, but an inner instinct did not fully trust her words.

"It is already printed, Anja, next to my flower collection, which I must attend to."

He left his wife to her inward solitude. Music was her escape; caring for his flower collection was his.

Chapter 20

Judith saw Warren walking ramrod straight along the corridor. He smiled at her as she approached him.

"Okay, what's that look for and you look fairly relaxed to the point where you have me on edge."

"I slept well; I think the body got to the point where I had no option and it needed to recover. I have also had another bend over the table and get reamed session from the seniors. It hurt them more than me, bloody careerists promoted above their capability and experience. I am pleased that I was never interested in a career; it allows me to concentrate on the job. What's the post?"

"One of these days, you'll pick up your post."

"Why? You have done a good job, Judith."

"You know that you will pay a price for that statement."

"Yes. Where's the letter from?"

"Weissenborn, who do you know there?"

"No one. Let's have a look in the office, Judith."

Warren pulled on blue surgical gloves, took his steel propeller letter opener from his draw and sliced the envelope open. A neatly folded letter fell out onto the surface of the desk as he tipped it upside down. They both looked across the table at each other and inwardly guessed who it was from, neither wanted to say. "Judith, pass me a plastic bag out of that cupboard and do you have any eyebrow tweezers?"

Warren carefully opened the letter as Judith peered over his shoulder.

"Winter thaw. There's nothing else on the paper, Judith."

"It's another victim, either a planned victim or one already in their sadistic loop."

"It looks like we can expect another body to surface next year, Judith. Christ, I feel sick to my stomach. Whoever is involved here has just changed the goalposts. Three confirmed murders and now a fourth is on the way. This is the first letter, which we have received and marks a change in their thought process."

"When was it posted, Warren?"

"Last Friday. No doubt with intent to ensure we have a good start to the week. My good day did not last long; at least we will not be looking at a decaying corpse this side of Xmas. That's the only advantage I can see out of this, Judith."

Warren stared at the letter and could hear the rattle of Judith's keyboard.

"Weissenborn, Hessen, 370 kilometres, South West of Berlin. They are now going for control of the police. It makes sense to send a letter from that far away only to reduce the possibility of tracing the source."

"Let's get this logged, Judith, and over to Astrid for an examination and see what she can come up with by the end of today."

It was close to the end of the day; Warren read his email and saw Astrid on his list. He picked up his phone and dialled Judith.

"Judith, where are you now, precisely?"

"Precisely, I am on the way to the toilet. Why?"

"I've just had confirmation that Astrid has finished her analysis."

"Okay, I'll meet you there but needs must."

Astrid saw the two of them through her window walking towards her office, "Judith, Warren."

Judith noticed the softer change of tone towards Warren and caught Astrid's eye. She realised Judith had picked up on the change of body language.

"What have we got then?"

"Well-spoken and together, you two have worked together too long, you ask the identical question."

"Sit down over there, opposite the screen. I'll just plug my laptop in."

"You said initial, Astrid."

"Because no formal report has been written."

"He really is good, Judith; it's easy to see why he needs a partner. How he survives in the outside world amazes me."

Judith clocked the silent momentary look between the two and wondered how deep their history was. Astrid carried on.

"There's, not a lot. This person is going for control, another feature of a psychopath. He or she is more confident and with confidence, mistakes follow."

Astrid smiled; it was obvious that she was enjoying the moment.

"The cut marks on the spine, it's a fingerprint and if you find the knife, we can match it. The envelope has been cut; it is homemade as you can see from the scissor marks. I could match those to the cut marks. You handed me the letter, what you both did not see was, what was on the inside of the envelope. It was printed in advance of folding and sealing the envelope."

Judith and Warren's bodies ran cold as they saw what was on the screen.

'Dear Warren, Judith, welcome to a world of justice where people do what others have failed. A fourth will meet justice. Natural causes, free to die.'

Silence fell around the room absorbing what they had read. Warren was first to speak as he noticed Judith putting her hair into a ponytail.

"Someone is doing their homework, how the hell did they find out our names?"

Judith looked up and across to Warren and then Astrid. She felt it necessary to divert the subject that someone has taken time to find their names and possibly her daughter's.

"What else, Astrid?"

"The font we know, Arial 10, the type of ink we know, we should be able to identify the range of printers, but we will need to contact the manufacturers. There is no printer code on the paper, so someone is considering details but not detail enough. There are no prints, the glue used to seal the envelope, we can analyse, but it will probably be a standard, which you can buy in most shops. There is one item on the letter, a minute detail but possibly a big mistake."

Astrid flashed up the next slide, again she smiled. Judith spoke.

"Okay, what is it, Astrid? It looks like something out of an alien movie."

"All of this is control, this person has thought and planned what to write, how to write it, but it is impossible to risk mitigate all possibilities in life. Lawyers can make a good living based on these human weaknesses. It is pollen, only a few grains but a silent witness. I've sent them over to the botanical gardens in Dahlem for identification. There was nothing in my database, so possibly it is a rare species. Somehow, I cannot see this person taking a computer, printer and paper outside. If it is rare, then we have a possible collector of flowers. Perhaps, the person had handled the flower shortly before he wrote the letter or he placed the letter next to his collection, who knows. We will have to wait for the answer, close of play tomorrow night."

"Okay, what does it mean, natural causes, free to die, Astrid? We are dealing with a serial killer."

"What exactly that means, Judith, I think we can only guess."

Astrid caught Warren looking at her out the corner of her eye. She knew he would be looking for a lateral thought from his friend.

"I'm not trained in this area but openly I feel someone is bored and looking for a much bigger thrill. Not content on seeking revenge on men for an undisclosed reason, there is a wish to now openly tease the police. It's on a more personal level; your names are mentioned and it makes it more inclusive as if you are now part of their personal circle. As for the free to die part of the letter, perhaps, the victim will die of his wounds; my view is they will indirectly murder him. Torture him and then let him die. Just my thoughts."

Warren looked at Judith; she could see the solemn look on his face at the thought of not been able to prevent a fourth person from torture and a prolonged death. A marked change from the man she had seen shortly after lunch. The letter had served its purpose and it had changed the chemistry of their thought process, her thoughts crossed to the safety of her daughter.

Chapter 21

Vincenzo, strapped to the wooden chair, with a ball gag in his mouth, struggled to swallow his spit. His arms, legs and head were bound tightly to the chair with tie wraps. He scanned the room and noticed the tan brown Formica clad table in front of him. Two books, one without a cover were lined up squarely to the edge of the table along with a bunch of white and red flowers in a vase. He could feel the breath on his neck of someone standing behind. A soft, quiet voice spoke, it was Anja.

"I see you've come around, back into our world. It's only a sleeping drug, but it gives us time to move you around. Fear and prejudice keep us safe. Anywhere we go, shopping, in a restaurant, out for a walk, when we see a dangerous situation or someone we do not like, we remove ourselves from it. Human beings like control, to be in command, except we control the situation, which you know. Tell me what is it like to not be in control? I believe it is a strange experience for you, especially under the control of a woman. Men should respect women, see them as equal, a partner and laugh together. What sort of a man believes when he controls a woman that he is a man. That sort of man is weak, a pathetic specimen of the human race and is an insult to men. You belittle women, you control them, and you make them inferior to you. That does not make you a man and…well; now you live in uncontrolled fear, the two great masters in our life, fear and pain. You looked at the books, wondering, are you? It's my husband's hobby; everyone needs a hobby, stress relief. The books contain flowers, rare, pressed flowers, but the best part, one book cover is made from human skin. He already mentioned to you that he requires a cover for his second book, do you remember? I saw you looking earlier at the books. Your chest is damaged; that's our fault, it was a mistake on my part, I got carried away, I am sorry for that, and at least the scars are healing. It looks like we will have to take the skin from your back, but then again you do not know if we are lying. Either way, you live in fear of the unknown."

Anja traced the scar over his chest with her index finger, around his side to his back. Vincenzo felt her trace a square out on his back through a gap in the chair.

"It does not really matter that much. There's plenty of flawless skin on your back."

Vincenzo felt a cold edge of a blade run across the back of his neck and down his spine. He clamped his eyes shut, fear once again set as his heart pounded as he panted for breath. The feel of the blade disappeared; he opened his eyes. Anja stood before him, clad in running leggings, her long blond hair draped over her shoulders, "I was deciding where to make the first incision to peel your skin. The fear, I see in your eyes would have been in the fear of the women you've beaten. I should have brought a mirror so you can see yourself. Perhaps, I should place one in front of you. At least then you will have your own company. You're in my world now, one where you cannot control the ending. It's a different world now to my sister's party. Who would have thought that you would have ended up here? My sister never liked you; she only tolerated you for Filippo. It's really impolite to look at women's tits when they open the door. She told me."

Vincenzo's mind raced, he remembered the party. He was now confused, what was the reality of time.

"I need to prepare a new book for Stefan. He should be here shortly."

Vincenzo could see out the corner of his eye, his captor moved closer to the side of his face. He felt her breath on the side of his face, then on the back of his neck.

"Don't worry, death will not come easy to you; I guarantee that we will not kill you…directly."

Unable to scream outwards or move, Vincenzo swallowed the scream as he felt the shallow incision of a blade across his back.

"I think that's enough, I'll tend to your wounds. We need to prevent an infection from occurring and prolong your life but not for your benefit. The area, which I've marked, is for his cover, it's a present for my husband."

Vincenzo drifted in and out of a world, which was no longer real. The morphine kept the pain at bay and the hallucinations provided an escape. He felt the breath once more of his captor on his cheek and the gentle smell of White Linen perfume embraced his nasal senses. The soft-touch of a hand caressed his shoulder, like a mother caressing her ill child.

"This morphine will keep the pain at bay while we slice the area of skin off. You will scream inwardly with pain as it burns through your body when the drug wears off. You're probably wondering and hoping that all of this will come to an end and someone will rescue you. You may also be wishing for death. What's really going in inside your head, it's hard to tell when I look at you. Perhaps, I should have not put your blindfold back on so I can look into the soul of your mind. How many times did you look into the eyes of the women you abused? The gateway to the soul of the body and did you get that feeling of power as you saw them cower. You never cared about their soul. The brain is a powerful tool to imagine images, you're probably wondering what you look like now. Helpless, scared, strapped naked to a chair. Maybe I should take your blindfold off and bring you that mirror. What did you mumble? It is really impolite to mumble."

Silence fell in the room and Vincenzo struggled against his head restraint as his felt the searing pain of a whip against his chest. The smell of perfume caressed his nose once more.

"You really are impolite."

Vincenzo heard a second set of footsteps in the room. They were heavier and he could hear the unclear whispering in the room. A deeper voice, the voice of Stefan and the stink of cigar smoke filled his nose.

"Anja, I've been reading the article you mentioned. It is quite interesting, the subject of torture from the mediaeval times. You were perfectly right, people were so cruel but inventive in those days. They could extract the maximum suffering from their victims whilst prolonging their life. It was really educational; people should always be willing to learn. Vincenzo is a lucky person; we attended his wounds, provided him painkilling medicines, and prevented infection. None of that was available then. Should we tell Vincenzo of his future? I am sure he would like to know how his story ends. I think it's only fair for him."

Stefan stood next to Anja and looked at the broken wreck of Vincenzo and removed his blindfold; she stared directly at him.

"The summary is that we will not murder you. How do you feel now, remember do not mumble. I bet there's a complete momentary sense of relief caused by the dopamine and endorphins flowing through your body at the good news of an ending. Don't worry, that is a normal reaction for everyone when we hear good news but…sometimes, good news is short-lived. Whatever happens, do not forget, you are responsible. The victim of your actions, this is a result of the path of life you choose, your problem. Here's the summary of your ending, so you know what to expect when you wake up. In medieval times, they would soak victims in honey and then cover the victim with ants and encase the living torso. Imagine it, these small creatures crawling and eating in every open orifice and wound on your body. You will sleep well the night before, when you wake up you will have no choice but to suffer the pain. The morphine will wear off and your last moments of suffering will be without pain relief. You do not know when, perhaps tomorrow, next week, but it will happen. See, I told you that we wouldn't kill you directly; your body will die from shock."

Vincenzo felt the needle go into his left arm and his world disappeared into the darkness.

Chapter 22

Anja stood with Stefan, before the sturdy wooden panelled door to Vincenzo's house. She paused before sliding the key into the lock.

"What's up, Anja?"

"Not sure, there's a strange smell, the pungent smell of death clinging to the inside of my nose."

Anja noticed his face cringe at the thought, "Anja, we have to go on. We must find his passport, suitcase, personal effects; it needs to look like he has gone on his holiday."

Anja opened the door and both looked at each other. The repugnant smell of death swirled around their noses.

"Don't throw up, Stefan, the last thing we need is to leave DNA. It's coming from over there. I'll look around the door. Christ, there's a decaying Cocker Spaniel."

"What was he going to do with the dog when he went on the holiday, Anja? Hopefully, he had not arranged for someone to pick it up."

"He's the type to put it on the street and leave it. I don't think we have anything to worry about, but this was a mistake and hopefully, there is no price to pay. We are lucky his house is detached and no neighbours have reported anything. We should have visited his house earlier, at least then we could have rescued the dog."

They pushed the door open fully and looked at the muzzled decaying dog, whose flesh was hanging between its ribs.

"Poor bloody thing was trying to get out, Stefan; look at the claw marks on the door, his lead only let him reach that far."

"Poor thing has starved to death."

"Sad, this I did not even think of...what a sad ending for such a beautiful dog. This was not part of our plan; an innocent victim. I'll have to remember to inform Vincenzo when we get back, this is all his making."

"Let's move away, it absolutely stinks. The decay and also the pool of dried faeces and urine, it's lying in. Look at the maggots crawling inside."

"Maybe, Vincenzo should lay in his body fluids."

"Anja, there's no time for remorse or reflecting on future planning for him. We have a task to perform and I wish to spend as little time as possible here. Let's look around and take what we need. I'll look around here and you search the upstairs."

Anja walked into the bedroom and looked around. She noticed his passport, wallet and boarding card on the dressing table, but she was more interested in exploring the room. The double bed was neatly made with a floral rose bedspread, not what she had expected from him. The sheets were creaseless and pulled tight over the mattress, which pleased her. She opened the wardrobe doors and shirts were individually hung. She liked the order, control and already she started to like the disciplined way Vincenzo lived. The door to the en-suite was open and she could not resist the temptation to explore further details of how her victim lived. The glistening white tiles provided an air of cleanliness. The mirror opposite the double walk-in shower provided the air of a much larger room. She noticed the red toothbrush and gently stroked it whilst thinking that it would never be used again. She smiled inwardly at the degree of control that she had over her victim and the power to walk around his house at her will. Anja remembered the passport and wallet and walked over to the dressing table and noticed talc dust on the side table. It bewildered her for a moment; such an orderly man had not cleaned this mess. He must have been in a hurry to go out. The night he came over, he must have showered and then use talcum powder. Anja wiped her hand across the corner and looked at the powder on her latex glove mesmerised like a child, looking at their first ladybird. Stefan shouted for her and it broke her concentration, she grabbed the passport, tickets, and wallet, and left the room. Stefan was waiting for her at the bottom of the stairs with a suitcase and laptop.

"Are you sure that you can hack into his laptop?"

"Are you into exchanging insults today, I've already hacked into it. I turned the Wi-Fi off to ensure there was no time trace left. The hard drive I will send to the police. They will be interested in the pictures of minors on the drive, Anja and that will use up more of their resources."

"That makes me sick, that warped, twisted scum of the earth, he will suffer in his last few days."

Stefan looked at his wife; her eyes were cold and dead. He knew she would exert revenge on Vincenzo and he wondered again, what were the limits of his wife?

"Let's go, we've been here too long already. The suitcase, tickets, wallet and passport we can burn, or dispose of, so there is no trace."

"It's a shame that he will never live here, Stefan. It's such a nice house to leave, what a waste but that's his problem. Just thought, it's too late now, but we could have brought him a picture of his dog. Perhaps not, the imagination can be more powerful. Vincenzo can suffer until the end of this week, Stefan, then I want him out of our house, it should not take him long to die, once he is encapsulated."

Chapter 23

Vincenzo drifted back into his surreal cruel world and tried to focus. Drugged to prolong his suffering, delirious, hallucinations; he no longer knew the reality. He could feel the bindings on his wrists, ankles, around his forehead and his mouth was still gagged. Sweat ran down his face, his body felt clammy, sticky, his focus became sharper and he realised that his body was encased in a plastic suit. Unable to scream outwardly, the primal emotion ripped through his body as he saw the ants crawling around inside. Adrenaline flowed around his body and in a desperate panic, Vincenzo started to thrash, trying to free the shackles whilst letting off an inwardly muffled scream. Anja and Stefan sat behind the Formica table; listened and watched the rapid panic breathing and thrashing of the body of their victim. They remained silent as they relished their victim fight for his sanity. Anja with her long blond hair, patterned leggings and black tee shirt walked towards Vincenzo. She stood before him and pulled the drip out of his arm. The soft voice, a tone that he feared, spoke. He looked at her; she could only see the fear in his eyes.

"The look I see now, is that the look you saw in your victims? Don't worry, you will die and be alleviated from this suffering. It will take a while for the morphine to wear off and then the pain will rip through your body. All those open wounds. The ants will crawl into every fresh wound and orifice in your body. You will suffer in pain and then delirium as infection sets in. Possibly, you will have a heart attack, we would feel cheated, but a quick end for you. Do you see the books over there, the smaller one on top, I know your vision is blurry but do try to focus. The book cover you can see is made from parts of your skin; we spared your back and took it from your thighs instead. Now, you will really suffer. You see this tube, it's so you can breathe, this bag goes over your head and then we will fill it with ants. If you wish we can glue your eyes together so the ants do not crawl into them. Why spoil the show, you should be allowed to see everything. In case you're wondering what happens next, we will be upstairs enjoying a meal and a glass of Cognac. Later, my husband will be fucking me hard and deep from behind, without a thought for you."

Vincenzo enjoyed the brief moment of being able to breathe normally as the gag was removed from his mouth. Anja forced the breathing tube into his mouth and fastened the buckle. Vincenzo closed his eyes tight as the sticky sweet solution was poured over his face. Anja pulled the plastic bag over his face and zipped it closed. His eyes smarted as he instinctively opened them and the ants crawled into his eyes and up his nose.

"Enjoy your solitude in darkness, Vincenzo. Stefan, I need a shower before we have something to eat and drink, you have made me feel dirty." Anja and Stefan shut the door to the bunker, switched off the light to allow him to suffer, alone. Vincenzo was alone in the dark with his pain, screams and his thoughts for company. The ants crawled into every open wound and orifice.

"How long do you think it will take him to die, Anja?"

"It depends, it can be a couple of days, but I forgot to close the nasal cavity, so probably not too long. Can you pass the Cognac over, Stefan? Oh, it's nearly empty, let's finish the bottle tonight, a celebration. Would you like a glass?"

"Of course, it's rude to celebrate alone."

"I would hope for a heart attack if I was him. The ants will crawl into his eyes, up his nose, in his ears and into his lungs. Maybe that's a mistake, next time, hopefully, there isn't, we can seal up the eyes, nose and ears. Deprive him of more sensory reception and prolong the suffering."

"I've ordered some new flowers, a Chocolate cosmos from Mexico. I need to add some more petals to my new book. When should we check on him, Anja?"

"We can go back in a couple of days and dispose of the body. The temperature is sub-zero and it is expected to be for a few weeks. The lake will start to freeze over in a couple of days."

"I wouldn't like to be the one who discovers or examines the body, Anja."

"Someone will, it cannot be prevented. I feel sorry for the innocent person who does, that picture will stay with them for the rest of their life. Why don't you take your Cognac, book, press some flowers and relax. I plan to take a long hot soak in the bath and later do my nails. We will check on him tomorrow."

Chapter 24

Anja and Stefan stood at the bottom of the stairs in silence and looked across to the tortured encapsulated body of Vincenzo. Anja walked across to the body and looked at the breathing tube, which she had inserted into his mouth.

"Looks like the ants have completed their work. They are crawling out of the tube so they must have at least crawled into his throat through his nasal cavity. We need to get this scum out of our house; it's starting to feel contaminated. We'll drain his blood out down at the lake and then slice open his stomach to slow down the build-up of gases. Bring the polythene sheets and tape so we can wrap the body. I don't want a mess when we drag him through the house."

Anja unfastened the restraints from Vincenzo as Stefan prepared the floor in front of the chair with the polythene sheets. Anja pushed the body off the chair on to the floor and as the skull cracked against the concrete floor, Vincenzo let out a feeble moan.

"Christ, he's still fucking alive, Anja, how the hell can that be after what he has been through."

"It's amazing what the body can survive through the torture and the will to live. You have to read the books about people who survived, it fascinates me. Believe me, his body and his mind will be in such a state of delirium, he has no idea what is going on. Anyhow, it is irrelevant, in the next few minutes, he will be dead and no one can live without blood. Let's drag this thing down to the boathouse; I'll go ahead and prepare the pulley and rope."

Stefan pulled the trolley along the covered walkway; Anja was waiting for him with the rope.

"I'll bind his feet and you can hoist him over the tub. Even if he is still alive it'll give me satisfaction to split his jugular open and watch the last drop drain from him like a pig being slaughtered."

Anja drove the knife into his throat turned the knife, ripped the jugular open and watched silently as the crimson red flowed into the bucket.

"We can dispose of this in the drains, Anja. Let's split his stomach open to prevent any build-up of gas and then lower him into the boat. I'm starting to get cold and hungry, there's a heavy frost due tonight and I want to be back before it is too late."

"You and your stomach, don't worry, I've the cooker on a timer and I've dauphinoise potatoes in the oven. Lower him into the rear of the boat and I guide him down, Stefan."

"Be careful, you do not want to slip on the gangway planks, Anja."

Stefan lowered the body into the boat and Anja untied the rope from around his ankles. She stood and looked at Vincenzo lying on the deck like a slaughtered animal.

"Anja, what're you thinking?"

"Nothing, I have no feelings for this piece of meat. Let's go, do you know where?"

"There's a corner, a few kilometres from here, where the trees overhang the lake and the reeds also cover the shoreline. The water is deep enough to submerge the body and shallow enough to freeze over quickly."

The lake was motionless and the ripples from the bow of the boat disturbed the subdued evening reflection of the trees. There were only a few other boats out catching their last chance before the lake became impassable. Anja looked out across the stillness of the lake; the peacefulness on such an evening brought her an inner peace of tranquillity. She felt unperturbed as she turned around and faced her husband. He had a feeling what was coming.

"It's time to move on, go somewhere else before our luck runs out. The one mistake that we've made is all our killings were in one quadrant. The police will be focusing on this area, Stefan."

"Quiet, Anja, on such a still evening, sound travels a long way on the water. Then let's back off, stop, it's easy to get too confident and believe we are untouchable. We've never gone looking for a victim, maybe we will never meet another; perhaps, one will come along in two or three years. Either way, I agree, it's time to stop; leaving the country is a good idea. We've enough money in our secondary accounts; we could also sell the house when we're away. Now, it's time to get rid of our friend, we're here."

Stefan throttled back the engine and put it into reverse to slow the boat down. The reeds brushed up against the hull as the boat came to a standstill. He looked to check if anyone was visible and then rolled the body over the side. The surface of thin ice cracked as Vincenzo sunk. The boat gently rocked from side to side as they stood and watched the body sink out of view.

"How deep is it here, Stefan?"

"Just over a metre, Anja, there is no water flow so the ice will form quickly. There is also plenty of shade from the winter sun, so this area will be the last to thaw."

"Let's get out of here, it is dark, I'm cold and I need a hot shower to warm up and cleanse myself before we eat."

Stefan dished out the Dauphinoise potatoes onto his plate; the smell of the spices that Anja had used swirled around the senses in his nostrils. He looked at his wife opposite and remained silent.

"What are you looking at, Anja? We've been married too long, you're thinking about the future."

"I know that we mentioned Cape Verde, but…Africa, central Africa, African coast, new life, new adventure, new names, new start."

"Do you have anywhere particular in mind?"

"Not yet, but we can both work as doctors for some charitable organisation. First, we should explore Africa and take a long-deserved holiday."

"And how do we get there without leaving a booking trail. Everything is logged, traced these days via damn computers and smart phones."

"That part is easy; Thorsten, the pilot who can fly anything from a kite to a Boeing 747. He still does work for Filippo and when he was younger, he used to also fly goods around Africa."

"What type of goods?"

"As long as he got paid goods, but he drew the line at weapons. He can fly us out of Germany from a local unused airstrip, not far from here. Since it is Europe…no border control, we land in another airport, TBD get out and then straight into an executive jet. No passport control, no one knows that we've left the country, except him, and he never asks questions."

"You said never asks questions. You've already approached him."

"Doing homework upfront, risk mitigation, whatever you call it and what harm has it done. I have invited him over for a meal on Friday night."

"We're a team, Anja; we take decisions like this together. You should have mentioned this to me."

Stefan knew there was no point in discussing it any further and would have to come to terms with the proposal. He knew, time would run out and leaving Germany was the only option.

"What about the practice, Anja?"

"I'll organise a replacement for at least a year. You can resign, or we can both wrap everything in. We can spin everyone a story that we are off to Australia, Indonesia, anywhere except the truth."

"And your older sister, Melanie, how would you feel lying to her?"

"Leave that up to me, Stefan and do not interfere. That's my relationship."

"Anja, she will know when her sister is lying, it's probably best not to tell her anything."

"Which part of keep out did you not understand?"

Stefan felt rebuked by the tone of Anja's voice. There was something defensive about the conversation and he could not place his finger on it. His gut feeling told him that Anja was hiding something and also planning. He knew it was worth pursuing but not at this moment and changed the tack.

"Before we do, let's torment the police, Anja, send them the hard drive from Vincenzo's computer."

"Sure, let's give them something to think about, a dilemma, especially when they see the pictures of children on his drive. They'll have to open up a whole new line of enquiry. Such guys as Vincenzo never work alone, they turn my stomach."

Chapter 25

The bell rang and Anja opened the front door to Thorsten. He had put on a few pounds since the last time she had seen him but at 1.90 tall, he dwarfed her. He wrapped his arms around her and lifted her off the floor. Stefan appeared as he placed Anja back on the floor. "Great to see you, we really do not see enough of each other; we're pleased that you could make it."

"You know that's not so easy, Stefan, flying here and there. Sometimes, I'm not sure which side of the world I will be on in two weeks."

"I have one quick question? When is your next flight?"

"In seven days, long haul, Argentina, why?"

"So we can share a bottle of Cognac Remy Thorsten XIII tonight."

He knew Stefan was a connoisseur of Cognac and his eyes lit up at the thought of more than one glass. "I see you are interested, I can tell by your eyes."

"Too damn right, I am Stefan."

"Come, before we eat, let's us all go through to the sitting room."

Thorsten's towering frame followed Anja to the sitting room whilst Stefan collected and placed the three snifters and Cognac on the distressed mahogany table. Thorsten looked at the unopened bottle.

"How long have you had this?"

"Not long, in fact, it's the second bottle from a collection of six, which I bought."

"Why six?"

Stefan looked up and over his glass as he poured the first drink and smirked.

"It saves me a trip to the shop."

Thorsten shrugged his shoulders.

"Good enough reason."

Anja raised her glass to make a toast.

"To the future, where ever that is."

Thorsten swirled the snifter and delighted in the aroma, which swirled around his nasal senses.

"You certainly can select a good Cognac, Stefan. The future, you mentioned the future, Anja and also when you called, you mentioned that you wish to hire my services."

Stefan was still enjoying the aroma as Thorsten looked across the table and focused on Anja.

"Do we talk now, Anja, or after the evening meal?"

Anja flicked and tucked her long blond hair behind her ears, turned and faced him square on.

"We can talk now so that we can enjoy the meal and another Cognac without talking business. Stefan can listen and interject in between savouring his drink."

"We're looking to hire a pilot and plane. We're planning a long sabbatical and wish to travel to Africa. Not quite sure where yet, but we would like to leave in the next couple of months and not via, let's say commercial airlines. The date is approximately the end of January, the start of February. We will confirm the date, but we will need flexibility, plus-minus two days."

"Flexibility costs extra; it is possible, as long as it is not Congo."

"Why Congo?"

"Memories of when I used to smuggle goods from South Africa over their borders. I was invited to spend the night in a cell at the request of the local police. They thought we were smuggling guns."

"Were you?"

"Thank God, no, we were offered the opportunity. We were smuggling food and getting paid in diamonds. Have you any idea how hard it is to get rid of unregistered diamonds. Anyhow, I was allowed my clothes back the next morning after striking a deal with the local police, who were very polite the next time we flew in."

Anja knew this tone and even Stefan tuned in to this new story.

"The next time they took our plane and we had to drive over the border. So please not there. Anyhow, the answer to your question is yes, it will cost, will not be cheap. Cost, approximately ten thousand Euros per flight hour. Once I have the details, I can provide you with an accurate cost."

"The cost is not a problem."

"I suggest that I hire a light aircraft and pick you up from an unused airfield. There are dozens in East Germany, fly somewhere in Europe and then board a private jet to Africa. Fly internal with a light aircraft and drop you off somewhere. It's not too complicated to do what you want, I will not ask why, but I have the feeling we will not see each other again. Right now, I'm interested in a change of subject. The Cognac has triggered my appetite, Anja, what's on the menu?"

Chapter 26

Olaf had never liked the attitude of Vincenzo, his next-door neighbour. For several weeks, he had noticed no lights on in his house and the routine seemed to be out of sync. A brief walk along Vincenzo's driveway and a look through the letterbox had led him to phone the police. Later that day, two policemen knocked on his door.

"Afternoon, I believe you are Olaf Niemann and you reported unusual behaviour regarding your next-door neighbour. May we come in?"

"That's right, please come in and sit down."

"So, what do you want to report?"

"That's the whole point, nothing, there has been no movement. The routine of his house is unusual."

"A long holiday? How well do you know your neighbour?"

"I don't, we keep our distance around here from him. The guy is an arsehole and we speak rarely."

"What do you mean?"

"Wrong attitude, self-centred and an attitude towards women that stinks. More than once he had put his girlfriend out of the house, the arguments were unbelievable and eventually, they would get less. He's a control freak and treats women like shit. His girlfriend, I have not seen for several months, if she had any sense she's escaped. There was always something going on and now nothing, it seems unusually quiet."

"What's the man's name?"

"Vincenzo Rossi; I have no idea what his girlfriend is called."

"His attitude, what do you mean by this?"

"Around here, we're a friendly bunch and once a year we have a party, autumn festival. He moved in a few years ago and naturally, we invited him and his girlfriend. The way he spoke to people and especially women and his girlfriend…well, it ended up one of our group thumping him. When he went to retaliate, he was faced with more than one person. Since then, none of us has spoken to him. It's not him I'm bothered about; it's his girlfriend, in case anything has happened to her. He can go to hell."

"You mentioned earlier, an unusual pattern to the house."

"There has been a couple of times when the lights were off for several weeks but this time it is over two months, possibly slightly longer."

"We'll take a look over to see if there's anything suspicious."

The policemen walked down the drive and their instinct indicated something was not right. The house looked cold and dead.

"Hans, let's walk around the house and see what we can find. Remember, we cannot enter unless there are suspicious circumstances."

"I'll go this way, Dirk."

Only a couple of minutes passed when Dirk's radio buzzed.

"Come around to me, I've found a reason for entry."

Dirk saw Hans looking through the hallway window at the flies buzzing around. In the corner, lay the decayed corpse of a muzzled dog.

"Looks like the next-door neighbour's instinct was correct, Dirk. I'll phone the vet. We'll not enter until he is here and I'll also phone the local locksmith. If there is no evidence of foul play, we will have the owner registered as a missing person. My instincts tell me there is more."

One hour later, Hans and Dirk entered and searched the house deliberately, leaving the dog to the vet. There were no signs of foul play.

"Dirk, it looks like the neighbour is right. Did you find anything?"

"Some photos, I'm assuming an ex-girlfriend."

"Why ex?"

"One was in the bin."

"Any names?"

"None that I could find, I'll have a chat with the other neighbours, can you speak to the vet, Dirk?"

Hans left the house and saw Olaf walking towards him.

"Did you find anything?"

"Nothing of foul play except his dog is dead."

"Do you recognise this person?"

"That's his girlfriend, well, the woman who was at the party last year."

"Do you have any idea who she is?"

"I have no idea, but I remember her dialect was Berlin, the distinctive 'Icke' sound. She is a genuine Berliner Flower, born and bred."

"Any family that you are aware of or do you know anyone who was friendly with them?"

"No, but ask the other neighbours. So, are you reporting him as a missing person?"

"We'll be filling out a report of our findings and take guidance, but probably yes. We will be back in touch, at this moment, I have to ask you to vacate the scene."

Hans saw the vet drive away as he walked back to the house. Dirk was waiting for him next to the swimming pool.

"What are your thoughts?"

"Not sure, Hans, if there is foul play here, something's not right. There are some women's clothes in the house, maybe the ex has done a runner, but to leave a dog to die, that's out of the ordinary. There is no woman registered to this address."

"That's not a first; my daughter is living with her boyfriend and she still uses my address. My suspicion is that, he is missing and she has left him. The question is where? Let's file him as a missing person and distribute it around the precincts."

Chapter 27

Winter was coming to an end and the path along Grose Krampe was starting to thaw. The icebreakers had cleared a waterway in the lakes and the odd boat could be seen in the distance.

The temperature had surfaced above zero, the lack of wind and the sapphire blue sky had brought people out of their houses for a Sunday afternoon walk. Silvia and Chris had recently moved to the area and had, with their stubborn Cocker Spaniel, Harry, decided to explore their new area. Chris threw the ball in the hope that Harry would play the game and as usual, he just sat, looked at him as to why he threw the ball.

"Why do you even bother to try, Chris? You know him, his attitude is; if you throw the ball, you go and fetch it for him. A dog is a man's best friend, therefore, you fetch. You never learn."

"I know, but I live in hope. The next time we pick a dog from the rescue centre, throwing a ball is a test. If the dog brings it back, it's in with a good chance of coming home with us."

"Back off, my dog, change the subject; we've only had him for two years. He's family and one of the reasons why we moved out of the city."

"I know and I love him to bits, he just frustrates me."

"It's his character, look at him, those eyes and his big floppy black and white ears. Go fetch, he's waiting for you to retrieve his ball. I'll go; you're more stubborn than him."

"No, why spoil his routine, I'll go."

Harry and Silvia watched as Chris walked into the distance to the edge of the water. The ball had landed next to the reads. She noticed him pick it up and saw Chris froze as he stared at something not far from the shore.

"Hurry up, stop daydreaming, he's seen his ball now."

The scream from Chris pierced through Silvia like a knife and she saw her husband stumble backwards. Instantly, Harry ran in his direction followed by

Silvia. He stood there frozen; Silvia wrapped her arms around him; he was shivering, not from the cold but from fear, seeping all over his body. His face looked white as the snow, as the blood drained from his skin.

"Chris, what's wrong?"

He could no longer control the shock and his body took over and wretched. Silvia could only watch the automatic reaction of her partner's body and felt totally useless. Chris stood up and wiped the traces of vomit from his mouth.

"Here, take a drink of water, Chris, rinse your mouth. Are you okay?"

"Does it fucking look like it, sorry, Silvia."

Another couple walked up to them to see if they were okay. Before they could even ask what was wrong, Chris answered them.

"Over there, under the ice, I'm not sure, there looks like an arm, a body in a plastic bag, black, decaying."

Silvia looked directly at her husband as they contemplated what to do.

"I only wanted to walk Harry, Silvia, that's all, a nice walk in the afternoon. Where is he?"

"He's standing behind you."

"Come here boy."

Chris wrapped his arms around Harry for security as Silvia and the couple looked on. The women looked at the two men. "Manfred, you have dealt with enough emergencies in your life. Have a look at what it is."

At two metres tall, Manfred looked down at his wife. He had been free willingly volunteered by her and put in a position of not being able to refuse.

"There're some bricks over there, we'll need them to smash the ice to break free whatever it is. Susanne, get me that branch please. I'll need something to stop, whatever it is from floating away."

Manfred threw the stones and the thin ice shattered; the bloated corpse with its exposed black decayed limbs, torso and head, still encased in plastic, surfaced.

Manfred looked at the group, who out of morbid curiosity had moved closer to the edge.

"Chris, I need some help to pull the body and secure it."

Chris, still in shock looked across at Manfred. He knew that he had to help him and could not leave him alone.

"Don't look directly, I'll do that, don't think too much about what is there, and switch off. I've seen some sites, burnt bodies, when I was in the fire service. Just react and do. We need to bring the body to the shore to secure it so the police can start their investigation. We cannot afford for it to drift away. Worry about the shock later, right now, you are doing okay. Nice dog, by the way, I'll bet he's stubborn as hell. How long have you been married? I bet this is one afternoon walk that you will never forget."

"Silvia, my wife's name is Silvia and he's Harry, yes he's stubborn."

"You have a Berlin dialect, moved from the city for fresh air. I'll bet you never thought life outside the city could be so interesting. Keep the branch there so I can pull the body onto the reeds."

"Children?"

"No, and married seven years."

"The dog? Let me guess, you had little say in that fact."

"He's a rescue dog. I was at work one day when I received an email asking what I thought. Harry was already on his way home. We're planning children next year, another reason to move out here." Manfred pulled the body to the shore. Chris felt himself drawn to look at the remnants of a human being. They both knew the image they saw and the repugnant smell would stay with them for the rest of their lives. Manfred looked at Chris.

"Thank you, go and check on your wife."

"The police?"

"He's dead, you're in shock; we all are. I'm a bit too old now for this type of thing, but I have seen…well, too many, one reason I went into retirement. I need a few minutes to clear my thoughts; my wife knows to leave me alone for a short while. The body is going nowhere; we need to move away from here, we have a hot drink in our flask. For the next few minutes, we need to think about ourselves, calm down, and then I will phone the police. These minutes will make no difference to the corpse or any police investigation, but it will help our sanity. Chris, there's a bench over there, get a hot drink. I'll join you shortly."

Manfred phoned the police and within a few minutes, the siren could be heard in the distance. The group watched the two officers walking along the partial icy path. Manfred walked over to greet them and indicated to the officers the location of the corpse. The young female officer returned and looked ashen white at what she had viewed. She looked at the group and down at Harry who had sensed something was wrong. She leaned down and stroked his head, Harry moved closer and snuggled into her. That small moment brought a sense of normality to the horrors they had all witnessed and would never forget. The young female officer looked up at the group.

"It's cold; you are all in some state of shock. It's not what you would have expected for a Sunday afternoon stroll. It's best if you all go with my colleague to the car where it is warm. He will take your details and we will send an officer around later today for a detailed statement in the comfort of your own home. Do you all live local?"

The group nodded in agreement.

"If you have a car, it is best not to drive; we will arrange to take you home and collect your car. There's nothing to do here for you and I'll organise a support officer. What we've all seen today will never fully leave us."

Verena, the young officer stood and watched the group disappear along the path. The silence, loneliness and cold enveloped her like a wintery blanket. Alone, her blood ran cold as the image of what she had seen flashed through her mind. The sound of the ice creaking broke the silence and sent shivers down her spine. It would only be a few more minutes before the whole area would be swarming with officers to start the initial investigation. Her mind started to wonder if someone local was responsible. They may have heard the sirens and she wondered if anyone was watching.

Chapter 28

Warren's desk phone rang as Judith walked into the office; he nodded and raised his eyebrows to acknowledge her as he picked up his phone. She noticed his posture slump as he listened; his solemn look on his face indicated it all. Warren put the receiver down and briefly, stared out of the window to compose his thoughts. Judith knew him well enough to leave him alone for a few seconds.

"Why the hell can people never find corpses early in the morning? Is there some sort of unwritten rule?"

"What's up?"

"A fourth body has been discovered at Grosse Krampe, near Langer See. I should say they've found something that resembles a body. The local police are there now and have secured the area. They started the preliminary log and survey and taken initial statements from the group who found the body. It was a couple who were out walking their dog; the other two helped them secure the body."

"Have they disturbed the scene?"

"Secured the evidence was the term they used, Judith. It was either that or they allowed the body to float away. One of them is an ex-fireman, so at least he was aware of what he was doing. Remember the letter, Judith, 'the ice has thawed'. Why do I feel that I'll spew my guts, again? Let's take a bottle of water and grab some mints from the vending machine on the way to the car. Christ, when will this come to an end?"

"It's in the same quadrant, Warren, there is a pattern and whoever is doing this, is making mistakes. Each body is discovered in the water, tortured, each one worse than the other."

"Finish your coffee first, Judith. Two more minutes will not make any difference and it will allow us to collect our thoughts."

"What's the phrase, less speed or something?"

"More haste, less speed."

"That's it."

"Maybe they will realise they are making mistakes and stop, or move on, Judith. Since no one would be prosecuted, the latter would be the worst of the two evils. This case has to break and somewhere, there is a link, a name that connects this all together."

"Like a game of solitaire. You have fifty-one cards out and only one unturned. Turn that card over and then the option of auto complete is given."

"Good analogy and it will come. Either way, we cannot sit here and describe analogies, Judith. We have a cold evening ahead of us and Doc will be waiting."

Judith and Warren saw Doc in the distance exit the tent as they walked along the frozen footpath. Suddenly, they saw him bend double.

"If Doc is spewing, then I have no chance, Judith."

Judith walked over to him as he stood up and Warren decided to keep a safe distance.

"You look a bit green, Doc?"

"Not as green as our friend in there. It's time he brought this to a conclusion, each one is worse as if there is no limit to the imagination. Brought any of those mints, Judith? I detest the taste of vomit on the back of the throat."

"If I remember well, Warren, you've a weak stomach. I noticed you kept your distance."

"Only when it's gruesome."

"Then both of you keep out of the tent, the man who found the body, I would not be surprised if he required sedation for the shock. I suggest that you only look at the pictures, that way it keeps the decaying, rotting smell of death out of your nostrils."

Judith and Warren looked at each other in disbelief that things could actually get worse. Let's sit down over there on the bench. Doc adjusted his glasses as he sat down and looked across to the forest on the other side of the lake.

"It's so peaceful here, the beauty of Mother Nature and yet the scene of a horrific crime, two opposites in life. Another three months, and this whole area will be green, teeming with new life. Each year, Mother Nature brings new life to the area, it's like...the world each year has a new chance. I've seen some scenes in my life, memories that I wish I could erase. This one, as you say in your language, Warren, takes the biscuit. Only God knows what, whoever is responsible, what they will do with a fifth."

He knew what Doc meant, but felt the phrase was not quite appropriate for the situation. Doc carried on rambling.

"I will take to my grave what I have seen today, I am still too young for early retirement. My problem is that it's in my blood to find that tiny clue that will provide justice to make this world safer. It's a drug for me; it drives me and always will be. If I lose that drive, then I know it is time to move on. I've no doubt that I will do the full stretch, my wife has a different opinion, and she wants me out."

Judith looked at Warren, they both realised that he wanted to talk to create a momentary breathing space to come to terms with the sight he had seen.

"His stomach was slit open, in the form of a cross, it allows the build-up of gases to escape and thus the body remains submerged longer. The plastic suit he is wearing was also split open."

"What plastic suit, the body was wrapped up, or what?" Doc ignored Judith and carried on talking whilst looking across the lake in the direction of the lifeless trees opposite, "He has also a full plastic face mask on with a tube inserted into his mouth to allow him to breath. His body has been sliced in different areas, skin removed. Inside the bodysuit... excuse me." Judith pulled out the paper handkerchiefs she had in her bag and also passed Doc another sweet. Warren struggled and managed to suppress the knock-on effect to join Doc.

"His body had been, still is, covered in a sticky substance and there are dead ants all over in every orifice, including his face and eyes. I have no doubt they will also be inside his lungs."

Warren could not hold back any longer the picture, Doc had just printed in his mind was too much. He threw up before he even reached the lake bank. Doc glanced at Judith and a weak half-hearted warm smile looked at her.

"I told you that he has a weak stomach, Judith. It is best to give him one of your magical sweets."

Judith threw the mints towards him as he turned around and wiped his mouth.

"What are your initial thoughts, Doc?"

"Mine, Judith, this guy has been tortured, how he survived to the end, you can never underestimate the survival will of the human body. You have to read history books about prisoners who were tortured in the Second World War. Informally, the torture took place over several weeks. The fact he was encased like something from a medieval torture book indicates he had survived the other tortures. Human beings are only limited by their imagination. Hopefully, he died of a heart attack but sometimes, the will to survive is powerful, the autopsy will reveal this. His tormentors, or tormentor, kept him alive for their own perverse, twisted pleasure, that I am sure of. As per usual, the official report will contain the information."

"Hang on, Doc."

"Welcome back to the party, Warren."

"We had a letter sent to us that stated he would not be killed. If he died of a heart attack, then that person is true to their word."

"In a perverse sort of way. You need to keep digging for someone with professional medical knowledge. No one can survive the pain he went through without been kept alive. They would have died simply from shock and blood loss. We'll get him back to the lab and I'll work with Astrid to see if we can find that tiny clue. My instincts tell me that whoever is doing this is highly intelligent and the chance of finding that clue is nil. Warren?"

"How long?"

"Your standard question as ever, Warren. At this moment, all I can say is several weeks, maybe longer. The water temperature would have slowed down the decomposing progress and before you ask, unofficially there are enough similarities to make this your fourth body. At least, no one has been disembowelled yet, maybe that's to come. It never ceases to amaze me what humans can do to other humans. Whoever is doing this is planning it really well, but no one is perfect and humans make mistakes. I need to go back to the tent and finish up. I'll leave you two with the peaceful scenery." Warren and Judith watched Doc trudge back to the tent.

"This I didn't want, Judith, no one did, a fourth body. The investigation so far had led us to this corner and they are all connected via water. Someone either did a lot of research or has local knowledge and I will go for the second option. There is no other reason for a boat to come here, no sandy beaches to ground your boat on, no jetties or coffee shops. This area is also sheltered from the sun, so there is no reason for anyone to stop and soak up a few rays. Look at the few boats over there, the main route is West to East and vice versa. Coming from that direction, this cove is hidden by those trees. Unless you know where it is you would sail past."

"Suggesting, they came from the East."

"I am trying to think logically, but it is only an idea, Judith."

"I have no reason to disagree. Either way, we still need concrete evidence that will stand up in court."

"What now, Warren?"

"Convene the team tomorrow morning for an initial update and then wait for the autopsy results. I do not envy Doc and Astrid."

Chapter 29

Doc and Astrid entered the autopsy room and the pungent sickening smell of the corpse swirled in the air sacs of their lungs.

"Doc, any time one of us needs to leave the room for fresh air, it is okay."

"Let's do the basics first, Judith, measure, weight, hair colour, age. Then let's start to dig deeper, samples behind his nails, X-rays, scars, and then we will start to remove this plastic suit, starting with his face. Last, we will dissect the chest and then the organs. How the hell… never mind let's get on with it."

Astrid noted in her voice recorder what she found while Doc perused the body like a second pair of eyes to ensure as much visual evidence was gathered as possible. The first forty-five minutes passed and Astrid followed Doc out for fresh air.

"It'll take a long time to get the smell out of our noses, Astrid. A dead body has its own unique smell, but this one, I will never forget. It never amazes me as to how sick and twisted the human race can be."

"You just have to look at wars for that. Let's go back in to complete the X-rays and then the dissection."

Astrid cut open the plastic face mask and carefully peeled it back while Doc recorded his observations. The ants were stuck to the sticky treacle-like substance covering his face.

"Stop staring and take a sample of the substance, Astrid and these tiny creatures. Start with his eyes. This is medieval torture, nothing new for mankind."

Astrid wiped the eyes clean and lifted the right eyelid and noted several ants inside the eye. Doc noticed her flinch.

"Know any good ant jokes, Astrid?"

"What?"

"You know like, what do you call a hundred-year-old ant, antique, or what's the world's biggest ant? Elephant. Those sorts of jokes, I am open to any deflective, defence humour today. Let's take the tube out of his mouth and see what we have and create a dental record."

"You mentioned medieval, Doc?"

"The victim would be covered in honey and then trapped or encased unable to move. Vermin would then eat the body while the person was still alive. Insects were also used and they would eat, burrow and breed inside open wounds. They would also pour honey onto the victim's face, especially the eyes, ears, nose. The victim would be force-fed to keep him alive to prolong his suffering. Delirium would have set in, septic shock and dehydration would have brought about death. Look, needle marks on his left arm, my thoughts are he was kept alive as long as possible on a drip and also with pain killers. My God, he must have been screaming inside and praying for death. You've gone quiet, talk to me."

"I've no answer, Doc; my mind is totally numb as to how someone can do this, or even in the past. Let's show him some respect and wash his face before we proceed. Then we can remove the other plastic...where the hell do people buy this sort of stuff from...don't answer, I know, the Internet. Let's get on and remove this and complete our external investigation. Then we can crack the chest open and perform the internal investigation and take organ samples."

Two hours later, Astrid and Doc walked out of the autopsy room, the smell of rotting flesh clinging to their clothes and the inside of their noses.

"I need to scrub and change, Doc, I'm going for a shower and these clothes are going in the bin."

"I will draft the initial report from home and forward it to Warren. I've already informed him that he will receive it tomorrow. I am pleased he had the sense to keep away today so we could concentrate. I'll see you tomorrow."

Astrid let the hot water flow over her hair and around her body as she tried to come to terms with the images she had seen. The ligature marks on the ankles and wrists, the patches of skin sliced off the thighs and torso, the ants in his eyes. Her mind felt numb at the thought of a person tortured, strapped and kept alive. She stepped out of the shower, dried her hand and noticed a missed call from her sister. Her heart sank and her chest tightened, there was no option, her sister would be waiting to tell her the news about their father. Warren's phone vibrated on his kitchen bench.

"I need a friend tonight."

He knew from the tone of her message, Astrid needed support. Within a few seconds, the reply appeared on her screen.

"I'll be there." Astrid sat on the bench as the tears slowly flowed over her cheeks. This day, the case, this news, the relief that her father was no longer suffering and sleeping, she knew she needed time out for her sanity. She looked at her mobile and dialled her sister.

Chapter 30

Astrid opened the solid wooden door to her flat and Warren stood before her with a bottle of Talisker, 18-year-old.

"If you don't like it, we can always revert to wine."

"Whisky is fine, especially a Talisker, you are probably one of the few people in the station who knows that I like whisky. It was something I discovered after the wall came down."

"You're not okay, are you? I've known you long enough to read your feelings in a message. Your smile is not there and you look stressed. I heard from Doc that it was a tough day."

"My father is sleeping. Cancer, I kept it to myself and bottled it up as a way of controlling the situation, keeping life as normal as possible."

"I'm so sorry to hear it, Astrid."

"Come through and bring your bottle friend with you. Hold me, just hold me tight. I need the feeling of your security."

Warren felt as if his ribs were about to break as she wrapped her arms around him. She snuggled her head into his chest. He felt her tears through his shirt as her body trembled with grief.

"You really are not okay, are you?"

"No, and it is a day I want to forget, I received the news after we completed the autopsy. Doc had already left. A shit day all around, did he get in touch?"

"Yes, I received the email on the way here; work is off the agenda tonight." Warren felt Astrid shrug a laugh as she released him from her clinch. "Here's a tissue, it'll do a better job than my collar. How are your mother and sister?"

Astrid looked up at him and smiled.

"You're the only one who knows, let's grab two glasses, open that bottle and sit in front of the fire and sod the measure. My sister has told my mother, she probably doesn't remember now, bloody Alzheimer's. At least his suffering is now finished."

"I remember he went for treatment before going on holiday last year."

"We've known each other a long time, Warren before the wall came down, and we worked in a circle of trust. A trust and friendship that still is as deep today. I'm not going sick, yet; I know, screw the case, visit your sister and visit your mum, I can hear all your thoughts. There's a serial murderer out there and once the report is completed with Doc, then I'll take time off."

"Doc can…"

"No, I need to do it for me. Despite the news and what I've seen today, work will give me some normality, a sense of completion. It's the future I'm scared of, how to handle it. He was my rock and strange after what I have been through and seen in my life…I suddenly feel lonely."

"So, you'll be at work tomorrow?"

"Later than normal and then I need to take a few days off to help my sister."

"Take off what you need and when you need it."

Warren noticed Astrid top his glass up past the double mark. He knew where he was stopping tonight. She needed support and company.

She handed him the glass and looked at him.

"Yes, but in the guest room."

She smiled at him; her eyes were still full of sadness. Warren smiled back and looked into her sad hazel eyes, "To your father, Astrid, and also to the first night, I met you."

"The night when Gabi brought you around, despite your training, you looked like a rabbit in the headlights."

"A long time ago now, Astrid and I had a lot more hair."

"Pass the bottle over and don't worry, I've headache tablets for tomorrow. Come here, next to me, you're too far away, I need the feel of security." He moved over to the settee and Astrid snuggled into him as he put his arm around her. A few minutes later, he could feel her body becoming heavier. The news of her father and the stress of the day had taken over her consciousness. Warren placed the glasses on the table and carried his exhausted friend to her bed. He wrapped the duvet around her, turned off the light and headed to the guest room. Warren lay on the bed and he could feel himself relaxing as a moment of peacefulness flowed through his body. For a brief moment, the pressure and stress of the case had taken a back seat.

Chapter 31

Warren walked into the office ramrod straight, looked directly at Judith and apologised for his lateness.

"Morning, you can sit down if you want, you look down for some reason."

"Mildly put, Judith. Astrid's father died yesterday, I stopped around there last night."

"I am sad to hear about that, I'll get in touch with her later. Are you okay?"

"I will be when we arrest these bastards or someone. Astrid will be at work later to finish a report, she wants some normality. Personally, I think she is in shock and I may take the decision if she does not, to put her on the sick."

"Change of subject, something more upbeat. Missing persons, perhaps, this will lead to turning the last card over."

"What? Sorry, carry on."

The mood Warren was in, Judith knew better than to tell him it was reported two weeks ago.

"Missing persons, Vincenzo De Simoni, lives in Erkner. A neighbour reported no movement in a house for several weeks to the local police. They investigated and found a decaying dog in the hallway. The owner of the house was no-where to be seen. I bet you a free night out in Berlin, the prints from our victim match prints in the house."

"Ring Sarah; you have cheered me up, my treat to two bottles of wine. Our last victim used to visit the gym there, it's too coincidental, Judith. Have you already triggered forensics?"

"Already done, they are on their way. May I suggest we join them?"

Warren and Judith stood in the porch-way between the marble pillars to the house. They both noticed a middle-aged policeman walking towards them.

"Morning, I'm Hans, one of the policemen who took the call. I understand you are in charge of this case. What do you want to know?"

"From the beginning."

"The missing person's name is Vincenzo Rossi. His neighbour reported him missing, after several weeks. Apparently, he was not the most popular neighbour in this area and with a less than acceptable attitude to women. When you look at the distance between the buildings, it is no wonder it took several weeks to report something."

"The missing person list, when was it reported?"

"Nearly two weeks ago by the neighbour. We investigated it and entered the building via the kitchen door when we saw the decaying dog. Apart from that, there was nothing else suspicious. It is not the first time someone has wandered off and disappeared. We called the vet, had the door repaired and put him on the Missing Persons list. Since then, we ran some family background checks trying to find someone to contact, amongst our other priorities."

"I understand what you mean; it will receive the priority now. He may be no longer missing; we recently found a body, murdered. Until otherwise confirmed, this is a murder investigation and this house is part of it. Carry on."

"Age 47, we checked the local registration office and we have started to pull bank records. His last transaction was November 9th at Freiheit Fünfzehn, Koepenick. In addition, he had also booked a flight with Lufthansa and was due to fly on the 10th to China. There is no car on the drive; we need to check if he has one, perhaps he sold it. In the normal routine of life, he would have come home. I cannot imagine anyone leaving dishes in the sink and a muzzled dog to die before they left the country," Judith interjected.

"Was he a member of the local fitness studio?"

"Yes, he was."

"You seemed keen to get that question out."

"Our last victim was also a member, Hans. Your missing person is the fourth."

Hans looked blank at the two of them and for a few seconds, silence fell between them as he realised he may be involved in a serial murder case.

"What else did you find out about him?"

"More than once we had visited this house, he had a bad habit of disrespecting women. When the crunch came, none of them would press charges against him. We have also spoken to a few neighbours in the area and it seems that he kept himself to himself, mainly because the neighbours kept their distance. I'll send you both a copy of the bank and phone records later when we have summarised them."

"It will be appreciated; it's the exact date of his last transaction we are interested in. It pinpoints the exact date and time of his disappearance. Good work."

Judith looked across at Warren as Hans disappeared. She knew from the nod of his head what he was thinking.

"Such an officer is few and far between, a person who owns the problem and knows what questions need to be answered in advance. Willing to take a risk and not worried about a career. Let's get suited up, Judith and have a look inside his house."

"Gunther is over there in the corner, Warren. Let's have a chat with him first and see what he has found and where we can tread."

"Judith, Warren, welcome, I assume you want an update and where you can look."

"Whatever made you guess that?"

"You are a man of routine. At this moment, there is not much out of the ordinary. Lots of fingerprints, which we are collecting and now we are working through room by room. Some match your victim."

"Have you found any suitcases, flight documents? We understand from the bank records that he was planning a flight with Lufthansa and was leaving on the 10th of November."

"Nothing, Warren."

"What about a computer, Laptop? He has Wi-Fi; I have a signal on my phone."

"Good point, Judith, unable to find one, which seems unusual. There is the power cable, next to the table, nothing else."

Judith and Warren looked at each other waiting for confirmation of what they were both thinking.

"I cannot confirm it but my initial summary is that someone was in this house after he disappeared. In addition, none of the locks were damaged, so someone had a key."

"Can we have a look around?"

"Sure, Judith, you are both kitted up, just don't move anything."

Warren and Judith looked at the solid wood mahogany table where the laptop could have been.

"He's perfectly correct; the question is, who and when, Judith. Let's head upstairs; there are too many people here."

"I'll go for whoever did the killing took his luggage and travel documents to make it look like he had travelled. And whoever was here was not aware of the fact that he had a dog."

"Look over there, the corner of the dressing table. Its talcum powder, someone has wiped the corner, the same as in the flat from Andreas Steinbauer. Whatever the reason, it is a commonality with the last crime scene; the hand movement is the same, left to right." Warren raised his eyebrows and tilted his head to one side indicating he was looking for a response from Judith.

"You are looking for my thoughts. It is someone who likes control, order and discipline in their life. That person also likes to achieve their goals, possibly a perfectionist fear of losing control could still be a man or a woman. Either way, they have left the same trademark."

"Let's have a look in the kitchen, Judith."

Judith spoke first as both of them stood in the corner and perused the kitchen.

"I'm pleased the dog is gone, that is one sight I would not have liked to see. Hans is right, Warren, no one with an ounce of decency would leave a muzzled dog to die or a sink full of dishes, when they are leaving the country. What was he planning to do with his dog?"

"Some people do not care. The last sighting of him was at Freiheit Fünfzehn, which gives us a fixed date of when he was alive. The spreadsheet, which Marleen prepared, we need to check to see where his name appears. Can we cross-reference his telephone number and details of the people who used the fitness centre?"

"Possible. We can use Gunther's laptop, Warren. I have it via email on my phone and I can send it directly to him."

Judith felt him peering over her shoulder. She knew the information, which he was after, but he would have to wait a few more minutes.

"You really have no patience, do you?"

"Not when it comes to a serial murderer, Judith. Do you have the graph yet?"

"If your computer skills are better or you can deliver the email quicker, please feel free, a couple of minutes."

The silence between the two of them was disturbed by Hans.

"We have found a name, Lena Rhode, on an old phone receipt, but no address yet."

"Good work, push for an address. Why have you never changed your role?"

"You are not the first to ask, I am content at the level I work at. There is enough oxygen to breathe at this level and no high-level politics, which you find."

"That I can understand, again thanks."

Warren looked down at the screen, which was still loading the spreadsheet.

"I want to look at the outliers and also if her name is on the list. If it is, we have an ID and the fitness centre will have a photo and address."

Judith turned her head at looked up at him out of the corner of her eye.

"Really, what a surprise, I would never have guessed that would be the question."

"Any particular colour you would like the dots in?"

"Just press and show the graph, I'll take whatever colour shows up."

Judith and Warren stared at the graphs of the cross-referenced information. "Explain, Judith, it will save me trying to interpret it and prevent a headache. At first glance, it looks like a five-year-old has been let loose with a pen."

"This cluster here, here are the times and dates when he went to the centre."

"Are any of these people a member of the fitness studio, Judith?"

"This group here, he would never have had any contact with them and especially, our last victim."

"Whose names are appearing in the same time frame? Was Lena a member?"

"I've already narrowed this down and there is one person who does appear in a similar period and age group, Anja Stegemann. There are others, but most of them on average are fifteen years younger. As you can say, she stands out from the crowd, but slightly. Two seconds…there is her name, Lena Rhode; we need to pay her a visit. Her name also corresponds to Anja and overlaps when she was there without Vincenzo. There are other names, but their attendances times are similar."

"Is Sabina Karsch on that list, Judith, the girlfriend of one of our victims?"

Judith typed their name into the search function and nothing appeared. She noted the frustrated seconds of silence from Warren.

"What the hell is the damn connection between all these women? Remember Sabina, Judith she mentioned that she had met a woman in the cafe at Friedrichshagen. Do some background checks, Instagram, Facebook, whatever social media is in fashion these days and pull her history. Find a picture of her and confirm if that was the woman in the cafe. Perhaps, a second visit with a photo may jog their and Sabina's memory."

"We should visit Lena, and also revisit Sabina and Mila. As you once said, we should look at the past for our future, perhaps, the link is now there."

Chapter 32

Judith walked into the office and saw Warren standing with his back against the wall. His face was solemn and full of concentration as he stared at the whiteboard opposite. "Warren, you've nearly run out of space."

"I know. Do you remember when I said one name would crop up time and time again?"

"Yes."

"I am trying to see that link; I want to see if a name ties up somewhere, between them all. Whoever is arrested I want them for all four, Judith, but we may have to forgo that for the second body unless we get a confession. Perhaps, I am starting to wear horse blinkers, which is dangerous in this job but I keep coming back to one name, Anja Stegemann. Let's keep concentrating on her if only to take her out of the equation and take my blinkers off. How was your morning?"

"I spoke to Sabina and she is fairly certain the woman who she talked to in the cafe was Anja. Not a positive identification, but a high degree of certainty."

"Her name crops up again, on the member's list at the fitness centre and overlaps with some of our victims. The last three corpses had one thing in common; they all abused women. If we could identify the second victim, I am sure that he would fall into that category."

"Sabina provided me with an address of an organisation in the middle of Berlin that helps victims of abuse. I would keep your blinkers on for a little while longer. I checked with that organisation and Anja used to work there."

"But a female mass murderer, Judith?"

"Not unknown, but I still go for two people working together. The corpses Warren, one was well built, one person would really struggle to move such a body. Let's talk to the first survivor, Ines, again, see if we can find that link from the past."

"Agree, but if we find it, we will still need more concrete evidence before we can charge anyone, Judith."

Warren saw Judith looking across to the window.

"Hopefully, you've an umbrella, look at the weather."

"It's only water, Judith and my car is near the door. It might calm down by the time we get there."

Judith looked at him, rolled her eyes and nodded.

"I see you still live in hope from time to time. From here to the car park; the rain will stop."

Ines's house was only a half-hour drive across the city and after avoiding several tree branches on the road from the mini storm, they pulled up outside her flat.

"That was a typical Berlin storm."

"What do you mean?"

"The rain here is nothing like the storm, which we left behind. I hope she's in."

"There's only one way to find out, Judith."

Judith ran across the road to avoid the rain as much as possible and rang the bell board.

"Hello, is that Frau Boettcher? My name is Kommissarin Hellwig and I'm from the Mordkommission and I wish to ask you a few more questions regarding the death of your former boyfriend."

Judith could hear the voice of a man in the background.

"It's history, she has moved on."

Judith waved her hand to Warren and indicated him to come over.

"What's up?"

"A man answered, mentioned it is history and then hung up."

"Since when did you take a diplomatic stance in the pursuit of a murderer?"

Judith rang the bell again and waited; after a third attempt, the man answered.

"Which part did you not understand; its history, the door is closed."

"I understand that it is your choice but we're investigating another murder and you may be able to help us. You can do it under your own free will or we'll arrest you for preventing the course of justice and you can answer our questions down at the station, your choice."

Silence followed and a few seconds past until the buzzer signalled and the noise of the door latch indicated open.

"Sometimes nice does not work, Judith. What floor?"

"I've no idea, Warren, but at least it's only a five-storey block."

Ines stood at the entrance to her flat on the third storey. They both stood once more before the slim petite woman, who had now dyed her hair light purple. Warren spoke first.

"It's being a while and we're sorry that we have to bring back bad memories."

Ines looked up at him in silence and Judith took the opportunity to divert her thought process.

"I see that you have dyed your hair. It's something I've thought about for a while but sometimes it is best not to upset the stuffed shirts and older generation at the station."

Warren cast an eye at the quip from Judith who would pay a price for the remark.

"This is difficult, come in, you can meet my husband, he knows about some of the past but no detail. Please, keep this simple; let's go into the sitting room. I thought this was all behind me."

Judith and Warren walked into the room and were greeted by her husband who was close to two metres tall.

"Hello, I'm Peter, please sit down. Ines, if you want, I can go into the kitchen, if you want to keep it private."

"No, maybe it's time that you knew some more details."

Judith looked sympathetically at Ines.

"Does the name Anja Stegemann mean anything to you?"

Ines looked across at her husband; he could see the deep sadness in her face caused by this intrusion of her past.

"Anja, a very emphatic woman, she's one of the reasons why I left my boyfriend. Years of abuse, physical and physiological, she saved me; it's not easy to move out of an abusive relationship. She helps to run the group for abused people; the centre is near Alex Platz."

"Abused women?"

"Abused people, Judith, there are also men out there who are abused by women. I eventually moved on, I met my new husband and realised what a true relationship is. After my ex was murdered, I visited Anja for a few months longer for support."

"When did the visits stop?"

"Approximately two years ago. There comes a time when another door opens and it gives you a chance to move forward but what happened never goes away. It fades, time does not fully heal, but it makes the past more bearable."

"Do you still have contact with Anja?"

"Not for a long time, Judith, like I said I'm moving forward. I hope she is still helping others. Why are you interested in her?"

"You're probably aware that a fourth body was discovered. This brings with it a new list of names and some of these are linked back to the other murders. So we have to go through the names again one by one to eliminate them. The time is moving on and we apologise for the late visit but you've helped us to clarify a question."

Ines closed the door behind Judith and Warren and turned to her husband.

"Should I phone Anja?"

"No."

"Why not? Or are you trying to control me?"

"Ines, back off that's not acceptable, it's not about control; it is about being rational. Her name has cropped up in a continuing investigation. If she has no involvement, there is nothing to worry about. If she does know something and you have phoned her, it could be interfering with an investigation. We don't want another visit, we move forward and keep putting distance between the past. Phoning her would bring us more in contact with the past. It's your decision, whichever way you go I will support it, you know that. Hot chocolate?"

Ines looked at her husband who waited in silence for the answer he wanted. She knew he was right, although, part of her still wanted to put control over a past that she had lost. She had that opportunity, but she was unsure what good it would do them. She could feel her husband's relief when she gave him the answer he was expecting.

"And two biscuits, chocolate."

Judith and Warren looked out of the window in the car whilst Radio 91.4 played music from the eighties. "Okay, I believe that you think Anja is involved."

"And her partner, Judith. I checked him out. He works as a nurse at the hospital. If she is the one, this level of secrecy cannot be kept from a partner who you live with."

"But you cannot figure out the motive or a concrete link to the victims."

"Yip, the most she had is passing contact at the fitness centre, and it's irritating the crap out of me. She's the link in the chain from the past; the only piece that is missing is the connection to the second body. I'll start with pulling out her complete history and then her husband. Tomorrow can you do some discreet diplomatic digging into the support group?"

"No problem, Question, it's late and I came on public this morning?"

"Yes, I'll play taxi driver and take you home to Biesdorf."

Chapter 33

Judith drove along Frankfurter Alle, the architecture of the GDR socialist boulevard never failed to impress her. She hoped the few flakes of snow, falling and melting on her windscreen would be the last. She yearned for springtime, the light nights and warm weather. The winter had been hard and since the middle of December, the temperature had rarely gone above zero. The traffic was moving slowly and she checked the time, hoping she would not be late for the appointment with Frau Steinkopf.

Thirty minutes later, Judith stood before the panelled glass door and rang the bell to the centre. An elderly stocky woman with rimmed glasses walked along the corridor and greeted Judith.

"Afternoon, you must be Kommissarin Hellwig."

"Hello, Frau Steinkopf, it is okay to call me Judith, thank you for finding the time for me."

"Time I have, my children have left the nest and my husband died three years ago. I've plenty, which is why I'm involved with this group. Please, follow me and we can discuss it in my office."

Judith noticed as they walked along the corridor, a male caretaker cleaning the herringbone wooden floor. She thought this strange and her thought process was distracted by Frau Steinkopf.

"This way, my office is over there."

Judith sat and looked at the white office and furniture, which would not be out of place in a hospital.

"You can say it, I can tell by the look on your face you're wondering about the colour scheme."

"It is strange."

"It's terrible, I've no idea what was going through the architect's mind. Perhaps, he saw it as a work of art and forgot people would actually work here. Anyhow, my first name is Karina, what would you like to discuss? I'll provide

175

what information I can so long as it does not overstep the mark of my professional responsibility."

"That's understood, if I require more detail I will approach via the formal route. There have been several murders in the last two years, four in total. There is consistency in the approach of whoever is committing these crimes and we believe that we've found a possible motive. I admit it is not solid, but it has formed a pattern, which we're now investigating. Three of these women were in a male relationship and were abused both physically and mentally. There will be a fourth involved but we were unable to trace that person. Two of these women attended this centre, Lena Rhode and Ines Boettcher. I'm certain when, if we ever found out who the second body was that his girlfriend probably attended this centre. Do you know if any of these women were friends or associated together outside of the group?"

"Not that I'm aware of, I can check when they came. If they did associate outside that I would not know."

"Do you have a list of people who help out at the centre?"

"Yes, but for professional reasons and data protection I cannot provide this unless you apply for it formally."

"How long do people typically stay for help?"

"It varies from a few weeks to months; it all depends on many factors."

"The women I mentioned."

"Again, it is personal records that I cannot provide unless…"

"I know; request them formally. What's your role here, Karina?"

"I don't get involved in the personal details with the women, I'm simply not qualified. I look after the running of the centre, the finances, I organise appointments, liaise with the company who runs the building, raise money, wash the dishes, clean up, lock up. I joined here approximately two years ago. Dr Anja Stegemann was already supporting this centre. She left the centre a few months ago, the end of last year. She certainly would have known the names, which you mentioned."

"How did you find her?"

"Caring, professional, emphatic and a stickler for detail. She was also obsessed with cleanliness up to the point where I used to think that it was an obsession with her."

"Why did you join the centre?"

"I needed something in my life after the death of my husband. All my life, I had worked on European Projects worth millions of Euros and some people struggled to find funding to run centres. I felt that I needed to help people, who need help and I had time to spare."

"I noticed you've a male caretaker, I find it strange. I would have thought this safe haven for women would have been male free."

"We share the building, the room across the corridor is for alcoholics and there is also another room for LGBT advice. We also provide a twenty-four-hour helpline and in the event of an emergency, anyone can bed here for the night. Unfortunately, I have no say in the hire of staff with the cleaning company. There was one occasion when a woman who attended the centre bumped into her ex. He was doing the cleaning and had broken his restraining order and had deliberately found a job in the building. He was dismissed the following day."

Judith went quiet and her heart skipped at the thought of her next question. She opened her bag and placed a picture on the desk.

"Do you know this man?"

"Yes, he looks slightly different but that's him, Alexandra Sagradov from Ukraine."

Judith knew by the quick positive answer that she now had the name of the second corpse.

"What do you know about him?"

"Not a lot, I do not get involved in the details except when someone wants a sympathetic ear. The last I heard he disappeared. A woman mentioned it one night during a coffee break. He had suddenly stopped trying to contact her. That would have been, roughly one and a half years ago."

"Do you know where she lives? We would like to speak to her in the course of a serial murder investigation. You have also identified the second corpse."

"The only details, which I can provide is Mila Metzger and she lives in Hohenschoenhausen. I have her address on the computer, but you can check via the registration office. They will not be bound by client confidentiality."

"Karina, you've been most helpful and thank you for your time. I hope your organisation continues in the work that it does to help. The world would be a worse place without people volunteers."

Judith sat in her car and pondered at the break in the case of finding the name of the second body and Mila. She relished the moment; it was a result, which she had not expected. Judith took her phone out of the bag and dialled Warren.

"Evening, Alexandra Sagradov is the name of the second corpse and Mila Metzger who lives in Hohenschoenhausen was his girlfriend. She attended the centre at the same time that Anja Stegemann worked here."

Silence fell whilst he tried to take in the news that he had just heard.

"Warren, are you still there?"

"Just trying to comprehend what you've just said, eighteen months I have waited for that answer. How certain is she of the name?"

"She positively identified his picture. He used to be a cleaner in the building and deliberately found a job there so that he could follow his girlfriend. Mila turned up one night, the following day he was sacked. The same pattern as the others, the aggression suddenly stopped. Anja Stegemann knew these women. She no longer works at the centre, but she worked there for over two years and left at the end of last year."

"Let's trace Mila via the registration system and can you visit her? Perhaps, it is also time to visit Frau Anja Stegemann and her husband."

Chapter 34

Judith parked her car outside the high-rise flats in Hohenschoenhausen and hoped the lifts were working. She rang the bell and as the buzzer sounded to open the door, she breathed a sigh of relief as an elderly couple walked out of the lift. A minute later, she was standing outside the open door to Mila's tenth-floor apartment.

"I am Kommissarin Hellwig from the Mordkommission and I am here concerning Alexandra Sagradov."

"This is a visit I never thought I would have after all this time."

"Have you eaten; I have some cake and something to drink, if you want. You look stressed and tired."

"Chocolate cake?"

"Of course. You mentioned that you wanted to talk about my ex-dickhead, Alexandra. Hopefully, you found him in a crusher."

"A crusher?"

"I was walking past a lorry the other day when they were crushing the rubbish. I had a moment of reflection and thought that would be a good ending for him."

"You really hated him that much."

"Rot in fucking hell as far as I am concerned. When I look back, after what he put me through. He's never bothered me for a long time; at least, he's disappeared off the scene. I thought he had gone back to the Ukraine to be a man, now I know his ending and finally he is out of my life. Why do some men think they are not a man unless they can control a woman? And women want equality? I'm long past the point of hatred; it takes up too much energy. Once you move away from a relationship like that you realise what you've missed, equality with men, they can stuff that as well."

"I have a picture and I would like you to see if you can identify the body."

"This week gets better, my ex is dead. Let me look. That's him; except the hair is the wrong colour; he had it dyed black then. Strange picture; the features do not quite look the same but it's him. Where did you get this from?"

"It's digitally recreated, we found his body and we have been unable trace him until by chance on another investigation. I ended up at the centre for abused women."

"Did you ever have men problems?"

"I did, then I realised men are not really my sort of thing, well sometimes, not often. You don't seem too phased by the fact he is dead."

"Not really, he's out of my life, there are still one or two lockers in my head where he haunts me. Now he's gone, you have confirmed that it feels sort of empty, a strange feeling, which I cannot describe, sort of a shock. Why now the visit?"

"Four people have been murdered, three women were in an abusive relationship and from what I know and you have told me, you were as well. What happened after you moved out of the relationship?"

"Moved out, not the best choice of words. He put me out…on the street, one in the morning. Except he forgot to take my mobile off me. Something inside me snapped. I expect he thought I would go back knocking on the door like a submissive little child. I phoned the police and it was they who knocked on the door. His face was priceless, they evicted him and I stopped the night in the flat. Early the next day, I got up and went back to hotel mum and dad. From there, I moved on. He tried to get in touch, several times, police were involved and then suddenly, it stopped. I found out later that someone had taken over his flat. I thought he had done a runner and gone back to Ukraine, I didn't really care too much at that point. I know now the reason why he disappeared and there is no fear of him coming back into my life. It is not often someone knocks on your door and is the bearer of good news."

"Where did he work?"

"The bank in Wildau but depending on meetings he would travel into Berlin, Friedrichstrasse."

"Did he have any brothers, sisters, family?"

"There are none, which I was aware of. He once mentioned that he was adopted and he had no idea who his real parents were."

"What about hobbies?"

"Fitness studio, he used to meet a few friends at Erkner, we lived in that corner of Berlin for a while."

Judith made a mental note; it was not the first time the studio had popped up in the investigation.

"How long were you together as a couple?"

"Phew, a long time, four years. I was lucky to get out. My parents had waited helplessly for that day and then supported me. Without them, I don't even wish to think what my life would be like. I know what it is like now and I'm content, it'll be a long time before I'll let a man into my personal life. I've male friends and that's where they stay. Strangely, none of them have tried it on and they are a mixture of gay and hetero."

"Do you know anyone who would want to kill him?"

"That's an open question, probably a long list of ex-girlfriends and their fathers. My father and mother will be pleased with the news, but kill him, he's not capable. He's in a wheelchair, so you can take him out of your enquiries. Alexandra upset a few people over the years as he removed me from my friends. The social circle we were involved in was his group. Even there, I cannot remember him pissing anyone off to the point where they would want to kill him."

"How bad was the abuse? If you don't mind me asking? I'm only trying to build a picture to understand if there's a common theme."

"That's easy to answer, if I say I do not wish to talk about it because of the memories, I think that's enough information for you."

"Did you know Dr Anja Stegemann?"

"Yes, I did, long blond hair; she worked at the centre in the help group. I've no idea what she does for a living."

"I'm pleased that you've moved on, it must not have been easy and also for your parents. I've enough information for now, as and when the case develops, I may be back in touch."

"Please, keep me informed and if I can help, I will, it sounds like he pissed off one person too many. I will be always grateful to that person."

Chapter 35

Warren saw Judith in the canteen and caught her eye as she walked over with her lunch tray. She had hoped for a moment of peace but that had now disappeared. He watched in amusement as she clambered onto the high chair in her tight skirt.

"I know what you're going to say Judith, only a man could have designed such a stupid chair."

"Too damn right, what was he thinking when he designed this type of canteen furniture. I went to visit Astrid last night. She's doing okay and the funeral is next week."

"I know I called her last night. I'll never understand why it takes so long for a cremation in Germany. She said she will return to work in two weeks. It has hit her hard, the case and then the death of her father was the straw that finally broke her. Too much stress coming together in a short space of time. So what did you find out about Alexandra Sagradov, Judith?"

"His girlfriend wished he died in a crusher. She was out for a walk, saw one and thought it would be a good ending for him. He was an abuser; she managed to come out of a violent relationship. He put her out on the street, she phoned the police and from that point, she moved on. She went back to her parents and then eventually, he disappeared. She never followed up to find out why. He was out of her life and even more now that he is dead. She identified the picture I showed her and confirmed she knows Anja Stegemann."

"And him?"

"Getting there, finish your chips before they get cold. There's a link; he used to go to the gym at Erkner, the same one. Don't choke on your food."

Warren looked directly at Judith, what she had just told him was a hard connection, which fed back into their investigation. He felt wordless at what he had just heard.

"You can speak if you wish."

"I know, you wait this long for a hard break, you know it will come and when it arrives, the moment is surreal. We now have a group of men who abused women and a solid link back to Erkner. There is one doctor, who is linked to the fitness centre and the centre for abused women. Her name is starting to pop up too often, Judith. We don't see her husband's name appearing. Everyone has a turning point in their life, what was hers? How is her husband involved?"

"An open question, maybe the thrill, power ultimate act of love for his wife. I'll leave that one for the couch doctors. Shall we interview her?"

"Difficult one, we have her name linking her to certain places and people, Judith. What we need is harder evidence and what is the link that connects Vincenzo? If we slip up, there is no doubt she will know every hole to crawl out of. Plus, I'm still struggling to believe we are dealing with a female serial murderer. We need to interview them both; how and, when we do it, is the question. First, may I suggest we visit the bank where Herr Sagradov worked, let's find out more about his background. Then as part of a general door to door investigation in the area, we pay Frau Stegemann and her husband a visit? Uniform can visit the other houses so they are not singled out for a visit."

Chapter 36

The secretary opened the dark wood-panelled door to the bank manager's office. Judith and Warren looked at each other and mentally compared their office.

Herr Richter greeted them before they were halfway down the office.

"Please, let's sit over there; it's less formal than sitting in front of my desk."

The leather blood-red Chesterfield was a long distance from the chairs in their office. Herr Richter sat opposite, cross-legged and each arm stretched out on the arm of the chair. Warren noticed the open body language and wondered if the approach to sit here had been a deliberate act.

"I understand you wish to talk to me about one of my ex-employees regarding a case, which you are investigating."

Warren noticed Judith unfold her arms, he knew from her body language that she was about to fire the first question.

"That's correct, his name is Alexandra Sagradov."

"He resigned from the bank. It must be about two years now, perhaps more, around about that timescale. If you wish, I can provide you with the exact date."

"Can you tell us more about him, his persona, why he resigned?"

"Why are two detectives from the Mordkommission sitting in front of me?"

"We would be grateful if you just answer the question."

"There are a lot of employees in this bank, some you want to forget, some you remember and some you forget. He fell into the first category and I wish he fell into the last. One hell of a worker, dedicated to the job, confident, successful, he became arrogant and felt he was indispensable. Eventually, he overstepped the mark of professionalism."

"What was his work ethics like? How did he perform his professional duties?"

"He achieved results, he upset one or two people, nothing personal, that happens in a workplace, more so in a competitive environment, people clash. He drove his team to meet their key performance targets, bonuses depended on it, fail your target, fail your bonus. It is one of the best ways to maximise achievement. If people do not achieve, they do not get paid, only successful and talented people achieve rewards."

Warren could feel himself seething as he looked across to Herr Richter and could not resist interjecting.

"So, to understand your work ethics correct, someone who may suffer from depression, for any reason, or may have lost a child and cannot perform one hundred percent, how do you handle such a situation?"

"Why is that question relative to the case?"

"We are trying to understand a larger picture and require an understanding of the culture he worked in."

"We are not totally heartless, we invest a lot of money in our staff, without productive, proactive employees a company is nothing. The employees are the company."

"Until they do not make enough profit and then throw them out to maintain shareholder value."

"Not fully correct. That person would be removed from the high-pressure area to perform. Then that person would be given a lesser role, which unfortunately means a reduced wage. We try and help out staff to the best we can, care of duty but some people cannot be helped."

Judith glanced at Warren from the corner of her eye and knew she must interrupt. She knew one thing that he loathed; people being used as a disposable asset.

"Tell me, Herr Richter, was there any issues on his team. How diverse is your bank?"

"Several different cultures, languages, a mix of women, men, gay, LGBT, across different ages and sexes. That is where his problem started, changing the status."

"That's one hell of a racist and homophobic statement all rolled into one. What's behind it?"

"Alexandra. The world is changing, more open and the workplace has to alter to be more accepting and supportive as society changes. We are talking about human beings. A wind of change swept through the bank, a more ethical approach, before you both say anything, banks do have ethics. We do not tolerate any abuse of bullying or discrimination, unfortunately, some people cannot adapt. Alexandra was one. People felt more open, they felt they could report an incident without fear of reprisal. This trust in the reporting system, which we installed and change in diversity cost him his career. He was asked to resign."

Warren and Judith looked blank at each other at what Herr Richter had just told them.

"The younger generation do not easily tolerate the social values that some of the older generations grew up with. They are more open and willing to report their opinion. We had been watching him for a period. I and the seniors did not like the lack of change in his attitude, he felt threatened as if he was losing control. A younger female member of his team fresh from university reported him for inappropriate sexual comments. We decided to investigate and took an open approach. We simply sent out an email to all employees asking people to report sexual harassment at the workplace. His name crept up several times and some of it was quite abusive and towards women. It was duly investigated and he lost his job. Apparently, this had been going on for several years; much to say that I am ashamed of. The decision to have a more open diverse culture is the correct way forward."

Judith fired the next question before Warren had the option.

"It sounds like you made the correct decision, his girlfriend reported him to the police for violence. I admire the women who reported him and stuck to their guns. Did he upset anyone enough at the bank to murder him?"

Silence reigned around the room at what Herr Richter had just heard. He looked across to the two of them and remained speechless.

"Murdered?"

"We will spare you the details. Did anyone here at the bank have a grudge, hatred, deep enough to kill him?"

"That's a hard question, Kommissarin Hellwig and carries a lot of weight. No-one that I am aware of, what relationships took place outside of work, I have no idea."

"Did he bank with you? If not, can you let us know where his wages were sent? We would like to have a look at his bank records."

"That's not a problem, he banked with us and you can have statements. I can email them to you, or you can have paper copies."

"E-mail will be fine, Warren, any further questions?"

"For the moment, no, but we may wish to speak with the women who made the complaints. We'll be in touch."

"My secretary will provide you with the statements, which you requested. If you wish to interview anyone, contact me or my secretary and we will arrange a place for you. I hope you find who you are looking for."

Chapter 37

Judith parked her Grey VW outside the rustic double garaged English style house, which had a breath-taking view of the lake.

"This looks like a very spacious house, Warren; one I could only dream of, hopefully, they have some traditional English furniture inside."

"Both, you and I on our combined wages couldn't afford such a house, Judith. Hopefully, they're at home."

"Only one way to find out, it is old fashioned, but works every time, let's knock on the door." Judith walked up the marble steps followed by Warren and they both stood on the pale grey marble entranceway gazing at the exuberance.

"I think that lever to my left is the bell. It's all slightly overkill here. The type of overkill, which I could live with for a while, Warren, in fact, a long while."

"It doesn't necessarily mean that you will be happier."

"I would like to try it to see if it works."

He looked at Judith as they heard the sound of the lock turning and the solid oak door opened. Judith looked at Anja who was the same height, her long blond hair tied up in a bun.

"Good morning. Are you Frau Stegemann, Anja Stegemann?"

"Yes."

"My name is Hauptkommissar Fischer and this is Kommissarin Hellwig, we're conducting door to door enquiries regarding a series of murders. We would like to ask you and your husband a few questions."

Warren watched her body language to observe the reaction. Emotionless, she stood before the two of them and a few seconds of silence past before she invited them both in.

"My husband is not home and will not be for a few hours. Come, we can sit in the kitchen and have a coffee if you want or perhaps, you both would like something else to drink?"

"No, we're fine, thank you, but thank you for the offer."

188

Judith looked at Warren and raised her eyebrows.

"Please sit over there and make yourselves comfortable."

Judith ran her hand over the soft white leather bar stool.

"I take it there are no children in the house."

"God no, that's the last thing I would need running around my house. They would only get in the way of my life and mess up the house. I like to keep my house pristine."

Warren could feel the more he stayed the less he liked this superficial woman. They were here to ask questions about a serial killer and she stood before them in a position of superiority and confidence. It was not the defensive body language that he had expected when someone turns up at the door and wishes to discuss the subject of murder. He fired his first question.

"We are investigating a murder."

"Did you know Alexandra Sagradov and Ines Boettcher?"

"Him. He had a restraining order and in order to get closer, he found a job at the centre. The police were involved, check your records, but then he disappeared. We never heard anything from him or the police. Ines attended the centre."

"Did you ever see those persons outside?"

"No, I work as a professional."

"Are you aware that he was a member of your fitness centre?"

"Not that I was aware of."

"How long did you work with abused women?"

"You already know the answer to that."

"Please, it's just to confirm."

"Approximately two and a half years."

"Do you own a boat?"

Anja looked down at Judith and the change of tack in the questioning. "Most of the people in this area own a boat. Yes, we do, it's at the bottom of the garden, and we've a jetty. I'm sorry for the pause; you caught me out with the change of tact on questioning."

"Apology, it was not my intent. The rape case you were involved with four years ago, the victim ended up committing suicide after the trial collapsed, were you aware?"

"Yes, I was, and it still plays on my mind, that bastard walked free thanks to you lot not preparing the case correctly, so-called technicality. Thanks to

189

Schengen, he fled across all the borders. God knows where he is now. There are too many men in the world who are an insult to men and too many of those bastards walk free. Why is that relevant?"

Both noticed the pause as Anja tried to compose her anger. She walked over to the sideboard and looked at a picture of her sister and noticed how dusty the sideboard was. With her left hand, she wiped the dust off the corner of the unit in a sweeping arc movement.

"The damn cleaner has missed this, that's not what I pay her for."

Judith and Warren noticed the movement, looked at each other and said nothing. Judith carried on her questions.

"It is relevant to explore all corners of a case. One quick question before you answer my last question, are you left or right-handed?"

"Left, why?"

"Curious."

"The police, you lot screwed that case up big time."

The change of her tone of voice to assertive was noted by both of them.

"Failure to disclose evidence to the defence, you lot opted not for the truth but to provide enough evidence to prosecute. Except the defence team found out and he was acquitted. Who the hell prosecutes you lot for fucking up. If you read your case notes carefully, you will find she later attended the centre where I helped out. That is one you missed off your list, not doing a good job today, are you?"

Both noticed the sudden change in tone, which was now bordering aggressive. She stared down at Warren, her face full of hatred for what he represented. Judith interrupted to stall Anja in her onslaught.

"Were any of the women you knew at the centre, a patient at your Dr's practice?"

"Patient confidentiality."

Warren was fed up with sitting and looking up at Anja; he stood up and walked to the window to stretch his legs. Anja looked at him.

"It's only polite to ask if you want to walk around someone's house."

He deliberately held back a response for a few seconds to ignore her controlling comment and turned the conversation to his advantage.

"You said that you have a boat."

"At the jetty, at the bottom of the garden, a Bayliner."

"Can we have a look please, besides, I need to stretch my legs; the stool is uncomfortable."

"I'll take you down."

Judith and Warren looked at each other. They both realised that despite her outwardly controlling calm manner, there was a deep hatred for a system, which had failed people. Judith followed them and noticed a flower collection as they passed through the hallway.

"The boat house, which you can see is mainly for bad weather and winter use. When the lake starts to freeze, we can winch it up, it saves having to keep breaking the ice around the boat. From here, you can go anywhere in Berlin. Sometimes, we disappear for the entire weekend through the city and to the Wannsee."

Judith noticed Warren starting to scan the Bayliner and boathouse. She knew she had to give him time and needed to distract Anja from him.

"That would take you through the Mühlendamm locks. I've never done a boat tour through Berlin. It must be a serene way to relax when you cruise the rivers in the sun at a slow speed."

"It is. There is one enjoyment of having a boat; there is only one pace of life, slow. You have no other option but to wind down from the stress of work. You were lucky to catch me in today. It's my half day off, Kommissarin Hellwig; normally I go to the fitness centre."

"The one at Erkner?"

"Correct."

"I would appreciate it if you keep your investigation separate from my work so as not to disturb my patients. If you require any further information, please do not contact me at my practice. If you wish to speak to my husband, you are welcome to return."

"Dr Stegemann, you're correct we'll try our best. I think we've disturbed you enough for today so we will leave you in peace to enjoy your time off work. If we do not strike a good work-life balance, it's unhealthy. At this moment, there is no requirement to speak to your husband."

Warren stared though the windscreen as they both sat in her car, he could feel his partner staring at him.

"Spit it out, Judith."

"She's cold, calculating, manipulative, highly intelligent, controlling and coupled with a deeply buried hatred of police injustice. She has compassion that comes out of the fact that she helps women who need help in a time of crisis."

"But."

"She has not got one empathic bone in her body. She could kill under the right circumstances."

"Most people can, when confronted with the right circumstance, Judith and that is the scary part. Luckily, most people never find themselves in that position. We need some more concrete evidence, at this moment, there are no forensic links."

"Two things, Warren, she is left-handed. She wiped the dust from left to right. Each time we have seen that it was always from left to right. Stand on the left side of a cabinet and create the same pattern with your right hand. You have to push; it is not a natural movement."

"You went into scan mode in the boathouse."

"Did you notice the overhead pulley system, why would they want such a system unless they were going to exchange an engine and how often would you do that? Besides, she looks like the sort of person who would have the work completed for her. She has a cleaner."

"Do you remember the pollen spores on the letter? Let's see what these pollen samples bring, a silent witness to a possible crime."

"When did you collect them?"

"On the way to the jetty, you both walked in front of me and I rubbed my handkerchief next to the flowers in the hallway. Hopefully, I have collected a few pollen spores which provide a match. We also need to track down her sister."

***

It was early evening before Stefan walked through his front door. The lack of aroma drifting from the kitchen was absent; this was out of the routine when Anja was off work. There was also silence in the house, he shouted for his wife.

"In here, the sitting room."

Stefan peered around the corner; Anja was propped up in the corner of the settee, sitting cross-legged with a book in her hand.

"What's wrong?"

"Contemplating when we should leave Berlin this week. I had a visit from the police today, asking several questions, door to door enquires. It is probably only a matter of time before they take us in for questioning, and has the forensics crawling all over the house. Whatever they have, has led them to this corner."

"Leave, it's planned for the end of next week, Anja."

"I know, but I mean leave now, tomorrow, day after at the latest. It's becoming too close for comfort and for the sake of a week, I have no wish to spend the next thirty years in a cell."

Stefan sat in the opposite corner and looked directly at his wife. "We both knew this time would come. We have the accounts set up in Dar-es-Salaam and a place to live. In principle, we could leave now. If the police are this close, then it is only a matter of time. What brought them here?"

"They visited the centre where I worked and from that, they have found names and identified the victims via their ex-girlfriends. Give it time and they will link Vincenzo, I saw them look at the picture of my sister on the wall. All they need to do is speak to her; luckily, they are not back until Friday. There are no forensics linking us yet otherwise we would have been pulled for questioning. I did see in a mirror reflection that the female officer took a sample of pollen from your plant collection when we were leaving the house to visit the jetty."

Stefan went silent and looked across to the cabinet in the hallway. He had placed the letter in the same area that he had sent to the police. Anja noticed the blood drain from his face.

"What's up, Stefan?"

"The letter, I placed it over there before I sent it. The police must have a sample of pollen; the sample they took will not take long to match up. Pollen, a hidden witness and it is their first piece of solid forensics. We need to leave tomorrow, latest. They will find all the forensics, which they require when they search the house."

"We can still sell the house later, or gift it to a foreign organisation, which will have us as directors."

"There's always a way, Anja, right now that's the least of our problem, I'll go around and speak with Thorsten and see if it is possible to leave in two days. Tonight is our last night here and we have to leave before your sister returns, she will confirm the link of the fourth victim."

Chapter 38

The evening rays of sunshine streaked across the disused Russian airstrip. Spring was starting to push its way through. The air was crisp and fresh as Anja rubbed her fingers along the shrub branch and stared at the fresh green buds. Mixed thoughts and feelings flowed through her body, especially about her sister, who would be home tomorrow. The move, the need to flee the country early irritated her; this did not fit in with her time plan. She hated the lack of domination over the situation, but soon she would be back in a country where she could control a new situation and rectify the past. The only question was when to inform Stefan of her true intent in Africa; that would have to wait until later. There was still the question of his devotion, which niggled at her. She looked across the runway at the derelict traffic control tower. The area had changed, the politics had changed; the Russian fighter jets no longer flew, now their life was moving into another phase.

Stefan walked along the edge of the runway and looked down at the rugged condition of the surface. Mother Nature was taking control and he wondered how Thorsten would land. That was not his only concern; along the edge were animal tracks from wild boar and wolves. He looked across the runway and saw that Anja had zoned out, he wasn't sure what she was thinking. The last few weeks had been difficult and the stress of fleeing the country had driven a wedge between them, Anja had become cold and distant. Stefan pondered for a moment and wondered if it was him, either way; the feelings between them both had altered. Would it be possible to enjoy another evening walk in the spring air? Or sit in front of the patio doors watching the burning red evening of Berlin? He knew he was dreaming of false hope and felt unsure about this new future, which Anja was controlling. The change was too abrupt for him and he had felt vulnerable for the last few months. He knew the unconditional trust and loyalty, which Anja demanded was in question and he felt unsafe. His plan to disappear out of the relationship would now have to be put on hold. Tonight was a necessary risk, a risk mitigated by the fact when the timing was right, he planned to leave Africa.

They both could hear the low drum of a light aircraft and looked along the runway as Thorsten taxied towards them. The cockpit door opened and his two-metre frame unfolded from the fuselage door.

"Evening, you two, I see you don't have much luggage."

Anja looked up at him and wondered how he fit behind the pilot's seat.

"We have enough for the journey. The rest you do not need to know."

"I'm interested in knowing the why, that's human nature but as far as I'm concerned, I don't wish to know. You are fare-paying passengers who have rented a service. I learned a long time ago in Africa, when I was smuggling, not to ask questions."

Thorsten looked across to Stefan.

"Brought any Cognac with you?"

"Travelling light."

"No worries, I've arranged a bottle on your second flight."

"Are you with us all the way?"

"No, I will fly you to the Polish Ukrainian border, internal Schengen flight. From there, a private commercial business jet on a humanitarian mission and then an internal flight. You will never leave the airport. It's a route that I have used more than once."

"I thought it would not be possible to land on this disused strip?"

"You are right, except I know where to land and it is not the first time that I have used this old disused airstrip. One thing is for certain, we cannot hang around, it will not be the first time that some local or dog walker called the police. Besides, if we wait much longer, I'll have some explaining to air traffic control."

The twin-engine light aircraft pulled up, Stefan and Anja looked across to the twilight of the Berlin silhouette. Soon they would cross over Frankfurt am Oder and into Poland, a few hours later, they would be near the Ukrainian border to change planes. They both looked at each other in silence. Stefan wondered when he would return, Anja knew she was going to even the score of her past history.

***

Warren and Judith looked at the double wrought iron gates to Filippo's house.

"Do you ever get the feeling that we took a wrong career route, Judith?"

"More than once, buzz the bell."

Only seconds passed when a male voice with a German Italian accent answered.

"Hello."

"Afternoon, my name's Hauptkommissar Fischer and I am with my colleague Kommissarin Hellwig, we're from the Mordkommission and investigating a murder."

A moment of silence fell before the sound of a latch indicated the opening of the gate. A tall greying man, approximately one ninety tall, smartly dressed, stood in front of the door as if he was greeting guests.

"This is all slightly weird, Judith, I've knocked on a few doors in my time, but never has anyone come out and politely greeted the police."

"Smart looking man, I bet he broke a few women's hearts when he was younger."

Filippo walked down the steps of his house to greet his guests.

"Hello, no need to show me your ID cards, I trust you. My wife, Melanie will be back in about half an hour, she has just popped out to get some shopping. We were away for a few days at Leipzig. Please come in."

Warren looked at Judith who shrugged her shoulders as he raised his eyebrows. Filippo took them through to the sitting room, which overlooked the swimming pool.

"I assume you both wish to ask questions about Vincenzo, my relationship with him, the night at the party, why I invited him, his history. I think that probably covers most of what you want to know. That is the only reason why I can think that you are here, but that was last year, or are you here for another reason, you mentioned, Mordkommission."

Judith and Warren looked startled at each other. They had come to expand their enquiries as a branch to Anja, but they had never expected the name Vincenzo to appear.

"The name Vincenzo Rossi, can you identify him from this photo?"

Filippo looked at the photo and handed it back to Judith.

"That is him, when was he killed?"

"Late last year, he was found locally."

Filippo sat down. Judith noticed he visibly looked in shock as the blood drained from his face. "Are you okay?"

"No, he was a long-term close friend, who I lost contact with last summer. I thought he would have got in touch after what happened; now I know the reason why. My God, that news I did not expect. We both went to school in Naples and then later to the same University. I qualified as an engineer and he qualified in physics. During university, my mother and father were killed and his family helped me through that period and supported me throughout my university studies. I therefore, owed his family a debt of gratitude. We moved to Berlin and he hated his job, despite the good wages he earned. We both started a small import-export business, quite successful. His parents died and left him a successful restaurant business in Italy. He sold it for a lot of money and planned to retire and disappear on his long-planned world tour. He had no set date to return and was due to leave last November."

"What about your wife, how did she find Vincenzo?"

Warren sat quiet and let Judith drive the questions as he observed the body language. "Vincenzo…let's put this diplomatically. Melanie cannot, sorry, could not stand him and disliked him intensely and also her sister, Anja. They found his politics too right-wing and disliked his abusive attitude towards woman. Unfortunately, for some women, they went for his looks, money and shit attitude. Only God will probably know why."

"What do you mean his politics?"

"Vincenzo had the belief that the elite should control the majority and only the qualified elite should be allowed the vote, no one else. His views became more right-wing as he got older."

"Not even disabled people."

"Not even disabled people and that's where it really rubbed Melanie's nose in it. The problem is the honour debt, which I owed his family. Eventually, after the party, the friendship ended, he upset one of my guests. The decision was simple, my wife or my friendship. He overstepped the mark of respect that day, not just for my house, but respect for me, my family and all the women at the party. He tried it on with a married woman and she put him on the floor."

Warren noticed a woman enter the room and assumed it was Melanie. Filippo turned and walked to his wife and kissed her on the cheek.

"These two people are from the Mordkommission and they're here concerning the death of Vincenzo, apparently, he was murdered."

"Good, one less extreme right-wing wanker to abuse women on this planet. I hope it was not pleasant."

Warren jumped in with the next question.

"So you had no love for him."

"Whatever gave you that idea, very observant, I couldn't stand the man. Before you ask the next obvious question, do I know anyone who would want him dead, the answer; a long list of women. Enough to keep you busy for years. Do I know anyone capable, no, but drop them a thank you when you find that person."

Filippo noticed the anger in the tone of his wife, it was more to do with the fact someone she distasted, had now, through a series of events brought the police to their doorstep. Warren carried on with the questions.

"After the party, there was no further contact with him?"

"You have met my wife. I had promised her no and I am the type of person when I make a decision, I stick to it. If you want, feel free to check the telephone calls, both internet, mobile and house phone. To be honest, after that night, I felt a sense of relief that I owed him no longer a debt of gratitude."

Melanie stared blankly at Warren.

"What is the intent of these questions?"

"Exploring facts in order to establish any possible links, motives, remove and prioritise facts within the case. You seem to have the same tone as your sister."

"Are you surprised after the case she was involved in, it cost a person her life. I recommend that you go away and read the information first hand from the source traceable documents to establish where you lot went wrong. Do your homework both of you and this time get the facts right and present all the evidence instead of selective. I am a defence lawyer and it is my job to make sure I can punch holes in your case; if I cannot then you probably have a watertight conviction. The defence did their job, your lot failed and he walked. It changed my sister; it broke her when she received the news of the suicide. You damaged more than one life."

"Just to set you straight, we will do what it takes to find and prosecute whoever is committing these crimes. The defence lawyers can have access to all the information they want because by the time we are finished, there will be no holes for the defence to find. They will only be in court as decoration. I will ask again, do any of you know if Vincenzo had any relationship with anyone who might want to kill him?"

Melanie spoke again.

"No, maybe check at the local fitness centre or the golf club at Motzen, he used to go frequently there."

"We will."

Filippo looked across the room to Judith and Warren.

"I hope you find him, no one deserves to die how he did. It is bad enough to lose a child but for parents to find out that their child was murdered…that is a picture no parent would want in their head for the rest of their life. Do you have any more questions? If not then I think we have all reached an end. If you have any further questions, which you wish to ask at a later date, feel free. Technically speaking, we cannot refuse unless we wish to be held responsible and arrested for preventing the course of justice."

"Thank you for your time and as you said if we feel that we have more questions, we will be in contact."

Warren looked at Judith and they both knew that it was time to leave and Filippo showed them to the front door.

It was only as Judith drove out of the grounds of the house that she let rip. Warren knew from the silence before that she was mad as hell and the outburst was no surprise.

"What a smooth-talking obnoxious, self-centred, pompous person full of his self-importance. He is now on my list of men, which I do not like."

"Am I on your list?"

"Yes, but in pencil, I keep rubbing you out. His name will be written in waterproof ink, what a slime ball."

He burst out laughing, he could not take his partner serious and Judith cast a cold friendly stare at him.

"Where did you learn all those words from, don't tell me the Irish Bar in Dresden."

"Wrong, I once had an English girlfriend whose boyfriend pissed her off. I wrote the words down hoping they would come in useful one day."

"Have you calmed down yet, what're your thoughts?"

"Honestly, I came away with no real feeling of suspicion. Normally, something does not feel right, gut feeling, you know what I mean but this time nothing. I think they're genuine people caught up in a web. At least, we know now that Anja knew all four victims."

"Let's head back to the station, when will we obtain the results of the pollen?"

"It is expected today."

Chapter 39

Warren and Judith found themselves once more on the pale grey marble slab entrance to Stefan and Anja's house. This time there was no answer as he tried the door, which to his surprise was open. Both looked in disbelief and they gradually entered the hallway. The house had an eerie silence as they walked along the hallway to the kitchen was the last and they noticed on the bench, two plain white china cups on a saucer and a bottle of Cognac with two glasses. Each cup had a spoon and a second bowl with sugar in it. A note was neatly folded and placed next to the cups. Warren read it out aloud.

'Dear Judith, first of all, I hope your girlfriend is well and Warren, we wish you all the best. Where you live in Karlshorst, Warren, is a pleasant area; your balcony has an enjoyable view. Biesdorf is also a nice area, Judith; we see you picked a new build flat, good choice. It doesn't take you both long to travel to work and Warren; you should really buy a new car. Take more notice of the world around you, you never know who is sitting in the same restaurant, past or future. Now, you are both wondering if we will meet again. We can almost imagine you racking your brains as to when one of you saw us. It was long before your first visit. You have noticed the house is empty and well done! Good detective work. Enjoy the tea, or Cognac, your choice, think of it as a goodbye present. Judith, I noticed that you took a sample of pollen from the plants. I saw your reflection in a mirror when we walked out of the house. If it wasn't for that, perhaps, we would be talking now, instead of you reading this letter, your mistake. Please, accept our apologies for leaving earlier than planned. Once we realised that we had made a grave error and you would match the pollen, that's why you required a sample, Judith, we had to leave. Please don't destroy the house with your search, there is no need. The plant, pollen…you've already made a connection, under the kitchen there's a cellar, which is not registered on the house plans. If you both turn around with your backs to the bench you will see a corner slightly ajar in the hallway. The steps lead to a cellar; there you will find everything you need, including books with pressed flowers. It was my husband's hobby as a way of de-stressing. The covers contain human skin so at least you can match the DNA to the victims, so at least the families will have some closure. We say some closure because they will find out their son's background. At least now some more women will be safer in this world where YOU THE POLICE FAILED TO PROTECT. You should also check the boat; it was useful for the journey through Berlin. Hopefully, now you both have some sort of closure and all the evidence you require to prosecute, except one item, where are we? Enjoy your drinks and do not worry, we will not visit the areas where you live again. Who could we torment if we killed you? Besides, you have done nothing wrong. You are only doing your job, albeit it is not very well.'

They looked at each other and a cold shiver ran down their spines at the thought of going down the stairs. "We're in a crime scene, Warren, evidence needs to be protected."

"Any contamination comes from us. I have shoe covers and I'm not waiting for forensics. Who or what is down there needs to be investigated and we are not sure if someone is there, therefore we need to check. That's all, nothing else."

"You're using that as a reason to go down and confirm what is in the letter."

"Yes, and it's justified."

Warren opened the door and descended the flight of stairs into the cellar. He noticed a pale brown Formica desk with a steel-framed laminated wooden chair behind the desk. Judith tapped him on the shoulder and they froze as they looked at the books on the table. Words failed them as their minds could not comprehend what they were staring at. Without moving, they changed their stare to the leather chair in front of the table complete with straps to fasten the victim to the chair. Warren noticed a bucket under the chair and nudged Judith.

"Whoever was in that chair was stripped naked."

"Please, there are enough pictures in my mind. Let's walk through that door over there in the corner."

The room opens up into another chamber with a wooden bench for a bed and a light facing in the direction of the headboard.

"This is what they used in some prisons for sleep deprivation, Judith. What is more interesting is the laptop on the bed. They mentioned in one letter that we would receive the laptop. I want that dissected today."

Warren looked around and noticed, Judith had wandered off to another corner.

"Look at this, a cell for standing room only, the walls are sharp concrete and above, whoever was here was strung up by the wrists. The cell is also used to simulate drowning, water comes over the head. The victim was probably blindfolded and then when it reached a certain level, it went out via that drain hole. I have seen this type of torture cell in a KGB museum."

"I had enough, let's get out of here, I need fresh air."

Judith and Warren sat on the garden bench completing at what they had just seen.

"What the hell, Warren."

"Hell, that's downstairs, we've just found it. People who want revenge on people are normal; it's a way of feeling that we've evened the score and regained control. This is a whole new level, brought on by a series of events. Remove any one of those…"

"What do you mean?"

"If the Police hadn't screwed up…"

"Fucked up would be a better statement."

"The guy had not met her sister-in-law; Stefan had not met Anja…"

"And men had not abused women. Some women are safer now, let's not forget that. This couple has disappeared, Warren, no idea where but far away. They are intelligent, unlike most criminals, they knew when to stop and flee, also they have money and are able to travel anywhere they want."

"Agreed, but we need patience now to find them. No one leaves a valuable house and when it's sold, we'll track them via the banks. The two of them will surface; it's a challenge for them not to get caught. Let's get forensics over, the laptop is my priority. After I know what is on it, then a visit to her sister's house. Let's see what tomorrow brings after forensics strip this place apart."

Chapter 40

Warren walked into the office after lunch and Judith was already waiting for him with the initial forensic results of the house.

"Good meal?"

"The canteen was at its best."

"Interested to take a walk and visit Astrid, she needs a friendly face."

He knew she was fishing for information, she couldn't resist it.

"Let's go, she can give us a summary, it'll be quicker than trawling through the file."

Astrid in her white lab coat was leaning over a microscope as they walked into her domain.

"I'll be with you in a few seconds."

She looked up and pulled her glasses down from her head almost as if to hide the blackness under her eyes.

"Since when did you start to wear glasses?"

"Today, we're all getting older; I was trying the microscope with and without."

"I like the style and colour, Astrid. We have an initial report; Warren would like a brief verbal summary."

"Reading was never his strong point, Judith."

Astrid caught the stare from her friend.

"Okay, the report contains initial information; it is live and will be updated as and when new info arrives, let's sit over there. First the book covers; they were made from human skin. The tested DNA indicates the covers relate to each victim. Each book contained pressed flowers, some of them are very rare but the Botanical Gardens will have to identify them all. The furniture in the cellar and the floor, we found evidence of blood on the concrete floor. Whoever was responsible went to great lengths to cover the equipment and floor during the torture. But as with any good cleaner, they always miss a patch. The wooden bed, we found hair samples jammed between the wooden slats. The DNA matches that of Vincenzo and Alexandra. To me, they knew their life would come to an end. It was a move, out of desperation that someone, sometime would find these to prove they were there. What the hell was going through their mind does not bear thinking about. We found a strand of hair belonging to Vincenzo on the back of the chair. This guy was definitely tied to the chair naked, the bowl underneath was used for defecation. We also found the acid; it was in the boat shed. There is enough initial evidence to confirm that all four bodies passed through this house. That's why I sent you the very basic initial findings. I am sure more concrete evidence will surface. We explored the house and yet have found nothing; the boathouse is something different. There is a machete and the cut pattern matches the pattern on the vertebrae of the third victim. We couldn't find traces of a blood splatter pattern, but we did find a trace of blood on some rope attached to a pulley. What we did find, near the jetty, and this is related to Vincenzo, was an ant nest. Now we know where they probably obtained these."

"Judith, are you okay? You've gone silent."

"Fine, Astrid, do you have a hair scrunchy? I need to put my hair in a ponytail."

"Top draw left."

Warren looked at his partner and knew she was stressed.

"Also, we found under the wooden bed and in the boathouse, a roll of polythene, obviously used to reduce contamination."

"The laptop, Astrid, what was found?"

"This guy was sick; we've found some internet history, paedophile. I would ban the internet just on the grounds of protecting children and stopping the worldwide spread of sickos. The laptop is now with the relevant department and you will receive their initial report tomorrow morning. I don't want to know anymore from that side of the investigation."

Chapter 41

Warren was sitting with one foot up, on his set of draws as Judith walked into the office.

"What's up with you? You look pissed off."

"I twisted my damn ankle dancing last night."

"Since when do you dance?"

"Four weeks ago, I am learning Salsa and Bachata. I am trying to find a way to distress and it was working until last night."

"You kept that a secret. Any further news?"

"Forensics did not take long to hack into the computer. There was another letter inside the laptop when they opened it up. That's the copy."

He slid the copy across his desk, indicating the urgency to read it.

"Do you want to read it first or grab a coffee?"

"I'll take the hint, coffee can wait. I had breakfast before I left."

'Do not watch if you have no stomach. No one should see what you are about too. The photographs and videos are from Vincenzo's laptop. You lot failed to protect innocent people again, this time children. Not very good at catching and prosecuting criminals, are you? Cannot even protect children from perverts. This makes our work more justified. The pictures are not pleasant, but there is enough information to launch a separate investigation. We know you will try and find us, go for the easy life and save your police budget, you will need the money for another investigation instead of around the world ticket.'

"I feel sick, Warren, the exploitation of innocent children. Many would probably say, Vincenzo got what he deserved."

"I'm starting to have less sympathy for him, that's for certain. Either way, Judith, whoever's doing the killing is breaking the law. Right or wrong, or whatever someone's viewpoint of the law, and what justice should be, we have to work in the framework of the law. Sometimes…well, my thoughts are different and I feel much the same way as you now. I live alone, Judith, but you have a daughter and a girlfriend, do you want someone to watch your family until this is over?"

"Strangely, I believe what they say in the letter. They have no motive to kill us; we're part of their control game. Remove us and then what will they do? They lose control. Still, I have a daughter and I need to explain this to Sarah. How? I've no idea; yes, I would like someone, especially, watching over my daughter."

"I'll have it organised, Judith. Let's look at what's on the drive."

Not a word was spoken between the two of them as he loaded the file. "Hell, he has over several thousand pictures and videos here."

Warren opened the first file and both stared at the screen. Only a few seconds passed when Judith spoke.

"Turn it off, these pictures; I don't want in my mind. It's bad enough dealing with our investigation. There're really some sick, twisted, warped bastards in this world. I know Vincenzo is someone's son, but I'm pleased he is no longer in this world. Not only are women safer but also children, someone has done them a favour."

"I'll contact the child protection unit, Judith and also let forensics dig deeper with the IP addresses. These people very rarely work alone; there'll be a network out there."

"Who wrote the letter?"

"Forensics confirmed it was Stefan's handwriting from other samples in the house. He is showing compassion, a sense of injustice against innocent victims and wishes to help those victims receive justice. My guess, he's the weak one in the relationship, his wife is the controller and has been supporting her. I would not be surprised if he was starting to doubt his wife. She's the lead, the one with the past and Stefan is her subordinate."

"What's your reasoning behind this, Warren?"

"I am just trying to understand their relationship. She has a hold over him, what it is, that I cannot even guess. Perhaps, her sister has an idea, or where they work. There is one thing we need to check, Judith, and that is flights. They mentioned, 'around the world tickets'. They are letting us know that they have fled Europe, Judith. Where is the question?"

"There is the big challenge, Schengen. They could have flown from anywhere in Europe, open bloody borders, freedom of criminal movement from Portugal to the Belarus-Polish border. We can start with the Berlin airports, and then work outwards. I have my doubts that they would have flown from an international airport, too traceable. Let's take them out of the inquiry, that should not take long and then the local airports. Even with them, I do not hold much hope. I'll set that rolling; in the meantime, I want to follow another lead, Warren."

"Clarify?"

"They look as if they left the house in a hurry, loose ends not tied up. We were close to them, they knew and ran. I believe they were planning to run. When was the question? They have wealth and probably contacts. If you wanted to disappear, how would you do it?"

"Check their social circle, all local airports and light aircraft flight plans first. These birds are long gone, God knows where; I want that bastard who flew them. We will start with her sister this afternoon."

Chapter 42

Warren and Judith stood before Filippo and Melanie's house and they were in no mood for his suave mannerisms. Melanie opened the door.

"Come in, Filippo is in the sitting room, you know where it is."

"Afternoon, what can we do to help you?"

He looked directly at Melanie.

"Your sister, where is she? She's disappeared with her husband."

"What the hell are you on about? Try to be a bit more polite and you may get a civilised answer. I haven't spoken to my sister for a couple of days, there's no answer on her home telephone or her mobile."

"Try to be less aggressive and direct with my wife."

"Filippo, Melanie can answer the questions here or formally down at the station. You included, your choice. Where's your sister, Melanie? I find it hard to believe that she never spoke to you before she disappeared and you knew nothing, not even an inclination."

"We all have secrets detective, what's yours? That's why they are called secrets." Warren briefly glanced across at Judith who raised her eyebrows as much to say that she really has no idea why we are here.

"Your sister and her husband are wanted for the murder of four people. Would you like to see the picture of the corpse hacked in half or the one, which was skinned, I have a few more. I'll leave the choice with you."

Silence reigned around the room and Warren saw the colour drain from Melanie's face as she struggled to contemplate the sister she loved with all her heart was now a prime murder suspect. Filippo, speechless helped his wife sit down.

"She's my older sister, who protected and loved me, I look up to her."

"And she probably still loves you."

Melanie heard Judith's soft comforting voice but the words washed over her. Her mind was numb, frozen with the thoughts of trying to comprehend the news.

He was in no mood to waste time, two suspects had disappeared and he wanted a lead.

"Your sister and Stefan, Melanie, if I think you or your husband are withholding information, or if I find out later the information you provided is false, I will charge you both."

Melanie looked and stared coldly directly at Warren.

"You really are an arrogant bastard, not sure if she would have liked you."

"I don't really care when it comes to catching serial killers and she'll like me less when I arrest her and her husband."

"Maybe, maybe not, she likes a challenge; she may even admire you if you catch her. Do you know what an accident is, I'll tell you. It's a series of events that happen in a sequence over a period of time. If any one of those events had not happened…the accident wouldn't have occurred. My sister would have been pushed over the edge by events, if one of those events had not happened you would not be here now."

Judith looked across at her partner who had remained quiet during the verbal onslaught.

"I agree with your analogy. I'll reiterate what I said earlier and I'm giving you both a second chance, if I find that you are withholding information, I will gladly and with pleasure arrest you both. The seriousness of the crime will be enough to put you both in jail. I don't think you are both interested in a change of lifestyle, sharing a cell smaller than your downstairs toilet. You're a lawyer, how far does your loyalty stretch. You said, 'pushed over the edge by events', Explain! What happened, with that statement it indicates to me that you know more."

Melanie looked across to Filippo; he knew from the look that there was an untold story between them. Their open and honest relationship was revealing a deep secret.

"Say it, Melanie, out in the open; we have too many years between us for whatever it is to damage our relationship. If it is such a deep secret, then you have had good reasons to keep it from me. I trust you on that."

Melanie looked up at Warren in silence and then turned her head towards Judith. "We lived in Africa for a period of time."

"How long?"

"Stop the interrogation, detective or I will run rings around you in a court and you will wish that you never set eyes on me. You are overstepping the boundaries of your profession. The facts, you want the hard facts. We came back to build a new life, my mother was raped in Africa, we moved back, she committed suicide and my sister fell into the wrong group of people. One night, let's say, accosted by a group of men and one of them was her so-called friend. He escaped because the police failed to prosecute. Our father had a complete breakdown and died of a heart attack. As you may have guessed by now, I and my sister have no love for the police. The one thing I do enjoy is being in court and obtaining a successful prosecution. They are probably in Africa; she mentioned it one day, almost as if she let it slip out. We were sitting around the swimming pool, we invited them on a holiday and then she mentioned Africa. It sounds like she was planning ahead; I have no idea if Stefan was aware of her future plans. After the party last summer and breaking the relationship with Vincenzo, we never saw him again. They're both qualified and would find work no problem. Where, I've no idea despite your threat of arrest. I'll leave that decision to you. It's up to you to judge if we know anymore. I can only guess that they would've not have left via a commercial flight, Stefan knew a few pilots, the type who can fly anything from a Cessna to a 747. He mentioned it before, more than once at a party."

"Names?"

"No idea, and that's the truth, your decision to believe me."

"Thorsten Zimmermann."

Melanie looked across to her husband in disbelief that he personally knew someone who might be directly involved.

"I mentioned it the last time when you were here that we had a small import-export business. Thorsten did a few flights for our business. He is a very talented pilot with years of experience, his home is his sky."

"Where can we find him?"

"I can give you his address but good luck. All I can say is that he will be somewhere on this planet, probably forty thousand feet in the sky. You will catch him at home, but it is a case of when? Before you ask, he is freelance and works for no particular airline. I take it you found nothing in their house to indicate where they went otherwise you would not be here."

"No evidence to where they are but we did find the cellar where the four men were tortured. Your sister- and brother-in-law whilst on their crusade seemed to have forgotten about the effect on other people who are involved. The young couple, who were out walking their dog and found Vincenzo, would you want that picture imprinted on your mind for the rest of your life? Think about what I said, the offer of arrest for you both still hangs in the air. Judith, I think it's time to leave, Filippo and his wife need time to think."

Judith looked at her partner as he sat quietly in the passenger seat. It was obvious that he was contemplating that they had lost their prime suspects.

"We need to visit where Stefan and Anja worked. Can you can visit the hospital and I'll visit Anja's place of work, then let's meet up later this afternoon back at the office."

***

Filippo poured himself a double whisky as he tried to contemplate what had happened. There was silence in the room as he sat on his leather relaxer chair and looked across at his wife. He knew despite what he said there would be an onslaught of feelings. "You're not okay, are you?"

"What the fuck do you think? Of course, I'm fine, having the best day of my life, hopefully, tomorrow is the same and I cannot wait."

Filippo sat quiet and took the outburst from his wife. He had known her long enough to know when she was boiling over and when he had to let her explode.

Melanie walked over the sideboard and looked at the picture of her and her sister on holiday on Majorca. She picked the picture up and flung it across the room barely missing her husband as it shattered against the patio doors. Filippo knew what was coming next and as with every time, his wife, without saying anything stormed out of the room, a few minutes later, the front door slammed shut. He knew in a few hours he would have to collect Melanie from somewhere. She needed to walk off, or go somewhere to rid the built-up anger, frustration and betrayal she was feeling. Until then, he knew he would have to sit and wait.

Chapter 43

Judith saw Warren walk past the coffee kitchen and shouted after him.

"Sorry, I was pre-occupied with thoughts, Judith. What did you find out at the hospital?"

"I spoke to a few of his colleagues who all seem to have a similar opinion. He is viewed as a kind man, who was willing to help others, when necessary but is a loner who is easily influenced. People said he was fastidious about: detail, precise with his job, a clean work record, polite but did not socialise too often with co-workers. He separated work from private life and only socialised at major events such as Xmas. He works also for fun and keeps reminding his colleagues that he does not have to work."

"Did he win the Lotto or something?"

"Close, Warren, he inherited over five million, his father used to play the game of stocks, shares and property. His father had made gradual investments over a long period and bought some property when the wall came down; you have to just look at the prices now. A lot of people made money when the wall came down."

"And a lot lost out and still do today, Judith. People in the East still receive fewer pensions than those in the West. Moving the politics to one side."

"I've certainly left a few people in shock that he is even remotely involved with the murders. You never know what your next-door neighbour gets up too. Who did you talk to, Warren?"

"Nurses, doctors, and the receptionist at the practice, some of them knew Anja previously; they used to work with her at the hospital. That's where she met Stefan, before setting up her own practice. They could not understand why he hooked up with Anja. They are two opposites, she is dominate, aggressive person in the relationship and a fanatic for organisation and cleanliness."

"What else did you find out? We can sit in the office rather than stand here in the kitchen."

"The kitchen is okay, Judith. Some of the staff was not too happy with her; let's say management skills, especially the men. She lived also for a time in Africa when she was younger and that confirms what her sister said. Her father was a doctor and probably the main reason why she became one. They seem to be a perfectly matched oddball couple. If she had so little respect for men, then why did they marry?"

"Leave that one for Freud, Warren. Meanwhile, we need to pull that pilot when he surfaces."

Chapter 44

It was eight o'clock in the evening, when the phone rang on the sideboard table. Filippo recognised his wife's number and wondered why she had not rung his mobile. He took a deep breath before lifting the receiver; he knew what was coming his way. There was silence, "Melanie. Have you calmed down?"

"You can find me in the Silberfisch, Oranienburger Strasse. Pick me up."

"That's a first, normally you walk it off and I pick you up somewhere. You're in the middle of Berlin and drunk. Red wine is it?"

"Did you work that out by yourself? Impressive husband, you should be a fucking detective and find my sister and that weed of a husband so I can kill them both. How the hell she can even get into bed with him beggars belief."

Filippo cringed; he knew by the soft calm tone of her voice that she had gone past the point of anger. It was rage, which he knew would pass. The level of wine left in the bottle would ease that concern by the time he picked his wife up.

"I figured the red wine part out because we are married. It'll take me about one hour to pick you up, Melanie."

"No hurry, the second bottle of red wine is on order."

Melanie hung the phone up and looked through the cellar windows at people walking past. Filippo shrugged his shoulders and looked for a second at the silent phone. He knew when he picked Melanie up that he would just have to sit, listen and take the understandable onslaught. Filippo walked along Oranienburger Strasse and he could see his wife through the cellar window. He looked at the sorry lonely figure; her sister had died in her, the trust and bond ripped out of her heart. She had every right to grieve what she was feeling. It was raw grief for the loss of her sister and no doubt, the memories of her mother. His heart sank as he walked down the stairs and turned to face his wife, who stared silently at him.

"The bottle is nearly empty, Melanie."

"Very observant, you need to order your own drink; the rest in the bottle is mine. Bastard sister."

"I've got headache tables for tomorrow."

"Put them in the bottle now; kill two flies with one swat. The pain is going to be nothing like my sister will feel if I see her again."

"I'll have a small beer and then we are going home."

"I didn't plan on fucking walking back."

The barman looked across at Filippo, who raised his hand as much to say that he required no help to calm his wife.

"Let's tone it down and just come home. It's starting to spoil other people's night in this pub. That's not fair on them. Do what you want back home, throw things around, smash whatever, I don't know, but you're coming home or you will spend the night in a police cell. Not good if you go to court."

"Let them try and prosecute me, I probably know the judge, I've won more cases than…"

Melanie looked square into the eyes of her husband. She never knew why but his patience and calm mannerism always calmed her.

"Take me home, Filippo."

The silence during the drive back surrounded Filippo. He felt his heartbeat raise at the thought of breaking the silence, knowing as soon as he spoke it may give his wife the option to vent her frustrations. He looked around at her, slumped in her seat, staring at the trees as they drove by.

"Shall we pull in over there and grab some fresh air. I do not want to take all this bad feeling home."

"Drive."

The command was clear and he knew better than to challenge it. Ten minutes passed, and Melanie turned to Filippo.

"She will surface…sometime. She will miss me, we are close, but it seems not close enough."

"Or close enough to ensure you were not involved, Melanie." He wished he could have swallowed his words, he realised he had just given his wife an opening.

"What flipped her, for Christ's sake, she's a fucking bloody doctor and her husband is a nurse who presses flowers for a hobby. We all want revenge at some point for something in our life…"

Melanie, let out a loud, piercing shrill of frustration and thumped the dashboard of the car, which took Filippo by surprise.

"Pull over, Filippo, now, I need fresh air, we need to talk before we get home."

"Good, it will save you from throwing things around the house. It's also safer for me. There's a place ahead, I'll pull in there and we can walk."

"Now! Or your car will be full of vomit."

Melanie opened the door and leant out of the car, Filippo walked around in time to hear the red wine splatter the ground.

"Here's some water, Melanie."

"Let's walk in that direction, Filippo, no reason, I need to move. Give me your hand, I'm not going anywhere until you hold my hand, I need you for balance. I feel betrayed, in grief, my sister died within me. How could she do what she did?"

"You can ask that question a thousand times, in years to come, you will still ask the question, but not as often. You will never find an answer, Melanie, even if your sister told you herself. She thinks and reacts differently, her logic process, her values have all been screwed up somewhere by her past, for whatever reason. Somewhere, the wiring short-circuited and with her medical knowledge, she used it to suit her needs when the fuse blew. There are a lot of ifs and buts. If Vincenzo had not come to the party, she would never have met him, maybe there would be no fourth victim, if your sister lived elsewhere, married someone different, had a different career, the list is endless. We cannot reopen the doors of the past, they are closed, Melanie."

"Stefan's excuse? Filippo, tell me, you seemed to be so switched on to how serial murderers tick."

"Probably simple, loyalty, no real idea, the whole thing is out of my scope of thought. I cannot get my head around what has happened, it's easier for me, but you will grieve for the loss of someone you love."

"Loved, wrong tense, Filippo."

"For the loss of someone you loved. Time will never heal this; it will make it easier for both of us. I do think you are right, at some point, she will be in touch. The question will be what will you do when she does?"

"Why did you let me drink the second bottle of wine, Filippo? I feel like I'm dying."

"The mood you were in, did you think I would run the risk of stopping you."

"We've known each other for a long time; you can read me like a book and know when to back off. Take me home, Filippo, I need my bed. Hopefully, tomorrow this feels like a bad nightmare."

"It's more your head I would be worried about, let's get you home."

Chapter 45

The Avanti twin-propeller plane sailed over the African plain, Anja looked across to Stefan who was still sleeping. She turned her head to look out of the window at the dramatic rosy sunrise. The brilliant orange glow of the sun would push over the horizon and Africa would come alive for another day. Anja felt a fleeting moment of childhood happiness flow through her body. The memories of her sister and parents were triggered by the sunrise. The sunrise meant a new start and a fresh chance for each day. Africa was her fresh chance to correct a past wrong, a thought of justice, which had been in her mind for several years, would now be paid with a life.

Anja looked down at the African plain and noticed a pack of Hyenas running in the morning cool sun. She knew of their reputation for eating everything, including the bones and paused in her thoughts as she watched the pack. The perfect way to get rid of a body and there was one from her past to dispose of, the Hyenas would leave no evidence. Stefan stirred; he opened his eyes, looked at Anja, smiled and curled up on the leather-bound seats. She knew that she had a score to settle in Africa. The pathway that life had put her on had started here, the rape of her mother and she would settle that score. The question was still how to bring Stefan on board? She looked across to her husband curled up on the seat who was snoring lightly. He knew very little of her past and she was losing trust in him. Perhaps, there would be two bodies but that would be his choice.

Chapter 46

Thorsten sat with open hands on the tan brown Formica table and stared directly at Judith and Warren. He wondered who would fire the first question. He felt at ease with his situation and he reflected on the time when he was interrogated by the police for smuggling. They both knew that they would struggle to prove that he assisted in their escape but hoped for an additional lead, which might track Anja and Stefan. This was their prime objective. Judith went first.

"Herr Zimmermann, you are a very difficult man to track down. When did you first meet Anja and Stefan and how long have you been friends?"

"We have never been friends, but then it depends on your definition of friends. I met them a few years ago at a party. Melanie and Filippo's house, from to time we have bumped into each other, once, twice a year, perhaps."

"You have a part share in a light aircraft, which two weeks ago you flew to the Poland-Ukrainian border, why?"

"You are correct with your research, before you ask the next question, I'll save you the time; I went there to have a look around, why not. If you find that strange, that is because you work and socialise in a different circle. I'll give you an example, I know people who lease business jets to go shopping. A small group of us flew to Iceland last month for a long weekend. At the end of the day, you buy what you can afford and I do what I can afford."

"How long did you stop there, in Poland?"

"You know the answer, it seems like you want me to confirm it, just for the record, as you say, three days. If you wish, I can provide a contact detail and address of who I visited." Thorsten knew this was a partial lie, his contact was trusted and it was not the first time he had used this route to help people with a new life. He knew it would be also extremely difficult for them to track the hired business jet. He had dropped them both off at a friend's private runway before flying onto his destination in Poland.

"What is your relationship with that person?"

"You could say, loose friend, sort of on the outside. We meet up from time to time, two, three times a year. It all depends on my flight schedule. I am a freelance pilot, 747 mainly, cargo aircraft. I also have several other flight licences for different types."

Warren had deliberately sat to one side, he wanted to watch and observe the body language, not only above the table but also below. It was always possible to look confident above the table but few people could control the language underneath. He had seen nothing to indicate his opponent was concerned with the interview. He was either comfortable with what he was saying or knew how to control his body language. Thorsten interjected before Judith could present her next question.

"To confirm, I am here of my own free will to answer some questions related to Anja and Stefan, but you have not informed me, why?"

"We will get around to that, but first, we wanted to establish your relationship."

"When did you last see the two of them?"

"A few months ago, we met up for an evening meal; I went around to their house. The conversation was general, nothing specific."

Thorsten drank the last sip of water out of the glass.

"We're investigating the disappearance of two people, Anja, Melanie's sister and her husband, Stefan. Your name appeared in our investigation when we interviewed them. Do you have any idea where they might have gone or anyone who may have a grudge against them?"

"None at all, they are both professional people, secure in their own status and wealthy."

"Have you ever been to Africa?"

Warren noticed no change in any body language.

"Lost count, I have been a pilot for over thirty years; the answer to your question is yes."

"Just to brief, well, maybe a gap in my knowledge of the Aerospace industry, how common is it to hire a business jet?"

"More than you think, some people buy these aircraft and use them, maybe two, three, four hundred hours per year. Some people lease."

"Out of curiosity, where did you get my name from?"

"Filippo mentioned your name in passing when we interviewed him. Apparently, you did some work for him, flying cargo for his export-import business."

"That's right, but you have left out his partner, Vincenzo. Complete jerk, but the pay was damn good."

"We had to pass on some disturbing news to them both regarding our investigation."

Warren looked at the body language; he knew where Judith was taking this line of question.

"You enjoy your job, your lifestyle; it certainly seems different from what the majority of us have. You require a lot of freedom."

Judith paused and Thorsten shuffled in his seat and tucked his legs around the chair legs for security.

"We're investigating a series of murders, you may be aware of them and we wish to question Anja and Stefan. If you are aware or have been involved in removing them from the country, then you are an accessory. You mentioned Vincenzo, his body was found, partially skinned, tortured with ants crawling out of his eyes."

Judith noticed the colour drain from Thorsten's face as she placed a picture before him. She knew there were two options, come clean, but nearly always people opted for the route of defence. He looked across at Warren and then back to Judith and knew he needed time to take in all this information. His freedom was on the line.

"If you thought I was involved, you would have arrested me and then questioned me. As you said, I am helping with enquiries regarding the disappearance of two people. I assume I am free to go."

"You are correct; keep it in mind what we have said. If we find a direct link, you will be arrested, if you are withholding, you will be arrested. If you assist with us then there may be a different route, Herr Zimmermann."

"I need to find some information, which may be of use to you. Information, which I cannot obtain here and it may take a few weeks. Africa is a large place. If there are no charges, can you escort me out of the building."

Judith returned to the interview room and Warren was standing with his back to the wall.

"What do you think?"

"Guilty as hell, but we have no solid evidence to link him to the fact that he helped, willingly two murderers escape Germany. He flew them out of Germany and then they were picked up by someone of a nationality, possibly, could be, maybe living in Morocco and then on through Africa. He genuinely probably did not know what the end destination was."

"He likes his lifestyle, Warren, he will come back with some information and assist. If we receive that from him direct, I doubt it, but we will receive some information and I believe it will be the destination airport."

"It was the correct decision not to arrest him, a risk, I know. Now the ball is in his court, provide the information or lose his lifestyle. Somehow, I do not think he will take long. He needs to go away, take stock of the situation he is in and realise there is only one route if he wishes to maintain his freedom."

Chapter 47

Warren gazed out of the window; Judith had taken a one-week holiday with her daughter to Croatia. The telephone rang and it was the front desk, a woman called Mila was waiting for him with an envelope. He headed off to the foyer, his senses of curiosity heightened as to why she was there. He looked through the window and noticed Mila sitting on the fixed blue plastic chairs, she seemed withdrawn and her cheeks were sunken, she looked ill. He opened the door to the foyer and joined her.

"Morning, Mila, what brings you here, it's a long time since we last met. Are you okay? You don't look well. What can I help you with?"

"I'm not too sure; I received a letter this morning, with another inside. One letter was asking about my health and hoping that I was moving further on with my life. It's from Anja, or someone was requested to send this letter. The other letter, which was enclosed, is for you."

"The thing is, what happened has not helped me move on with my life. It destroyed my new relationship. My ex was a bad person and I was lucky to escape and start a new life. He deserved something, but not the way he was slaughtered. No one deserves that type of ending and somehow, I know I am not responsible but somehow I am. I met him with open eyes, became involved, he was handsome and at first charming. If the relationship had never started then I would not be sitting here now. At least, I will die knowing he cannot harm other women and that is a blessing. I have incurable cancer. Sorry, my demons are rambling on, I have to leave."

Mila stood up and walked out of the door. Warren had no time to respond and for once he felt the male victims in the case had got what they deserved. He sat numbly at what the future held for her and felt as if his world had closed around him. He sat still on the chair and opened the letter from Africa. He could guess who it was from, but he could never prove it. The letter was from Africa,

224

Botswana and simply read, 'Dar es Salaam, East coast, one return ticket is required, male, near future, time not confirmed'.

Warren was convinced that Thorsten was involved and felt justified now for not arresting him. Anja had used him as a postman to enquire about Mila's health, and for whatever reason, it looked like Stefan was planning to return. For the moment he needed Thorsten free, he was the only link to Anja and Stefan. Whether he genuinely knew what they had done would be debatable. They both still had the house, bank accounts had been frozen, the ones that they could find. He needed to know when and where and the waiting game irritated him. The time would pass quickly allowing a second chance at justice. There were now two unanswered questions, why Africa, why that area and what started the killings? He felt that both were connected and now he needed to confirm if Anja had been in touch with her sister.

Chapter 48

Warren stood ramrod straight as he rang the bell. It only took a few seconds and Melanie was looking at his stern face. "I suppose you had better come in, it looks fairly serious."

"Withholding information from the police can be if it was intentional. Is Filippo home?"

"Change the tone, I have invited you in and I can request you to leave."

"We can do it at the station if you wish."

"He should be home in about half an hour. Do you wish to talk to him as well, we could phone him."

"Not yet."

"We can go into the kitchen."

"I'll keep it simple. Where is your sister and have you had any recent contact?"

"No too both, is the answer simple enough."

"Africa, Dar es Salaam. Does the name mean anything to you?"

Silence fell in the kitchen; there was no sharp reply from Melanie who now looked ruffled. No longer standing as the superior in the questioning, she sat down to be on level eye contact with Warren. He watched her bow her head as if she was collecting her thoughts.

"I never thought the name would crop up in my life again. Africa, it is on the east coast, it was one of the places where my parents worked, the last place before we flew home. Our father was a doctor and he worked at the local hospital for a short while. If she has gone back there, I can guarantee that Stefan does not know the history and has totally flipped out. It does not make any sense to go there, too many bad memories."

"Your sister flipped out, as you say, a long time ago, except you did not recognise it. She would not be the first to live a normal life in society with a secondary dark secret. Perhaps, Stockholm syndrome, revenge is driving her

226

there to that corner. I am no psychiatrist, maybe she needs to feel for the place to let her go. Who knows what is going through her mind."

A moment of silence fell in the kitchen, was Africa the root cause that caused Anja to cross the line. She wondered why Stefan followed suite, was it out of pure loyalty and totally unaware of the reasons. Two people who were protectors of life were now the takers. She knew Warren was right; it was one for the psychiatrists.

"Before you ask, why I did not inform you of that area, where do you draw the line at what information you pass on? I thought it was irrelevant. We were there for such a short period in our life."

"Well, it is relevant now, I have evidence that your sister and Stefan are there."

Warren heard footsteps coming towards the kitchen and Filippo spoke to Melanie.

"He believes Anja and Stefan are in Africa."

Filippo looked down at Warren who seized the moment to ask a direct question.

"You know who Thorsten is, are you aware of his relationship with them?"

"Yes, I am and yes I do."

Melanie looked up at her husband.

"Over the years, he became a loose friend to them. Why is he in the picture?"

"Following all lines of enquiries, but we believe they are in Africa. Did they mention at any time, or give an indication that they would go there?"

"Yes, we were next to the swimming pool, remember Filippo, we mentioned about going on holiday and invited them. Anja mentioned that they were thinking about Africa, she did not say where. So what happens now?"

"I don't think there was any deliberate attempt to withhold information. We all make a decision to provide information when asked and we provide what we think at that time is relevant. We will keep investigating; if there is any communication, inform me, otherwise, I will now view it as withholding information. Hopefully, they will return, sometimes the temptation of home can be too much. I have the feeling that you are close to your sister and you feel a certain sense of betrayal. I am sorry for that both."

"That is putting it mildly, the phrase you should be using is, were, not are close. It is not just me but also Filippo, we feel…never mind that is our personal business, not yours. If she, they get in contact, do not worry you will be the next to know."

Chapter 49

Stefan sat on the balcony with a glass of wine and failed miserably to kill the mosquitoes, which the light attracted. He reached down for the spray and wondered if it would be better just to use it instead of shower gel. The distant noise of scooters irritated him as he wiped the sweat off his brow.

Four months had passed since they had left Berlin, Anja had become withdrawn and several times he had approached her only to be rebuked. Within weeks of arriving, he had soon realised that she had detailed local knowledge, information that she had kept from him. He felt the trust, the bind of everything they had gone through was broken and she was growing distant from him. There was a reason, buried deep inside her that he was not aware of, he knew his wife, or he thought he did. It was not the new start he had hoped for, the culture, the humidity and heat, the list was endless. What he did not like, Anja seemed at home here.

Like an animal instinct, he recognised his wife's footsteps as she walked across the wooden floor. She sat down opposite, her face was lifeless, the eyes had lost their soul, he knew he had lost his wife and the trust between them.

"I need to apologise, it is not what we planned, is it? Or how it would turn out for you."

"For me? Where is this going, Anja?"

"I should have told you earlier. When I was younger, I used to live here with my family. My father worked here and eventually, we moved back to Berlin."

"We all have secrets, Anja, but this is no secret to be kept. Why has it not crept up in any of our general conversations?"

"Because of what happened here."

"You've lost me, we came here to escape, new life, you know the story, now there is a story here. Where has our trust gone, Anja, you've broken it."

"I need your help; I need your trust again."

Stefan knew where this conversation was going, even before she had told him why. His answer was direct.

"No, Anja."

"I've found the man who raped my mother."

For a brief moment, Stefan thought about leaving the room as his body struggled to comprehend what he had heard.

"Anja, you should have told me, we are husband and wife, but you've used me. We came here for a new life, a new start and you came here for revenge. We need to move forward, sometimes, the door needs to be closed, but not forgotten. Look to the doors that will open, we have the chance of a new start and you have blown it for your personal use. I know you will not rest until you have had your revenge. I'm finished; I'll not take part in any more slaughters."

"Did you not hear what I said?"

"Yes, I did and I cannot comprehend what your family and you must have gone through."

"That man destroyed me and my family and is responsible for my mother's suicide. That one man set the path of my future."

"So like our other justified victims you require one more in your campaign to bring you justice."

Anja recognised a resistance she had never seen before in her husband. She sat back and upright to bring more distance from her husband. Stefan noticed the change in body language.

"Which way is this going, Stefan, will you help or not?"

"You will do what you feel is right, that I cannot change. You brought me here on pretence of a new life. I bought into it, for reasons, which we both know. You lied to me, Anja, and all the time you had a hidden agenda to come here. You've lost my trust, do what you need, I will not take part in this act of revenge, but I understand your reasons and that is all the support I will provide."

Anja stood up, speechless at the lack of support from a man she trusted, the man she had opened too, who she could no longer count on for support.

"It's not a problem, Stefan, at least, I have your support. I'm going for a walk, I need to rethink my plan."

"Don't do it, Anja."

"Not an option, I will do what is necessary."

He looked at Anja's face; it was cold, emotionless and the soul of her eyes was vacant. She brushed past him as if her husband had never existed.

Stefan looked over the balcony and watched his wife walk along the street into the distance. She knew the areas where not to wander. He knew it was irrelevant to Anja if she had broken the trust, what was relevant was that she no longer trusted him. He gazed across in the direction of the sea, the promenade lights lit up the crest of the waves as they rolled onto the beach. He knew the trust was lost between them and he also knew what his wife was capable of. It was time to leave Africa; the only question was how much time would he have? He had already been in contact with Thorsten, now it was time to firm up a flight home. The trust had gone and now each a free agent, Stefan, in a land he did not know and Anja in a place she understood. He knew he had to disappear and quick, the loss of trust meant one thing, his life.

Anja turned the corner and noticed no lights shining from their flat. She knew in her heart Stefan was no longer there and opening the door would only confirm her suspicion. The emotion of betrayal was still there and the fact Stefan had gone was irrelevant, he had betrayed her. Anja slid the key into the door, opened it and listened to the silence. The balcony door was open with the curtains flapping in the gentle evening breeze. She jolted as the through draft caused the sitting room door to slam closed. Anja switched the light on; she noticed the open bedroom and wardrobe door. The feeling of anger had subsided and she wanted to even the score, emotionless, she looked around the room and noticed the flickering light on the laptop. Stefan had left in a hurry and Anja sorted through the internet history and email. It was not long before she found out that he was heading back to Germany. Anja stood in the shower and let the water flow over her body to cleanse the day off her. Her thoughts drifted to Stefan, she had never realised how easy revenge could be. Anja also knew where her old history drank; it had taken her a few months to find him. In two weeks, there would be free time, no work for a week, time to relax, indulge under the sun and a trip out to feed the hyenas. The visit to her past would have to be the first weekend of her holiday.

The train pulled out of Kostrzyn station and headed in the direction of the Polish-German border. Stefan looked out of the window at the former checkpoint and thanked Schengen; it was so easy to move around Europe, free of police checks. It would not be much longer before the train would pull into Berlin Ostbahnhof and back into civilisation. The journey had been long and he looked forward to a comfortable bed. Stefan stared at the passing countryside not taking any real notice of it and reflected on Anja. He knew what she was capable of, especially for men who had lost her trust and he wondered if he would ever be safe, even with a new identity. To leave the relationship was the correct decision, if only for his safety, but he wondered why it took so long. He knew he should have disappeared before Africa but the timescale was too short. That door was past and closed, he had new pre-planned doors to open. Stefan fixed his focus on the hypnotic passing of the fences. The killing for him was over; he had a new identity and money in a separate account.

The jolt of the train woke him up, tiredness had set in and his body had switched off. Although confused, not fully awake, he saw the sign for Ostbahnhof and felt relieved that shortly, he would be in a double bed. Stefan stood on the platform and breathed in the cool evening Berlin air: civilisation, regular trains, taxis, restaurants, German beer and a Bratwurst ran through his mind. A sense of relief flowed through him as he walked through the hallway full of shops and headed to the taxi rank. He looked at his watch; it was only 7.00 p.m. There was time for a shower and then head out to a restaurant to wind down from the long journey.

Stefan stepped out of the hot shower and wrapped a towel around him. He stood looking at the comfort of the bed and agreed with himself that a small beer from the mini bar was acceptable. The firm knock on the door caught him by surprise as he opened the door to the bar, no one was expected. Judith and Warren looked down as Stefan stood before them.

"Can I help you, I'm ready for bed, and I've just completed a long journey."

Judith looked for a moment at the medium-framed serial killer standing before them. She wasn't sure what to expect.

"Yes, you can help; we're looking for a man who fits your identity who has recently travelled from Africa. My name is Kommissarin Hellwig and this is Hauptkommissar Fischer, we are from the Mordkommission and investigating a series of murders. Can you confirm that you are Stefan Stegemann? We received an email stating that you are stopping at this hotel."

Stefan realised he had been careless exiting too quickly. The laptop history, Anja would have picked up the information. Thorsten sprung to mind; he booked the hotel for him. His instinct had been correct to leave; he had no interest in ending up as one of her torture victims. He also knew there was no point in lying, the truth would soon be found out. There was no option, Anja had her revenge and he knew if she had the chance, her revenge would be brutal and Thorsten was now a marked man. Stefan nodded his head and calmly confirmed his name.

"May I change before you bundle me in your car. I assume you have a lot of questions and wish to know where my wife is living."

"We know."

Judith was bemused by the calm, cool, emotionless attitude. The lack of resistance, the easy acceptance of his situation confused her senses. Warren stood watching, observing, the lack of his interjection indicated to Judith that he was enjoying the moment of this arrest.

"After we arrest you for the murder, I would prefer to use the word slaughter of four people, you will accompany us to the station on the suspicion of four murders."

Chapter 50

The hot evening air blew through the wooden slats of the beach bar. Anja sat holding a double Bombay gin, which was drowning in the melting ice. She wondered if Stefan had already been arrested. The coolness on her hand was welcome as she lifted the glass and gazed across the harbour to the lights of the distant ships. He was gone, out of her life, he had been a necessity to fulfil her aim and she had no remorse for using him. The spring day, when she had stroked the fresh buds waiting to leave Berlin, she knew she was not returning for a long time and felt distant from Berlin. She noticed the older tanned man looking at her sarong as it flapped in the breeze around her legs. He kept looking to catch her gaze, not in a flirtatious way, but as if he recognised her. That was her intent and why she had picked this seat. She felt confident, he didn't, nor did he look threatening as she remembered him. Anja downed the last drops of her watery gin and crossed over to the bar, it was time to grab another and flirt with her prey, who would not see the sunrise. She knew who he was, why she was here and what she would do.

Anja sat directly opposite him and introduced herself and there was no question of recognition, much to her relief. She realised there was no need for Stefan in her life, he was gone. This murder she would perform alone. Anja felt a sense of excitement, contentment and confidence that flowed through her body as she toyed with her prey. There would be no torture this time, the offer of a one-night stand would do the trick, and the poison would do the rest. The hyenas would be fed.